Prais~ ~~ ...

"Katherine Reay's writing shines in this modern tale that's sure to please fans of regency fiction. Admirers of Jane Austen, especially, will delight in the delicious descriptions and elegant prose as the protagonist is transported to the English countryside, taking readers along for the ride. Both cleverly written and nicely layered, Reay's latest proves to be a charming escape!"

—DENISE HUNTER, BESTSELLING AUTHOR OF
BLUE RIDGE SUNRISE ON THE AUSTEN ESCAPE

"At once sophisticated and smart . . . Clever and classy . . . Whether for the first-time *Pride and Prejudice* reader or the devotee with an ardent affection for all things Austen . . . *The Austen Escape* is an equally satisfying retreat into the wilds of Jane's beloved Regency world. In scenes brilliantly woven with Austen's classic characterization, Reay goes beyond courtship and manners to explore modern-day scenarios, grappling with themes of brokenness and loss, the weight of decisions and consequences, and the anchor of faith through difficult circumstances. As amiable as an Austen novelist could be—but with a pen just as witty—Katherine Reay proves she's ready to become Jane to a whole new generation of women."

—KRISTY CAMBRON, BESTSELLING AUTHOR OF
THE LOST CASTLE AND THE HIDDEN MASTERPIECE SERIES

"Wildly imaginative and deeply moving, *The Austen Escape* is Katherine Reay at her very best."

—BILLY COFFEY, AUTHOR OF STEAL AWAY HOME

"*The Austen Escape* has the remarkable ability to be both lighthearted and gripping. The dramatic elements are first rate, the characters even finer. Wonderful writing. Highly recommended."

—DAVIS BUNN, BESTSELLING AUTHOR

"Reay's sensually evocative descriptions of Italian food and scenery make this a delight for fans of Frances Mayes's *Under the Tuscan Sun*."

—LIBRARY JOURNAL, STARRED REVIEW, ON A PORTRAIT OF EMILY PRICE

"Another rich, multilayered story from Katherine Reay. This is a lovely tale that will nest in the reader's heart and won't let go."

—RT BOOK REVIEWS, 4½ STARS, TOP PICK! ON A PORTRAIT OF EMILY PRICE

"Romance novelist Reay (*Dear Mr. Knightley*) crafts another engaging and sprightly page-turning bildungsroman. The American-goes-to-Europe plot is a real chestnut, familiar but nicely revived by Reay, who hits a sweet spot between adventure romance and artistic rumination; the novel finds a fantastic groove where chick lit meets Henry James."

—PUBLISHERS WEEKLY, STARRED REVIEW, ON A PORTRAIT OF EMILY PRICE

Other Novels by Katherine Reay

Dear Mr. Knightley
Lizzy & Jane
The Brontë Plot
A Portrait of Emily Price

Katherine Reay

THOMAS NELSON
Since 1798

HarperCollins
PUBLISHERS
—— Since 1817 ——

Published in Nashville, Tennessee, by Thomas Nelson. Thomas Nelson is a registered trademark of HarperCollins Christian Publishing, Inc.

Thomas Nelson titles may be purchased in bulk for educational, business, fund-raising, or sales promotional use. For information, please e-mail SpecialMarkets@ThomasNelson.com.

Publisher's Note: This novel is a work of fiction. Names, characters, places, and incidents are either products of the author's imagination or used fictitiously. All characters are fictional, and any similarity to people living or dead is purely coincidental.

Library of Congress Cataloging-in-Publication Data
Library of Congress Control Number: 2017948841

Printed in the United States of America
17 18 19 20 21 LSC 5 4 3 2 1

For MBR and MAR,
A hero and a hero-in-training.
This one is for you both, with all my love . . .

[A novel] is ... only some work in which the greatest powers of the mind are displayed, in which the most thorough knowledge of human nature, the happiest delineations of its varieties, the liveliest effusions of wit and humor, are conveyed to the world in the best-chosen language.

—Jane Austen, *Northanger Abbey*

And for yours, Miss Austen, the world salutes you ...

Characters from Jane Austen's Novels referenced in *The Austen Escape*

Northanger Abbey

Catherine Morland–Catherine is very intelligent and kind. She is also naïve, as she has had little exposure outside of her narrow world, but she learns to think, question, and take ownership for her story throughout this novel.

Isabella Thorpe–Calling Isabella a manipulative gold digger wouldn't be off the mark. It would, however, not tell the whole story. Isabella is a beautiful young woman who relishes adoration and flattery. She craves attention. She also has no clue what she wants in life–besides wealth, of course.

Henry Tilney–Clever, perceptive, and kind, Henry is often a conundrum to those around him. He comes across as occasionally patronizing, but his gentle teasing and constant questioning come from a good heart.

Persuasion

Anne Elliot–A character Austen described as "almost too good for me." She is one of Austen's older and most beloved heroines.

At twenty-seven, she thinks love and her "bloom" have passed her by. Not so, dear Anne . . .

Captain Wentworth—An officer with courage, sense, and sensitivity. He is a new kind of hero—honored for his personal qualities and professional acumen rather than his birthright. Like many Austen heroes, he has a lesson to learn as well. He must forgive and conquer his own pride in order to find love and happiness.

Lady Russell—Lady Russell is a rich, well-meaning, practical woman who adores Anne Elliot. If her advice is misguided, it still comes from a true love for Anne and respect for her family.

Sir Walter Elliot—"Vanity was the beginning and the end of Sir Walter Elliot's character; vanity of person and of situation." That is all one needs to know of Sir Walter's character.

Pride and Prejudice

Elizabeth Bennet—Considered almost a perfect heroine, Elizabeth is lovely, smart, witty, wise, and kind. She believes her judgments are accurate and sound—and she is completely wrong. Fortunately for everyone, she discovers this. "How despicably I have acted . . . Till this moment I never knew myself." Unlike other Austen characters, once faced with this defect, Lizzy mends her ways and all ends well.

Jane Bennet and Mr. Bingley—These two simply belong together.

Lady Catherine de Burgh—If vanity is the beginning and end of Sir Walter, pride is the beginning and end of Lady Catherine. She tops that by being haughty, mean, and closed-minded as well—and gives a headache to everyone around her.

Emma

Emma Woodhouse—Handsome, clever, and rich. Three things everyone must know about Emma Woodhouse. One also needs to know she messes up a lot and gets almost everything wrong. In the end, she sees life more clearly and values friends better, and is rewarded with "perfect happiness" in her marriage.

Mr. Knightley—As a model of common sense and honor, one might find Knightley too good. Yet he marries these qualities with kindness, generosity, and such a devoted love for Emma that readers can't help but swoon.

Sense and Sensibility

Marianne Dashwood—Perhaps originally intended as a caricature of a person with a great emotional appreciation of the arts, Marianne matures throughout her story and brings balance to her life with a touch of sense.

Mrs. Jennings—A thoughtful and generous woman with the singular aim of enjoying the young people and seeing them all married. Her sense of humor can offend—Austen dubbed it vulgar, which her readers understood as common and unsophisticated—but that should be forgiven when weighed against her warm heart and solid good sense.

Edward Ferrars—A kind, honorable, quiet man. The important fact to note is that he was secretly engaged, for four years, to the young, beautiful, and opportunistic Lucy Steele. The aforementioned qualities kept him from breaking the engagement. Luckily, when he lost all his money, she did it for him.

Mansfield Park

Mary Crawford—Think of Mary this way: split the bright and brilliant Elizabeth Bennet in half and give all her wisdom to Fanny Price (*Mansfield Park*'s heroine) and all her sparkle to Mary. Mary leaves her story as she enters it, and causes great disruption in the middle.

Chapter 1

"How can I help?"

The world stilled. It wasn't the first time I wondered how one voice, one presence, could quicken the air and simultaneously stop all motion.

Nathan.

I offered a stiff and awkward smile as he propped himself against my desk. His knees bent and touched mine as he handed me a Starbucks cup.

"Thank you." I sipped and rolled my chair back a few inches to break contact. A clear head requires distance. "You can't. An engineer is only as good as what she designs and . . . my project is a failure."

The technology and math worked. The science worked. The breakdown was in the design. In the subjective, not the objective—it was in me.

Nathan nodded—a long, slow motion. I knew that look. He was trying to think up a plan, and if this had been another time or place, or I'd been another girl, I'd have hugged him for the effort. But I was ready to pay the price.

"It has potential," he said, "but Karen has other goals for the company right now. Even so, I'll talk to her."

I shook my head to clear it of his optimism and my lingering illusions. "There's no talking to Karen. There's no working with her either."

"That won't do, Mary." Nathan stared at me. "You've got to try."

"Why don't you plead for it yourself?" Moira said.

We'd spent the last half hour leaning against her cubicle's outer wall and staring across twenty other cubicles to the closed conference room door. I wondered that the sheer force of our concentration didn't burst it open.

"Karen will do what she wants."

"So you expect Nathan to do all the heavy lifting?"

"That's insulting and vaguely sexist. I can take care of myself." My look dared her to laugh.

She kindly banked her smile. "Good to know, as I was thinking more of insanity than anything else. What's that definition again?"

"Very funny," I said, but she didn't smile. "Fine. Doing the same thing over and over but expecting a different result."

"And so we wait." She, too, kept her eyes on the door.

"Nathan's suggestions weren't going to work. First, he wanted me to ask Benson and Rodriguez for help, as if I couldn't solve the problems myself. Karen would've jumped all over that. She's itching for a reason to fire me. Besides, she never would have approved their hours. And then Nathan wanted—"

"Stop." Moira held a hand to my face. "It wasn't so much about solving a problem as it was letting them in. We're a team. At least that's what that poster over there says." She pointed across the floor to where Lucas, our head programmer with an affinity for inspirational quotes, had hung

Teamwork Makes the Dream Work

"You help them all the time. What were you doing here last weekend?"

"Rodriguez needed a hand. It was no big deal." I waved away her comparison.

"For two full days . . . And he'd do the same for you in a heartbeat. You know I'm right."

The door opened.

My heart skipped a beat as Nathan emerged. It always did when he appeared. But this time he was coming from a meeting that determined the fate of my project and possibly my job.

He looked around and paused when his gaze crashed into mine. One steady look, then he turned away to speak to Craig.

"That was not good," I whispered to Moira. I rounded into my cubicle and flopped into the chair. "Karen killed it. Nathan looked like the grim reaper."

Moira's chuckle followed me. "Nathan is just a consultant who will soon be gone. You should have been watching Craig, the CEO who makes the final decisions."

"Wrong. I should have been watching my new boss. Karen will be CEO any day now. But—"

Another voice cut in with a soft "Hey, Moira."

"Nathan." Her brusque acknowledgment silenced and prepared me.

Nathan stepped into my cubicle as Moira exited it. He leaned against my credenza. "We should talk."

I watched Moira drop from view into her own cubicle, but I knew she was still listening. Everyone was. In our open office plan, everyone heard everything.

The overt eavesdropping used to breed gentle teasing and foster camaraderie. Now there was an odd silence. We strained to hear one another. Sometime in the past year, we had shifted from a mind-set of abundance to one of scarcity—any information you gleaned might be that charged tidbit that saved your job.

"Good or bad?" I worked to keep my voice low and unemotional. Any added professionalism was lost as the bun I'd twisted my hair into fell over my eyes. The wire had pulled loose for the third time that day. I was losing my touch.

My hair dropped into a straight curtain of dark brown. I blew it out of my eyes and found Nathan reaching for the red twist of wire. I snatched for it as soon as he straightened.

"It's electrical wire. The plastic coating makes for good hair ties." I bent it back and forth as if to prove my point.

"So I've observed." Nathan smiled. His smile, so unlike mine, was never stiff and always reached his eyes. Now it spread across his face and dug one dimple into his right cheek. For a moment, I forgot *We should talk*.

He gazed over the divider walls at the expanse of cubicles, then looked back to me. "Walk with me?" He was already moving away before I answered.

I yanked my hair into a ponytail, secured it again with the red wire, and hurried after him. Halfway to the door, one of my ballet flats slipped off, and I skipped along while pulling it back on.

Nathan didn't turn, didn't glance right or left; he just walked across the floor and out the side glass door. He stopped outside as if to let his body adjust to the Texas sun and heat. His blue oxford reflected the light. It matched the sky. It also made him look almost formal in WATT's uber-casual environment. I glanced into Lucas's cubicle as I hopped by—he wore what looked like pajamas.

My progress across the office had drawn all the glances Nathan had avoided. Walking outside always attracted attention, and gossip. I consoled myself with the thought that most folks would think Craig had tasked his consultant to kill his engineer's failing idea. Awful as that was, it was better than the truth: Craig's engineer had a hopeless crush on his consultant and now appeared to be racing after him. No one except Moira knew that one.

Nathan held the door open for me.

"Where are we going?" I straightened and smoothed my skirt.

He took a few steps from the door, closed his eyes, and drew a deep breath. "Don't you love it out here? You can smell that dry, crisp fall smell. You can smell the sun."

I stifled a smile. While running on the treadmill during my lunch breaks, I'd seen him out here doing this countless times. "To be honest, I haven't been out here much lately."

The whole office complex, ten high-rise buildings housing three times as many tech companies, was riddled with paths and ponds—a man-made oasis designed to promote creativity and relaxation. What had looked so clearly planned and artificial when WATT moved into the space four years ago had now grown in and filled out. It looked natural, beautiful even. I almost felt myself relax. Almost.

"Why not?" he asked.

"I've gotten into a bad habit of arriving early, staying late, and running on the treadmill at lunch."

Nathan looked straight at me.

"I'm getting fired, aren't I?"

"Despite your best efforts, no." He winked and resumed walking. "Let's circle the paths. Karen's voice is scraping my ears like those whiteboard markers you love. That high-pitched squeal can drive a person nuts."

"And it does . . . every day." I stepped beside him.

Nathan was silent.

"You could at least warn me so I'm prepared to face her . . . Do I need to dust off that Boston job offer?"

"Stop it." Nathan spun on me. "Unless you *want* to leave. I feel like you keep angling for an escape."

"With Karen in charge, I may not have a choice. So?"

"Do you ever feel like running away? Or is it just talk?" He offered me a sideways smile. It, too, felt like a question, but not the ones he'd asked. *Can I be real with you?*

He acknowledged my nod with his own and continued. "She got to me in there. Craig hired me to manage growth and reposition WATT. We've done that job well."

"But?"

"You all know this. His goal was to stay independent, maybe go public someday. Karen is pushing for a sale, and soon. That's public too, if you haven't heard it. Finance is running numbers. That's a whole different ball game." He looked back to the building. "For everyone here."

"I see . . ."

Craig, a brilliant physicist and engineer, thrived in the chaos of creativity. He had founded WATT, named for his childhood hero and the unit of power, on the principle that a few twenty-somethings with energy, smarts, and grit could make great stuff.

Not glamorous or sexy stuff, but bold and innovative devices that people wanted or needed to make the sexy stuff run better. Craig loved innovation. Karen loved strong sales and healthy margins.

For the first time I saw clearly the power struggle pulling at us. I also saw that Karen's vision was gaining ground. And that my project was a tangible symbol of the conflict.

"Golightly" was my pet name for it—a pair of glasses I'd started dreaming of years before the technology caught up with my imagination. One Friday night, when I was about twelve, my mom introduced me to *Breakfast at Tiffany's* and Audrey Hepburn's iconic character, Holly Golightly. I watched that movie dozens of times, mesmerized. I'd never seen a woman more beautiful. And although I missed much of the story in those early years, I caught the drama, the ukulele, and the sunglasses. I'd made my own ukulele out of cardboard and string, and now I'd moved on to the sunglasses.

They weren't as glamorous as Hepburn's, but mine did more than shield the eyes from UV rays. My Golightly glasses were self-contained augmented virtual reality glasses that embedded interactive 3-D images. They rivaled Microsoft's and Apple's offerings in an even slimmer format—at least that was the goal. Every prototype had failed—one exploded—and each one took something within me with it.

I walked past Nathan—my version of running away. "Back to batteries for me."

Two strides and he caught up. "What's wrong with batteries?"

"Nothing, except I didn't think my world would be dominated by them. I've been dreaming of these glasses for years." I stopped. "You wouldn't understand."

"Then tell me."

"There's no point." I shook my head. "You know what drives

me nuts? Out-of-the-box thinking used to be lauded around here. But now . . . no more risks? No innovation? I needed this one, Nathan. I can do it."

"I know you can."

I studied his face. "But not anytime soon . . . She cut funding, didn't she?"

He didn't reply, but one blink said it all.

"It'll be too late, you know," I said. "We can't circle back. The market will move on."

"I know that too, and I'm sorry."

We walked on in silence. I looked up in surprise when we reached the building again.

Nathan held the door's handle but did not pull it open. "Are you going to be okay?"

I pinched the bridge of my nose. "My allergies are horrible this fall." I lowered my hand and caught Nathan's expression— sympathy encasing pity. "Of course I'll be okay. Easy come, easy go, right?"

He narrowed his eyes. It felt like some offering, some connection, had fallen between us because I hadn't held it.

He accompanied me back to my desk and perched as he had before—as if we'd never taken a walk and he'd never delivered the blow to Golightly, and to me.

"Craig mentioned you had an advancement for the IR battery."

Back to batteries.

"I was playing around with Golightly . . . Double insulate it and we can cut the space between components. Everyone wants smaller devices. See, Karen doesn't get that; we need some ideas to generate others. Without—" I pressed my lips together. "Never mind. The lab is testing the battery now."

Nathan picked up a small wire elephant sitting on my desk and handed it to me. "Please don't let this derail you, Mary." He stood. "I've got another meeting with Craig. Will you be around later?"

At my nod, he was gone ... and my afternoon was suddenly free.

Chapter 2

"Easy come. Easy go." One swipe of my hand and six months' worth of wire animals skidded across my desk and onto the floor.

Moira leaned over the wall. "Easy? There was nothing easy about all that work, and stop killing your animals. They're wonderful."

I bent to pick them up, and one by one repositioned them at the edge of my desk. Duck. Giraffe. Two horses. A tiger complete with contrasting stripes. "It's embarrassing there are so many. Shows you how stymied I've been."

I picked up the last one, an elephant made of black 18-gauge electrical wire, and crushed it in my palm. "I was so close to the answer. I can almost see it. But . . ."

Moira snapped her fingers. "Then answer something else for me."

I pushed back from my desk to give her my full attention. "Shoot."

"Why haven't you grabbed that boy and kissed him already?"

I shot up and scanned the room, noting that most cubicles

were empty. "You can't yell stuff like that. You can't even *think* stuff like that. What if someone hears you?"

"Then we'd all get somewhere."

"Now?" I sat back down. "You want to talk about my love life *now?*"

"Seems a more fruitful topic."

I could still smell the coffee at that morning meeting when Craig first introduced Nathan to the team.

"He's thirty-two, so most of you may feel the need to call him sir, but listen to him anyway. He got his MBA at Harvard and he's brilliant at running a business. So while you keep pushing the limits, he'll keep our lights on and get WATT running smoothly as we grow—'cause that's what we're doing around here. We're taking this whole thing to the next level. And as soon as I hire another CEO to manage this beast, I'll get back to playing with you lot."

Craig rubbed his hands together, then slapped Nathan on the back. Everyone gathered around, a few called him sir, and then most drifted back to work. I stood frozen—overcome by a simple, clear awareness that something about him spoke to something within me. And we hadn't yet exchanged two words.

In the eleven months that followed, that feeling had only grown.

Nathan was smart, patient, clever, quixotic, and kind. He was a completely analytical consultant, ready to tear your business apart, who also quoted romantic movies, remembered everyone's birthday, and crooned ballads to our sixty-five-year-old office manager. He was a mystery and infinitely intriguing.

Moira interrupted my reverie.

"You knew Golightly was dead the minute Karen became your boss. You've had three months to digest it."

"She's going to fire me." It was the first time it felt real.

"Karen won't fire you. I run the numbers; you're too valuable." Moira walked around the divider between our cubicles and I twisted in my chair to face her. "And let's get back to the subject. Everyone can see the way Nathan looks at you. Why do you give him the Heisman every day?" She thrust one arm straight in the famous football pose.

I had to laugh at her attempt to cheer me up. Moira, dressed in four-inch heels and a tight skirt, knew nothing about football.

"He doesn't look at me any differently than he does you. And I don't give him the Heisman."

"If he looked at me that way, I might break my engagement. You're either a liar or a fool."

"I'm pragmatic. Besides, one: he'll be gone soon, and two: he's dating someone."

"He told you that?"

"He's mentioned Jeffrey's and Sophia's. Those are date restaurants."

Arms crossed, Moira drummed the fingers of one hand against her skin. "Nice assumption, Sherlock, but this isn't the sixth grade. Talk to him. Ask him."

"It isn't the sixth grade, but it feels like it . . . and I hated the sixth grade."

She pushed herself upright. "Invite him to Crow Bar tonight."

"Right. Look, it's already been a rough day and—wait. Tonight?" I scattered through the chaos on my desk to find my phone. "How'd it get so late? I'm meeting my dad at Guero's for dinner." I gathered my notes, my computer, and my second computer and shoved everything into my bag. "I'll never make it to South Congress on time. MoPac will be jammed."

"Nathan? Crow Bar? Call him and see if he'll meet you there after dinner."

I started to leave, then stopped. "Is it obvious, Moira? No one else knows, do they?"

Moira had every right to laugh. I did sound like a sixth grader. Instead her eyes softened at the corners with sympathy or pity. "You're safe. It's me, Mary. I doubt anyone else would pick up on it."

"Including him?"

"Definitely him. All shields are up and in perfect working order." The humor didn't reach her eyes or her voice.

As I walked away I felt her disappointment follow me.

"Safe isn't always best, Mary," she called out—vague enough not to raise listening ears, pointed enough to hit its mark.

I shot back. "But safe doesn't get her heart ripped out twice in one day."

Chapter 3

I inched down Texas State Highway Loop 1—known to locals as MoPac, after the Missouri Pacific Railroad that was there before the road. At ten miles per hour, I had plenty of time to replay every word, spoken and unspoken, from my walk with Nathan.

The sun had dipped to the horizon, but the heat hadn't abated. It was late October and Austin hovered in the high eighties and low nineties.

I pulled into a spot a few blocks south of Guero's, directly in front of Crow Bar, and crossed the street to the restaurant. As soon as I stepped inside, I spotted Dad's cloud of white hair through the mass of people. He always reminded me a little of Albert Einstein, and I was secretly glad he never cut his hair short or even brushed it much.

He wore his usual white oxford with *Davies Electric* embroidered in red over the pocket, worn jeans, and Ropers. He stood to greet me, and I reached up and kissed him. He smelled of home—WD-40, Clubman, and Tide.

"Hey, Dad. Sorry I'm late."

He twisted around me so I could take his stool. "You're right on time. I put our name in about an hour ago. We should be up soon." He nodded to the bar behind me. "I've been chatting with the bartender. Very nice fellow."

The light glinted off Dad's whiskers. They were scruffy, gray, and thinner than I remembered. He'd forgotten to shave again. He'd probably forgotten to eat today too.

"Have you gone through all those meals I made?"

Dad fought a grimace, and I almost laughed. I wasn't a good cook. I wasn't even a marginal cook. A friend had taught me five easy-to-freeze recipes a couple years ago, and whenever I was home I made double batches for my dad.

"Stop fretting," he said. "And don't let me forget—I made a new gizmo for you."

"You did?"

"Wait until you see what it does. You're going to love—" Dad stiffened, then his eyes lit. "That's us." He gently directed me in front of him to cut through the crowded bar.

Dad made me "gizmos" to solve small everyday problems or simply to make me smile. My favorite remained the toothbrush that self-dispensed exactly the right amount of toothpaste and timed my two-minute brush.

We sat at our table, and he opened his menu.

"Dad? What are you doing?" I pushed mine aside. "You never look at the menu at Guero's. You always order the Chiles rellenos."

"What, a man can't branch out?"

I wagged my finger at him. "There's something else going on here. Spill."

His eyes darted up and down the long page, then he gave up

and laid the menu and his glasses on the table. "Fine. You should accept Isabel's invitation."

I felt my lips part and my body slump against the chair.

"We already talked about this. You agreed with me."

He wouldn't meet my gaze.

"She called you, didn't she?" I closed my eyes. I should have expected it.

Isabel, unquestionably my oldest friend, questionably my best, had called a couple months ago with an invitation for a "trip of a lifetime"—a costumed Austen-style adventure to Bath, England. And while aspects of it appealed to me, brought back pleasant memories rather than painful ones, I concocted a few excuses and politely declined.

When I'd told Dad about it, he'd agreed. Work comes first, two weeks is a long time for a vacation, having a new boss is a tough spot to be in . . .

What I hadn't told either of them was the truth: I was tired, and on some level was easing my way out of my friendship with Isabel. Our relationship seemed to be stuck at age eight. The same dynamic charged between us—and that might have been fine, but somewhere in the last year it had darkened a shade and taken on an even more competitive edge than it had acquired in high school—which started over an incident regarding Austen too. So despite the temptation to hop on my first plane, take my first true vacation, and finally see something beyond the ninety-mile radius of my world, I'd said no.

That Isabel had rejected my decision and gone around my back to Dad should not have surprised me. That was standard operating procedure. She loved my father almost as much as I did. While her dad traveled to oil rigs and refineries around the world,

mine was the one who had attended her parent-teacher confer-
ences, picked her up from field hockey practice when she broke
her ankle, and was the name she wrote down as her emergency
contact every year. And if you want something, that's what you do:
you ask your dad.

"She needs you." Dad leaned across the table and rested his
hand on top of mine.

I could feel the calluses on his fingertips. I slid my hand to
my lap.

"I'm not saying she can't be a challenge. She lays claims to
things and no one else can touch them, but remember, Mary . . .
We had our problems, and God knows it was tough, but that little
girl had it even harder. Her mama left when she was only six.
Think of her life in England, her father traveling all the time, then
uprooting her to bring her to the States but still constantly gone.
She went home to a live-in nanny most nights of her growing-up
years. Can you imagine that? You had your mama, you had me,
and you had your brothers. Who held her when she cried herself
to sleep? Who paid attention? No wonder real and make-believe
got blurred."

As much as I wanted to protest, I couldn't.

Isabel had joined our second-grade class three weeks into
school. With her bright-blue eyes, gorgeous black curls, and lilting
British tones, she had every girl salivating to be her best friend.
At lunch on that first day, Missy Reneker, the most popular girl
in the class, with her Guess jean shorts and gladiator sandals,
pushed me off the bench to sit with the new girl.

Isabel, without missing a beat and wearing the coolest Beatles
T-shirt ever, grabbed my arm to pick me up and said, "Mary sits
next to me." That was it. Best friends. Even now, looking across

this table twenty years later, I had to admit . . . It was pretty much the best day of my childhood.

Dad smiled with an odd mix of compassion and shame. He rubbed at a stain on the linoleum tabletop. "I'll never forget how she helped you find all those pretty dresses. I had you working as an electrician's assistant every summer, and your mama was too weak by then to do stuff, but Isabel made things fun. She made them pretty. Your brothers and I . . . We didn't know how to do that. She even made the reservations and planned that party for your sixteenth birthday. Remember how she called all your brothers and told them to get their butts back home!"

My laugh morphed to a snort. That was a good memory. At twenty-three, twenty-five, and twenty-seven, all three of them complained the entire weekend, especially about being called to task by a "five-foot-two pip-squeak." But they showed up, each of them bearing a gift wrapped in newspaper—no bows. They had their limits.

Dad shook his head and continued. "We laugh that she's silly, but those things weren't silly. They were important, and I—we would've missed them. If she needs you now, that's what family does. We're there for each other."

"Isabel is family now?"

His eyes narrowed.

I raised my hand before he could reply. "I'm sorry. I didn't mean that."

And I didn't. Isabel *was* family and had been since the first day she came home with me after school. She was there for every occasion. And when my mom died two years ago, Isabel showed up at my apartment every night for almost three months, often waiting hours while I worked late. She always brought something—ice cream, a movie, chocolate, a magazine—to make me feel better, laugh, and forget for a while. She was the author of those easy-to-freeze meals. Dad was right—Isabel knew how to make things fun and pretty, even when they hurt.

"So you'll go?"

Before I could answer, Dad quirked a sideways smile. Deep lines trailed through his temples. He knew he'd won—again.

"Goodness' sake, girl, you should see your face. She wants to take you to some fancy English estate for a costume party, not torture you."

I lifted a single brow.

"Stop that. You'll have a great time. You love wearing skirts. Like the ones you used to wear, the pretty ones that swirled and bounced."

"Dad, those went out of style long ago."

"Your mom used to say pretty never goes out of style. Forget the skirts, Mary . . . This is a real opportunity for you. We could never afford to do stuff like this."

There it was—the vast, barren landscape that spread between Dad and me. Mom had been sick, and he'd worked to feed and clothe and send four of us to college. There had been room for little else.

"It didn't matter, Dad." I reached for his hand now. "I'll go."

His sideways smile evened out to a full grin. "Text her now."

"No cell phones at the dinner table."

"Don't be sassy. Go on, text her." He picked up his menu again. "I'll look this over while you do."

I pulled out my phone.

I'm in if the offer stands. Thanks for invite. Send me details
and let's get together this weekend.

"Happy now?" I dropped my phone back into my bag. "Or do you have more surprises? Because it's been a big day and I'm not sure I can handle any more tonight."

"You need more sleep." He laid down his menu.

I laughed. A smile and sleep were Dad's answers to everything—and he was probably right. "What are you ordering?"

He dropped his eyes. "Chiles rellenos."

Chapter 4

I pushed my way through Crow Bar's Friday throng to find Isabel seated, drink in hand, with an empty stool beside her. She'd texted back during Dad's tres leches cake that her weekend was packed and tonight was her only chance to meet. She'd wanted HandleBar; I was committed to Crow Bar. She only had fifteen minutes to spare; I couldn't change my plans. She would try to make it work; I would hurry.

"I'm sorry I'm late. Dad had a new gizmo to shove into my car, then he wanted to see the bats fly out from the bridge tonight. They'll migrate soon."

"They're still doing that?" Isabel pushed off the stool and dodged her head from side to side for her signature double air kiss. On any other Texan the move would seem pretentious, but with Isabel it was just what she did.

"I think it's hard to get a couple million Mexican free-tailed bats to do anything different. It's kinda their thing."

She pushed at the empty stool beside her and glanced down the bar. "I wasn't going to be able to hold this much longer. Do you know how many guys asked to sit here?"

"Five? Seven?"

"Ha-ha." She lifted my low ponytail and inspected it. "Did you do something with your hair? It's different. I love the colors."

I leaned back to draw it from her fingers. "Nothing new. It's the usual summer highlights that haven't faded yet. But you—"

"What do you think?" She pulled a chunk of black curls forward. "It's a little dark, isn't it? My colorist says it's very in, matte black, no variation whatsoever, but I'm not sure." She widened her eyes.

"It's dramatic, but good. I like it."

She twirled the section of hair. "You know me, I don't really care what it looks like as long as it's not dreadful, but he was so set on it."

I dropped onto the stool. "What are you drinking?"

She tapped the base of her martini glass. The liquid inside was clear with bright green flecks and a dark berry resting on the bottom. It looked like fall, but not quite Christmas.

"The guys at the end of the bar, the blond and the stocky one in the suit, ordered this for me. They wanted your stool. I suspect they thought this would get it for them." She slid it away from me. "I'd share, but the green flecks are cilantro. You hate the stuff." She stretched up and waved at the bartender.

"I don't hate cilantro." I leaned around her. "It just tastes like soap."

She blocked my view. "Don't look at them, it'll only encourage them. Here . . ." She twirled a finger at the bartender, now standing in front of us. "Hang on, someone's calling. Order while I get this."

Isabel pulled her phone out of her bag. I ordered a glass of Prosecco.

"TCG." Her voice arced, high and flirtatious. "How's your Friday? . . . I can't tonight. I'm out with SK."

SK. I hadn't heard that nickname in a long time. So long, I'd almost forgotten it. Part of me was surprised Isabel still used it, another part surprised it still hurt.

"I'll call you when I get home later? . . . Maybe . . ." She turned her wrist, checking her silver-and-diamond watch. "Sure . . . I'm actually near there . . . See you later." She tapped off the phone and laid it on the polished wood between us.

"You call him TCG to his face?"

"Not like that. Never. He saw my contacts list once and I came up with 'Tall Consultant Guy' on the fly." Her fingers flicked air quotes before she reached for her drink again. "He loves it."

Isabel's nicknames. Whenever anyone got one, they felt special—initiated into an exclusive club. She fed the image by keeping the translations tightly held secrets, objects of curiosity and mystery. I'd discovered mine years ago and TCG's more recently, by accident.

"You're seeing him tonight? Did you upgrade him?"

"No, but he's a nice guy." She watched me with a scrunched face. I couldn't tell if she wanted to say more or if the cilantro suddenly tasted like dishwashing soap to her too.

Tall, cute, quiet, a little boring, but sweet had been her dismissive description of TCG six months ago.

"I'm surprised he's still around."

"He doesn't take it any more seriously than I do. We have a few mutual friends, that's all; I may go meet up with them later. But while I'm here . . ." She raised her glass and tapped the rim of mine. "To Bath. To England. And to Jane." Her eyes lit with excitement. "This is it. The final piece of the puzzle. I can't believe my father finally gave in."

Isabel's dissertation, "Refined Escapism: The Twenty-First Century Appropriation of Jane Austen," had lain in limbo for the past couple years. She claimed she couldn't finish it because she hadn't experienced the "ultimate escapist experience." No grant would finance it, and her dad had staunchly refused.

"What made him agree now?"

Her pleasure wavered, and she trailed a finger around the rim of her glass. Her dad was never an easy subject. Whenever I doubted the saying that hate wasn't the opposite of love, I thought of Isabel's father and remembered—*indifference* was.

"Honestly, I think he's tired of me. He pointed out that most of my cohorts have submitted, even graduated already. He said he doubted I had it in me. Do you think I can finish it?"

"Of course you can. And if everyone has graduated, then your friends are a bunch of overachievers, because five years is fast. The average length for an English doctoral program these days is more like six or seven."

"How do you know that?"

"I looked it up." I took a sip of my Prosecco and waited. Isabel disliked silences and usually spoke into them quickly.

Not this time. I looked up, and she widened her eyes as if to say, *And?*

"It was last year when I ran into him at Christmas. He was on your case, so I found a few sites and sent him the links . . . I'm sorry, I shouldn't have done it. But you were really low. And he was behaving badly."

Isabel's bottom lip pouted out on her exhale. "I can't believe you did that for me."

"Well . . . someone had to tell him."

She took a pull on her drink and changed the subject. "Did you know his new girlfriend is thirty? We would've been in high school together."

"Is she the one I met last Christmas?"

"Different. This one's been around three months and twenty-two days. We had a fight about her last month. Don't you love that?

We barely talk, but he'll sure defend her. He started yelling in that horrid low way that I didn't respect his sacrifices, the decisions he's had to make, the life she brings to him—" She stopped and drew in a deep breath, then blew it out slowly, yoga fashion. "It doesn't matter . . . Thank you, Mary. Thank you for standing up to him and for coming with me."

I opened my mouth, but she raised a hand to stop me. "Please don't say anything. I know you don't really want to come, and it was kinda dirty pool to call your dad, but I had to. I needed family and that's you. You always have been and also . . . I owe you. I don't want you to be angry, but I did something. I . . ." Her eyes darted over my shoulder and she swallowed whatever she was about to say. "Oh. Your friend Moira is headed this way."

"I told you that. That's why I couldn't go to HandleBar. All the guys are coming here tonight."

The "guys" consisted of our little tribe from work—Benson and Rodriguez, WATT's two other engineers; our three physicists; a couple from the finance team, including Moira; and another few from marketing. We got together almost every Friday night.

I spun and waved to Moira. Turning back, I was surprised by the look of swamped loss pulling at Isabel's face. "You can stay if you want. You know you're always welcome. You know everyone."

She shrugged away the expression and my invitation. "No worries. We'll have plenty of time to talk, and I told you I couldn't stay. I'm already late."

She pushed off the stool as I reached for her. "Stay. Finish your drink at least."

"Friday night with engineers and physicists?" She glanced at the crew entering behind Moira. "Benson continues to look like a twitchy mouse, I see."

"Did you expect him to change?"

Rodriguez and Benson had come in together, and Isabel was right. Benson looked anxious. His eyes darted around the room. But I knew Benson. He wasn't anxious. He was taking it all in.

"He's just reveling in a Friday night. He's ready to relax, have fun . . . And don't smirk. Your pretentious academics don't rank any higher on the Friday-night-fun scale." I worked to hide my smile.

"You got me." Isabel grinned. "There was a debate the other day on whether Browning was a Merlot poet or more Pinot Noir."

"What does that even mean?"

"No clue. I said any poet above beer was pretentious and a whiskey one was more my style. No one appreciated that." Isabel gave me a quick hug. "I gotta go."

I noticed movement in my periphery. "Your timing is impeccable. Blond and Stocky just stood too. They look like they're leaving."

"Well, then . . ." She widened her eyes and added that flirtatious glint only Isabel knew how to manufacture. "They can walk me out while I thank them again. One can't be rude about these things."

Her parting laugh danced over the noise as she wove her way through the crowd. She paused at Moira and each woman gave the other a cursory glance and a sharp nod. I smiled—I always did when those two squared off. If they ever stopped sizing each other up, they might be friends.

Isabel now stood about ten feet away chatting with Blond and Stocky, and Moira joined me at the bar.

"You didn't tell me Little Miss All That was going to be here." When Moira heard how Isabel gave everyone nicknames, she'd returned the favor.

"There's something so painfully eager and needy about her.

She has to be everyone's focal point." She slid onto Isabel's stool and we faced the bar again.

"I decided to accept that trip she invited me on. Dad twisted my arm."

"Good for him. You need a vacation even if it comes with corsets—and her."

I opened my mouth to reply, probably to defend Isabel, when someone pushed into me from behind.

It was Isabel. She was back, hugging me tight and whispering into my ear. "Blond and Stocky come here all the time. When we get back from England, we'll come celebrate again. Maybe we'll both get free drinks."

"Maybe." I clasped her arms and squeezed. "But you promised you wouldn't set me up anymore."

She laughed and stepped back. I twisted the stool to face her. Sitting to standing, we were eye to eye.

"Sharing a couple drinks with two cute guys is hardly a setup. I'd never break my promise."

I arched a brow.

"Not until I forget it, at least." She flapped her hand in front of my face. "Never mind all that. I came back to thank you. This trip is going to be amazing. I'll forward you the link and our flight info."

"Do I need to do anything?"

Isabel shook her head. "It's all scheduled and paid for, but you should at least check out the website. It's gorgeous—dresses are supplied, hats, shoes, everything. Wait till you read about all the activities." She glanced at her watch again. "Now I really do need to run."

With that, she waved and disappeared.

I looked to Moira. "I don't think she ever doubted I'd say yes."

Chapter 5

I received copious e-mails and texts over the weekend. Isabel didn't have time to meet again, *much too overwhelmed*, but she did have time to send long lists of to-dos, to-packs, to-sign-up-fors, and to-read-up-ons. It was a good thing Golightly was off my plate, because I was now overwhelmed too—by Regency England.

Feeling a little bored on Sunday, I played with my dad's latest gift. It was an extraordinary dispenser made from antique kitchen tools, fine copper wires, and several porcelain knobs used for electrical wiring back in the 1920s. It dropped out Skittles for me—one every 2.2 minutes.

"I figure at fifty-four Skittles per bag, if it takes you two hours to eat a bag, you might stop at one," he'd said.

He had made it for work. He knew Golightly was giving me fits and that I either constructed wire animals or ate Skittles when concentrating. After dinner, while we dismantled some of its larger parts to fit into my car, I didn't have the heart to tell him of Golightly's demise. I simply gave him a kiss, a hug, and a thank-you.

So instead of measuring life at work, my gizmo measured cleaning at home. My apartment took half a bag, and my car a quarter. When I called Dad to report, we spent fifteen minutes pondering what we could measure in Skittles and how many each project might take. We determined cleaning his garage workspace would take at least three family-size bags.

"It's only noon. What will you do with the rest of your day?"

I looked around the apartment. I often worked on Sundays, not because I had to, but because I found doodling and design relaxing. There was no work. But there were lists.

"Isabel sent me tons of stuff about our trip. I need to sort through it all, and I think I better brush up on my Austen. Maybe grab a book or two."

"That'd be nice." I could hear him nod with each word.

He said little after that and we hung up, both lost in thought. Dad probably headed to the garage, his sanctuary. I grabbed my keys, headed for my clean car and for BookPeople on Lamar.

After riffling through the entire Austen selection, I chose its only copy of all Austen's novels in one volume. It was huge and heavy and smelled like leather. The woman at checkout turned it over and over in her hands.

"You can get these for free on an e-reader. They're in the public domain."

"I know and I probably will, but I love books. The weight. The smell. The bigger the better. It's a shame Encyclopedia Britannica doesn't print all those encyclopedias anymore. Weren't those the best?"

The woman sighed the equivalent of a *Whatever* and rang the sale.

I patted the book's dark green cover as if to soothe any hurt feelings. I'd gone over the top with the whole Encyclopedia Britannica thing, but books—heavy books—meant something to me, and at well over a thousand pages, this one was larger and heavier than my meatiest college textbook. I already loved it.

My mom had always insisted on paper, and because she couldn't do much but read, people gave her books. She loved them all—and the heavier, the better. She said they felt like blankets resting on her lap. Our house growing up was filled with electrical wires, brothers, and books. So purchasing a large book in her honor was only right.

I spent the rest of the afternoon and well into the early hours of Monday morning reading. Mom had first introduced me to Jane Austen in the seventh grade. She wasn't well that year and we spent much of our time together with me reading aloud. *Pride and Prejudice* was first, *Emma* next. But eventually I had my own reading to do for English classes, so my indoctrination into Austen's remaining novels was postponed.

The Austen I remembered was not the Austen I encountered now. *That* Austen was staid and challenging. And I'm sure my slow pace and mispronunciations must have driven my mother crazy—words like *reverie* and *supercilious*. She never mentioned it, though, or let her smile waver—Austen and I were her delights.

Mom's devotion to those novels made sense to me now. Jane Austen understood people, and she was funny. Being an engineer, analytic and literal, I knew I was probably still missing nuances and subtleties and most of her brilliance, but what I caught was captivating.

She wrote with such precision that a single phrase evoked an emotional response. She elicited laughter, warmth, and even a sense of awe. Across two hundred years, I recognized her characters in the here and now. She wrote about people I knew.

Northanger Abbey struck me most forcibly. I found someone

there so clearly drawn that I recognized words, phrases, even mannerisms. I finally put the book down at three o'clock Monday morning. I needed sleep. I would need a fresher mind to tackle all I'd found there.

I'd found Isabel.

On Monday morning, I stopped just inside WATT's front door. Karen was hovering outside my cubicle. Her frosted hair, cut precisely to the chin, shifted back and forth as she scanned the office.

Three hours of sleep were not sufficient for this ... I pulled my bag tighter on my shoulder. I could feel the instant she spotted me.

"Mary? A moment."

Rather than point me toward my cubicle or into a conference room, she walked straight past me and pushed out the door back to the parking lot. On her way past she offered the tiniest of smiles. She was playing with me. Giving me what I wanted—almost. I steeled my expression and followed.

Karen pointed a few feet away to a small gravel area, landscaped with cacti and other native plants, and stepped right into the gravel.

"Nothing is private in that building. How anybody gets anything done is beyond me." She shifted around to secure firm footing before looking to me. We stood eye to chin. I slouched to compensate.

"I looked for you Friday, but you were gone."

"Oh." I wasn't sure how to answer her. I wasn't an hourly employee, and I hadn't left until after six.

"I'm re-tasking you to battery improvements and the hearing device Benson is testing. It shows great promise. Ask him for his notes."

"It's his design. Shouldn't he—"

She cut me off with a wave of her hand. "He can stay lead if necessary, but at this point, I'd like to put him on some new ideas I've got. I've assigned each engineer a physicist and would like you to streamline development along those lines . . . Is there a problem?" Her tone held a corrosive note.

"We've never worked that way."

"WATT is too large now to work any other way. We need to eliminate inefficiencies and cross dialogue."

I opened my mouth to ask what that meant, then closed it. I suspected I wouldn't understand the answer. "I'll talk to Benson today."

"Good. Put all your designs for Golightly—is that what you called it?—on the shared server and let it be. We're done with it. Not a penny more, but if someone can glean insights from the time and resources you've spent, all the better. I hate to call it a complete loss."

"It's not a loss at all. Already ideas have come from the work. And Golightly has incredible potential."

"Not enough, Mary. We're entering the fourth quarter and we've got some quick improvements and advances to get out the door. Margins are solid on the battery line, and we can push a couple new iterations. I'm encouraging you to use your days and company resources wisely."

"I understand."

"You brought this on yourself, you must see that. You robbed everyone, robbed WATT by holding your ideas so tight. And now? We simply can't throw more resources at it. You must remember there is no I in *team*, but it's emphasized a great deal in *pride*. I doubt that's the reputation you want circulated, that you put yourself above the team and are the only one capable. It not only stifles synergy, creativity, and group cohesion, it causes irrefutable harm."

"That sounds serious."

She gave me a flat smile, unsure if I was agreeing or, as my dad would say, being sassy. I wasn't sure either.

She then crunched her way out of the gravel. I glanced back to my car, wondering how my *reputation* would suffer if I hopped in and sped home.

⟨✦⟩

I tapped the treadmill from eight- to seven-minute miles, then returned my gaze across the paths and park to WATT's building. The sun hit one spot on the blue-black glass and it glowed like a magnifying glass on a sidewalk.

Almost four years ago we moved WATT out of Craig's garage and into our present office space. We went from random casseroles a friend or parent dropped off to espresso for breakfast, sushi for lunch, and two state-of-the-art gyms packed with the latest equipment and floor-to-ceiling windows, so that while running, cycling, rowing, or stepping, we could look out onto these paths and ponds and feel tranquil.

I did not feel tranquil—and hadn't for some time.

A hand appeared before me. I pulled up and then stumbled. The treadmill raced on as I stretched for the emergency cut-off button. The hand hit it for me.

"Whoa." It gripped my arm. "Hey . . . I'm sorry. I didn't mean to startle you."

I hopped off. The ground moved beneath me; I wobbled straight. "You didn't."

Nathan slid his hand to my shoulder and held me firm. "I said your name three times. Where were you?"

"Pondering my future with Karen."

Nathan stepped back and looked around. I did the same. There were only three others in the gym. Two guys from Trillium and one woman from Stellnet.

"I heard about your morning talk. Was it that bad?"

"She was right. Nothing is private in this place. Who told?" I grabbed the towel off the side rail and attempted to press away the red and sweat from my cheeks.

"A couple people saw you talking as they arrived."

Nathan's hair needed a trim. Over the past month he'd cut his days at WATT from five a week to two. Other than our walk and talk on Friday, I hadn't really looked at him in a few weeks.

Standing here now, I realized how much I would miss his smile and the odd sense of excitement-meets-comfort I found in his presence. And his ear—I would miss the way Nathan listened.

"I'm to help Benson on his hearing device. We met this morning and discussed some changes. It's an amazing achievement really—the size of a few grains of rice. But that's not what's so bad... I keep replaying what Karen *didn't* say. It's more than one product, it's where we're headed that's at stake."

"That's a hefty conclusion to draw from things not said."

"But you don't disagree."

Nathan didn't answer.

"And ... she declared an all-hands-on-deck to prepare for fourth quarter, but stopped by my desk just now to make sure I knew it didn't include me. She actually wished me well on my two-week vacation."

Nathan smiled and addressed my insecurity rather than my

statement. "She wants to systematize processes so they aren't reliant on an individual. It's not personal, and it's the way corporations have run for years. In many ways, it makes sense. If all goes well while you're gone, it proves her point." He crossed his arms and stepped back again, bumping into the treadmill next to mine.

"But it's not the way we work."

"True, but she's the one who has Craig's ear right now, and that's right, she should. He hired her." He raised his hand to stall my counterattack. "She's got a long record of success, and he paid a lot to bring her on board."

I pressed my lips shut.

He smiled again. "No comment?" He tilted his head toward the check-in counter. "I thought you might need cheering up, and I knew this would be the last day I'd see you before you go."

I followed the gesture to the counter. There sat my favorite kind of cupcake, from my favorite shop. Hey Cupcake's Red Velvet.

"Call it a commiseration-congratulations cupcake."

"How did you know?" I dashed toward it.

"You lit up like a kid at Christmas when I brought cupcakes to celebrate Craig's birthday. I figured I'd hit upon something special."

"You did. Cupcakes surpass Christmas." I picked it up and held it toward him. "Share?"

At his nod, I headed to the outer doors. "Come on. We'll even go outside, just for you."

"How can cupcakes surpass Christmas? That's not normal."

I yanked several hand wipes from the dispenser and hip-checked the door open to lead him across the dried grass, the mulch walk, and the tinkling stream to the pond, one of the few with surface-nipping koi.

"It's normal when Christmas gets mixed up with life and . . . Let's just say it's not my top holiday anymore."

"It was nice and cool in there." He pointed back to the building.

I sat on the bench. "But you love the heat. It 'warms your bones.' Wouldn't you rather be out here?"

"You remembered that?" Nathan dropped onto the bench beside me. "I was cold for three straight years in Boston. I don't think I've gotten over it."

"I wouldn't know. I've never left Texas. Not even for a vacation." I peeled back the wrapper and pulled the cupcake in two. I held both pieces out.

"I won't take your notion of defecting to Boston too seriously then." He nodded to my offering. "You take the larger."

"They're the same." I studied them. One was a little larger. I offered the smaller to him and leaned back on the bench.

"Good choice." He chuckled and examined the bright-red cake. "Benson was championing you today. He said you've dug into a few of his projects over the past couple years and solved problems he hadn't anticipated."

I shrugged away the praise and focused on my cupcake—and waited. I knew Nathan well enough to know he was leading me somewhere.

Two bites and he spoke again. "Why didn't you ask him or Rodriguez to help you with Golightly?"

I narrowed my eyes at him. He caught it and lifted his hands, one filled with half a cupcake, in surrender. "I'm just curious."

"We both know you are never 'just curious.'" I dabbed some cupcake off my lip.

Changing the subject or stalling too long wouldn't work on Nathan.

"The math worked, so the configuration should've worked,"
I explained. "It came down to artistry. It's one thing to get help
with the objective, but the subjective? We've always 'owned' our
own projects here. A design bears our creative signature and is an
intrinsic part of the designer's professional identity . . . The failure
felt like something within me, and that got too complicated. I can't
explain other than I didn't, and maybe couldn't."

Nathan didn't comment. Instead he nodded as if I'd satisfied
his curiosity and nothing more needed to be said.

I followed his cue and bit into the cupcake again.

"This makes everything better. Thank you." Cream cheese
icing hit my nose. I rubbed it away.

"Craig saw me with the cupcake. He'd forgotten you were
going on vacation and got all twitchy. He'll miss you."

"I'm glad someone will."

"I'll miss you." Nathan's voice held no teasing. It was soft and
weighted. "I'm headed to Minneapolis to check out a new third-
party logistics facility with Craig tomorrow, then I'm done. I'll
submit my final recommendations and be off to a new client before
you get back."

"I didn't realize." I crumpled the empty wrapper. "So that was
a good-bye cupcake?"

"I hope not." He twisted to face me. "Aren't we friends, Mary?
At least that?"

I felt my lips part. *At least that?* An image of Moira and her
Heisman imitation floated to mind. Was she right? Had I missed
something?

"We're friends. And we'll see each other, at least I hope we will.
You should come out on Friday nights with us again. Will your
next client be in Austin?"

"Perhaps . . . And I might take you up on that invitation. Friday nights will be less awkward when I don't work here." He smiled at my expression. "Consultants and clients aren't a good mix socially. It's like regular staff feel I'm a spy or a lawyer bound to secrecy. They either say nothing or everything, and I'm in trouble either way."

"Did I do that?"

"Never. You stay right in that middle band. Half the time I'm not sure what you're thinking. Amend that—more than half the time." He faced forward again and took the last bite of his half of the cupcake. "No wonder you love these things."

I peeked at my watch. It was still set to my heart rate: 155. Faster than it beat during a good run. I looked back to Nathan, wondering if he could hear it. I could certainly feel it.

He glanced at me, and I bent over my watch to hide what I was sure my face revealed.

"I should go. I have a lot to wrap up in two days."

"Me too." He stood first.

I started to walk away until a quick tap turned me back.

"I am sorry, Mary. I know Golightly meant a lot to you and I know . . ." He gripped the back of his neck. "Talk to her, okay? Keep Karen in the loop on everything. She'll like that. She requires that. It might help smooth the way forward."

"I doubt it." I caught a sigh before it fully escaped. "Thank you, though. I'll get over it soon enough."

His face clouded.

"I will . . . I have to." I looked back to the building and felt myself falter. I wasn't sure if it was the heat, the run, or that I'd stood too quickly, but my vision swam in little stars. "You will keep in touch, right? Consider Friday nights?" I heard the slight panic in my voice and lowered it. "I mean, I'll see you later?"

Doubt flickered through his eyes as if he was trying to figure out what I was really asking.

"Sure."

We walked back in together, but I was focused on one thought and my need to remember it.

I'll get over it—and him—soon enough.

⟨𝄢⟩

The afternoon, a complete waste, was almost over. My desktops—actual and virtual—looked like those of someone about to go on a two-week vacation. Too clean. I'd also created two new wire figurines: a rhinoceros, complete with a tiny 22-gauge orange horn, and a bright-green bicycle. I was branching out.

Moira's voice interrupted my daydreaming. "Why the long sighs?"

I looked up to see her leaning over the wall. "I had another talk with Karen today, and it wasn't good."

Moira nodded.

"It's no big deal." I rolled my chair a few inches away. "How much can it matter? It's just a job, and engineers are always in demand."

Moira pulled straight as if what I'd said made no sense. "You keep telling yourself that." Then she raised an eyebrow and her voice dropped to a whisper. "Nathan's headed this way." She dropped out of sight.

I rolled back to my computer, and a moment later I heard a finger tap on the metal edge of the low wall.

"Hey you. I'm heading out." He looked down and canvassed my desk. "A rhino and . . . I love the bike. What stymied you today?"

I smiled and shifted the bicycle. "Boredom. We're waiting on a prototype of Benson's earbud and I have no projects of my own right now."

"Ah . . ." He propped himself next to me and picked up a giraffe made from 20-gauge black wire. "Henry in finance told me you gave him a bear for his daughter's birthday. Said it was her favorite gift. Will you make me one?"

"Take her." I closed his fingers around the giraffe. "Her name is Pandora." I laughed at his furrowed brow. "I made her while trying to work out Golightly's power sequencing. Like Pandora's box, each path led to endless problems. But"—I tapped his forefinger—"hope remained. Until now of course."

He handed the giraffe back to me. "Hope still remains, and I'll wait. You'll make one while you solve that sequencing problem. Because I know you—you're not giving up." He grinned. "You'll simply move it to your weekend ponderings. The wire creature that gets you there—that's the masterpiece I want. Maybe a trout?"

"A trout?"

"Any fish will do."

"That seems too easy."

"Who said your solution isn't going to be easy? I suspect it's right there." He tapped my temple so gently I sensed rather than felt he'd touched me.

He reached into his pocket and handed me a tiny brown paper bag. "I forgot earlier. I got something for you."

"You already gave me a cupcake." I shook out an oval-shaped stone. It was cloudy and unpolished, but cool and ground smooth. "Amber."

"I've had it for a while. It's the same as your necklace. I saw it in a shop in Clarksville and thought you might like it. The owner said it's a rubbing stone, a stress reliever."

"Thank you." I touched my ever-present necklace with one finger, his stone within my palm. It was a little larger than a robin's egg. Movement around us caught my attention. People were listening. They always were. I dropped the stone back into its small bag.

Something passed through Nathan's eyes. He scrubbed at his chin and nodded. There was an odd finality to the gesture.

"Thank you." I repeated the words.

"You're welcome." Nathan leaned forward and kissed my cheek. "Have a great trip and please keep in touch. Let me know when you're back."

Before I could draw a breath, he was gone.

Chapter 6

Friday night passed in another flurry of texts, a phone call, and an unexpected visit.

Isabel arrived around eleven o'clock. She was dressed in slim jeans, boots, and a black silk top. Her eyes trailed from my head to my bare toes. "You stayed in tonight?"

I waved her into my apartment, fluttering my hand toward the mess. "It was a long week and I needed to pack."

She stopped and rested her handbag and another bag on my high kitchen counter. "We've got trouble. I completely forgot you've never traveled. You need a passport."

"Like this one." I pulled it off the small pile I'd created on the same counter. "All you need is a form, two pictures, $349, and two business days."

"Of course you took care of it." She gave me a small bow. Dad always said if there was a job to do, I'd get it done and Isabel would make it look good.

I followed her gaze around my apartment. It did not look good. Usually neat and sparse, it looked like a tornado had struck. Gadgets and junk covered the coffee table; clothes were scattered across my bedroom, which we could see through the open door; and tonight's takeout containers still rested on the counters.

Despite Isabel's copious instructions and the fact that the estate was supplying my wardrobe, I had no idea what to pack or how much. She was right; I'd never been anywhere. The farthest I'd gone was from Round Top to Austin when I left for college—a ninety-minute drive—and I'd taken everything I owned.

"It's going well, I see." She walked toward my bedroom. Her boots made a firm rap against the wood floor. "Good call." She pointed to the discarded swimsuit and flip-flops that lay on the floor by my dresser.

She then noticed my unwieldy Austen book and reached for it. Her wrist gave from the weight and she grabbed for it with her other hand. "This thing is huge."

"I got to thinking about Mom. She loved real books, the smell, the weight. So last week I found the biggest copy I could. But for the trip, I also downloaded them all to my Kindle."

"She did love herself some Austen." Isabel turned the book over in her hands. "Remember how she'd prop books on her knees? She said they kept her warm."

"I expect they did." I pointed to the book and scrunched my nose to get the words right. "It is a 'truth universally acknowledged' that reading that whole thing in less than a week proves I am the best friend in the universe."

"Bravo." Isabel flattened her palm on the book's green cover. "And?"

"And . . ."

She sat, waiting for my answer.

"They surprised me. And to be truthful, I'm not quite finished with *Persuasion*."

"You'll like that one. But you can't expect to understand them fully with one quick reading." Isabel pushed off my bed and returned to the small hallway area between my front door and kitchen. She carried the huge book with her and placed it on the counter next to her bag. Reaching in, she pulled out six books and stacked them one on top of the other. "You'll need to spend more time with them." She leaned against the counter. "We'll trade."

My mom's six leather-bound copies of Jane Austen's novels rested behind her.

I backed away. "She gave those to you."

"Only because you showed no interest. Please, Mary. I'm trying to make things right." She put my copy into her bag. "Which did you like best?"

"*Northanger Abbey* was the most interesting. I saw a little of you in Isabella Thorpe." I said the name tentatively, in question. I had so many questions after reading that book, but none would come out well. Isabella Thorpe was not a likable character.

"The antihero?"

"That might be too strong. She was also beautiful and charming and—"

"We can talk about her later . . . I've got to go." Isabel headed the few steps to the door. "I haven't even started packing."

"Hey." I followed her. "I didn't mean to hurt your feelings. I only wondered when you read *Northanger Abbey* and if you liked Isabella's confidence. She's a fascinating character."

Isabel shrugged and looked thirteen again—a flash of vulnerability I hadn't seen in years. She pointed back to the six books on the counter. "Cherish those . . . The car will pick you up first, then swing by my place. I'll probably need the extra minutes. I'll see you tomorrow?"

She asked the last as if it were a genuine question. Isabel had often given me this feeling of heightened expectancy in the past few weeks. Statements had turned into questions and she'd taken on an indecisive stutter-start-stop that was at odds with her usual decisive nature.

It had started long before tonight and my clumsy Isabella Thorpe comparison. I glanced around my apartment as if the cause was material and I could find it.

"It isn't a question, Isabel. You know you'll see me. Is there something—"

She gave a quick head shake—decisive, even brusque. "I'll see you tomorrow. Be ready at noon."

And she was gone.

Chapter 7

I sabel slept most of the plane ride to London. I savored every moment—I watched a couple movies, read my book, ate all the warm nuts and chocolates, and discovered that the seats in first class really did recline into flat narrow beds. At one point I wandered the aisles and found that the entire flight did not have it so good, so I returned posthaste to my fuzzy slippers and Bose noise-canceling headset. Isabel's dad had clearly not skimped on any detail.

Now we sat in the back of a car heading to Bath and Braithwaite House. We had not mentioned the books again. We had not mentioned Isabella Thorpe again. We had not talked much at all. If pressed, I wouldn't know what to say—I was still surprised we were sharing Austen and a trip to Bath.

After all, Austen was another thing that Isabel had "laid claim to," as my dad so aptly put it. She had staked Austen out sophomore year in high school with a book report on not one but all six of the completed novels—which she delivered dressed in a period gown. Our teacher dubbed her his "most brilliant Austen scholar," and she had actually replied, "It was wonderful to read them again. My mother and I read them together when I was young. They meant so much to us."

She avoided me for days after that class. I never said a word, never told my mom or complained. I also never read another Austen. I doubt Mom noticed. There were other novels, other things to fill our time together. And in the end, she gave Isabel her beloved copies.

I glanced at her. Isabel faced the window and had for the past couple hours. She seemed deep in thought and much less excited than I thought she'd be as we approached her "ultimate escapist experience."

I counted fields and cottages as we dipped farther into the countryside. London had given way to pastureland hours ago. There'd been an uptick in traffic and interest around Oxford, but as the car dropped farther south to Bath, pastureland reclaimed our view. A light rain dampened the fields, the roads, and the car's windows, making the world look obscenely green and lush.

"It's hard to believe we're in a drought back home. I've never seen so much green. Is this how you remember it?"

"We lived in London and I don't think we ever left the city. If we did . . . No . . . I don't remember a thing. Isn't that odd? I was eight when we left, but not a single thing." Isabel stretched to see from the car's front window as we topped a hill. "Look. Bath."

The car's hum turned to a pebbly rumble as smooth road gave way to cobblestones. The driver's tired gray eyes captured mine in the rearview mirror. "I thought I'd bring you in on the A3039, then to York Street, so you can see some of the sights. It's a Sunday, so no shops are open yet, but some will be after noon. Welcome to Bath, ladies."

A low sandstone-colored city opened in the valley before us,

punctuated vertically by church spires. It was larger than I anticipated. From my reading I'd almost expected to find a Regency town.
Brigadoon come to life with horse-drawn carriages and strolling
ladies. I almost laughed at my own absurdity. It was two hundred
years later. Of course Bath would be modern, industrial, filled with
shops, cars, and even a factory spewing smoke atop a distant hill.

Our driver tapped his window as we turned the corner. I felt
reassured; Brigadoon existed—curiously well preserved.

"This is the heart of traditional Bath. Right there are the famous
Roman Baths, first used by the Celts, long before the Romans. They
are already open for the day; over a million tourists a year visit there.
And up here . . ."

I plunged toward Isabel as the car took a sharp right turn.

"Landsdown Road comes right into Bennett Street and the
Assembly Rooms." He stretched his arm across to the passenger
window. "You cannot come to Bath without visiting there."

He drove through a large roundabout with a sign announcing
The Circus, then steered into a gentle and broad arc to the right.
There stood a long, semicircular row of townhouses, completely
contiguous and—semicircular. It spread for what seemed like half a
mile and was the most extraordinary street I'd ever seen.

"Wouldn't it be fun to have a compass large enough to measure
this? It feels like a full one-eighty degrees. It's gorgeous."

Isabel shook her head at me, but she smiled.

The driver twisted in his seat and offered me a toothy grin,
minus a few teeth. "The Royal Crescent is beautiful, isn't it? It's
one of the finest examples of Georgian architecture in the country,
built in the mid-1700s. It looks the same today as it did then, and
some of them are private homes. Can you imagine that?"

"Honestly, no, but it is beautiful."

He turned out of the crescent and away from town. "Wait until you see where you're headed. Braithwaite House is a right gem. An American couple fixed it up and it is beyond something grand now."

Isabel pulled herself forward by the driver's headrest. "Is it far?"

"Less than a mile. It's one of the only estates in the county left with its full acreage. I don't often say it, but it was a good thing when those Americans bought the property. They kept it intact. A good number of estates have long been carved up by developers." He adjusted his rearview mirror to capture Isabel's face. "Have you been to Bath before?"

He didn't wait for her answer, but continued his monologue down Weston Road in a long, contiguous sentence. He had much to tell us and, if we were going to reach our destination in a few minutes, his time was running out.

I caught a sign for Braithwaite House. "This is it."

Isabel slapped my arm. "Okay, now I'm getting giddy."

"About time." My excitement matched hers.

She stretched farther ahead. "Look. Look. There's the house."

I held my breath as the large four-story home came into view. I blinked and studied it. Two stories. The tall windows revealed that it had only two stories, but very high ceilings. The beige-toned gravel drive, flanked by mature trees, turned and continued to rise to a car park at the side.

I mentally calculated the house to be at least fifty thousand square feet, but I couldn't see how deep it ran—meaning my estimations could be shy by several thousand feet, if not more. The front featured tall, rectangular, flat windows in the center and curved ones set in deep bays at the corners. I caught glimpses into the rooms where the sun shot through the glass rather than bouncing off it. And fireplaces . . . I looked up and counted eight chimneys visible from my vantage point alone.

"It's . . . it's massive."

The driver heard me and chuckled. "Here we are, ladies. Braithwaite House." He pulled the car to the front door and made a dramatic skid on the gravel. He then twisted to almost fully face us. "I've never been in, mind you, but they say the queen herself could stay here and not be disappointed."

I faced Isabel. "Are you ready? This could be your Pemberley or Netherfield Park, or even your Kellynch Hall."

Her face glowed. "I'm beginning to believe in my own thesis. Let's go." She gestured to the car door.

I climbed out, a sense of awe welling inside me. Colin Firth had never occupied a moment of my time; Downton Abbey never swallowed a Sunday evening; and even love, friendship, and zombies had failed to entice me into the theaters. But I agreed with Isabel—I was beginning to believe her thesis too. This was the ultimate escape and a luxury beyond imagining.

She stood beside me. Eyes fixed on the building, she grabbed my hand and squeezed tight. "It's perfect."

I followed her up the six broad front steps to the single-pane glass front door. It opened out, while an enormous wood one opened into the house.

Between the two open doors stood a woman, tall and elegant, dressed in gray with silver hair. Something about her glowed against the now graying sky—as if they were one and she was the brighter iteration.

Although she came from inside the house, she wore a deep-gray waxed coat and hot-pink rubber boots.

I felt her track my gaze to the boots and back. When our eyes met again, hers danced with laughter.

"Aren't they marvelous? I was crossing from the side garden when I saw your car." She pulled her hand from a gardening glove and stretched it toward me. "Welcome to Braithwaite House. I'm the manager, Gertrude. You must be Miss Dwyer."

"I am." Isabel stepped fully in front of me and captured her hand. "Isabel Dwyer. It's nice to meet you, and this is my friend, Mary Davies."

Gertrude nodded at the rushed introduction and peered at me over Isabel's head.

"It's lovely to meet you as well, Miss Davies." She cast her gaze beyond us to the driver. A single flick of her fingers conveyed he was to bring our bags in a side door somewhere to the left. She then retreated into the house and wiggled the same fingers to beckon us to follow.

"You are the third academic group to stay with us this year. You are the professor?"

"Doctoral candidate."

Gertrude continued. "First your Jane Austen Society of North America came to town last spring, then we hosted Harvard's English department in July."

"The entire English department?" Isabel's mouth dropped open.

I suspected the rest of her thought had fallen out. I bumped her. "UT's endowment is big too. Get tenure, then make a plug for this."

"Shh..."

Gertrude's pink boots squelched across the marble floor. "Come through to the Day Room—that's what I like to call it. I had Duncan lay a fire there to chase away the damp."

I lagged behind, not wanting to miss a single detail—the black-and-white checkerboard pattern on the hallway's marble floor; the oil paintings, landscapes and portraiture, that covered the hallway walls beyond the high arched front foyer; the door and window frames, with their unpainted wood polished to a deep high-gloss brown. The play of light was beautiful across the different colors and textures. A bevel in one of the windows caught an errant sunbeam and shot a rainbow across the floor.

Gertrude waited for me at the doorway of the small sitting room. Entering, I understood why it spilled green light across the hall. Its walls were covered in pale-lime wallpaper with white sprays of flowers. There was a single seating arrangement situated by the fire, composed of two delicate and feminine-looking chairs and a love seat. A small writing desk sat under the window, its chair set at an angle as if someone had been writing letters and had just left the room—maybe to check today's menu with Cook.

The Day Room, as Gertrude called it, faced the back of the house, where the gardens spread the expanse of a football field before dropping, perhaps into a valley, beyond our vision.

"The Stanleys decorated this as a lady's sitting room, as it would have been fashioned in the early nineteenth century. They used only historical papers and fabrics. It would have been called a drawing room, and back then one might find the lady of the house writing her correspondence at that desk in the mornings or painting screens near the fire with friends in the afternoon."

She seemed pleased with our rapt expressions—at least I assumed I looked as hypnotized as Isabel.

Gertrude continued. "The Stanleys are only the second owners in the house's history. Upon purchase in 2004, they put the house through a full five-year restoration. All work was completely in keeping with the Secretary of the Interior's Standards for Historic Preservation. And while these Austen offerings focus upon the Regency period, spanning from 1811 to 1820, or the Regency era, which encompasses a larger time period from 1795 to 1837, the main section of the house dates slightly older than that." She glanced to Isabel and broke into a self-conscious smile. "I get so used to that introduction I sometimes forget. You likely know all that."

"Not about this house."

Isabel's eagerness called forth a more relaxed smile in our host.

"Well, the house is older. Construction began in 1760, but it wasn't finished and situated with the Duke of Walsham's family until 1780, which puts it right at the doorstep to the Regency era. And in Bath, Regency is good for business." Her smile turned yet again. This one felt laced with cynicism.

I tapped off the years on my fingers. "Only the second owner in 258 years? It must have been hard for the Walshams to sell."

"Braithwaite was the family name and yes, I expect change of any kind is hard." She spread her hands flat as if offering us the house. "Today you'll find every service and amenity you can imagine . . . and tea. I'll send Sonia in with the tray while I register you."

Gertrude left us to ourselves, and I joined Isabel by the fireplace. I dropped into the blue-and-green armchair across from her and sank into its cushions. "Have you ever?"

"No."

We sat grinning at each other. I felt just as I did the first day we met in second grade—struck with awe and expectancy. Something new was about to begin.

"Thanks for inviting me. Really, Isabel, I mean that, and I'm sorry I pushed back. It was beyond generous of you."

She held up her hand. "We both know you pushing back was long overdue. Don't say any more."

I opened my mouth, but stopped at her whispered, "Later, Mary. There's a lot I need to say, but please, not right now."

I closed my mouth. Something new had already begun. "Later then . . . I wish my mom could see this."

Isabel nodded. "Me too. She'd love it . . . So would your dad."

"I'll need to take lots of pictures."

Gertrude returned with a young woman carrying a large silver tea tray. The scent of sugar and orange enveloped us. On the tray were balanced a small plate of sandwiches, another with slices of glazed orange cake, two teacups, and a beautiful teapot covered in butterflies.

My stomach growled before I could slam my fist into it. "Excuse me. That was rude."

"Not at all. You must be starved. But this might sit better than a heavy lunch." Gertrude reached to unload the tray before it was set down and gave a quick round of introductions.

Sonia, it seemed, was the young woman assigned to us. While she helped with serving, cleaning, and everything else, she was also available at any time of any day for anything we might need.

I felt my eyes widen. This was a role I hadn't anticipated: mistress with a maid. Was I expected to know what Sonia should do? She was only a few years younger than we were, and I certainly hadn't expected to say things like "Please arrange my hair" or "Please brush out my skirts" to a woman I might call a friend. I pushed out a weak, "Thank you. I'm Mary."

Isabel threw me a wry glance, as if I was already messing up the fiction.

Sonia, however, smiled as she wobbled the tray onto the table.

Gertrude was pouring tea midflight. Sonia stepped away from the settled tray just as Gertrude lifted the two full cups and handed them out.

She continued without missing a beat as Sonia backed from the room. "I've had Duncan take your bags to your room. As soon as you've enjoyed your tea, please go to the top of the stairs. You'll find the Green Room third door to the right. If you'd rather not go alone, I can guide you, but this is your home for two weeks, and we have found that letting guests find their way immediately helps them feel more relaxed." She tapped her fingers together as if checking off items on a list.

"We usually start the festivities the day after arrival so your first night is more comfortable. Sonia will meet you in the Green Room later to show you where everything is and take you on a tour if you wish. You will find dresses already in the wardrobes, and Sonia can assist if any need alterations."

She straightened from the table. "You'll find your visit here to be steeped in the stories and culture of Jane Austen. As you read on our website, many guests choose characters from her novels they wish to embody during their stay, but don't feel you must. Others simply enjoy the costumes, the carriage rides, and the long walks, then sit here and check e-mail, work, or watch television. There are televisions hidden in most of the common rooms. I can show you the panels and—"

"We won't be needing any of that. Right, Mary?" Isabel straightened. "For my research, I really would like us to stay as close to the fictional dream as possible."

"Most guests do. We had one private party who took over the entire house for a *Mansfield Park* re-creation. It trespassed into reality when one of the wives really did run off with another man."

I'm sure I looked shocked, but Isabel's eyes lit with excitement. She was forming chapters right before my eyes.

"I've made a list of some of our most engaging happenings and scheduled interviews as requested."

"Excuse me?" Isabel choked on her tea. "Interviews?"

"Your father asked me to arrange a formal interview schedule with the staff." Gertrude darted her eyes between us. "You didn't know?"

I reached for Isabel's cup as she struggled to stop coughing. An array of emotions chased through her eyes—shock, anger, resignation. "We haven't talked lately, but thank you." Her face hardened, but her tone remained calm, even gracious. "May I get that from you tomorrow?"

"We'll review it at breakfast." Gertrude waited on Isabel for confirmation, but she was miles away.

I stepped into the gap. "That's fine. Thank you. Is there Wi-Fi?"

Isabel came back to the moment in time to glare at me.

"I'll hide it," I promised, "but I will need to touch base with work. Two weeks is a long time to be gone."

Gertrude laughed. "We have a fully equipped business center with most common supplies provided, including charging cables, Ethernet, and HDMI cables too. We also have accounts with several server storage facilities for larger data needs. And the wireless signal is boosted throughout the house. You can check e-mail from the shower, if you wish."

"Larger data needs?" My interest was piqued.

"Business doesn't stop even for a holiday. I believe Mr. Stanley negotiated a corporate merger over whist one afternoon. The entire game and meeting were conveyed via a sixty-four-inch monitor on the back lawn . . . The Stanleys' desire is that you feel like a member of the family or a beloved guest," she continued. "There are no restrictions on what you may do or where you may go, and you need only ask for anything you desire. You'll find, along with your luggage, Duncan has laid your keys on the desk in your room. Your present attire is appropriate for tonight's dinner." She paused, then added with a warmer tone, "Then tomorrow, please pick a gown and enjoy all Braithwaite House has to offer."

"Thank you for making us feel so welcome." I felt the need to say something kind. For some odd reason, I got the impression that although Gertrude knew the speech cold, she didn't like delivering it.

She turned, then twisted on her boot's heel to face us again. "In case I don't see you out and about later, I'll tell you now that drinks and light appetizers will be served in the front parlor before dinner, and we will dine in the formal dining room to the left of the front door. After-dinner drinks will be served in the library across the hall—or I may move our party to the larger assembly room, as we have a Swiss family who arrived yesterday, and cards and games might be nice for the child. An Austrian couple checked in this morning and are staying the week as well. You will enjoy the Muellers. They are very pleased to be here, and I expect, Miss Dwyer, they will pepper you with questions."

Isabel frowned, as if chatting about Austen or trying to bring others up to speed might impinge upon her own immersion.

Gertrude didn't notice that she'd said anything displeasing. She simply nodded as if to say *job done* and left the room without another word.

Her withdrawal revealed Sonia, who had been standing behind her in the doorway. "I've checked your room," she said, "and your luggage is already there. There's a bell pull hanging near the desk. If you ring it after you have rested, I'll come straight up to answer any questions or take you on a tour."

I nodded, but there was no way I was ever going to pull some rope with the expectation that Sonia would come running.

Once she left, I raised my cup to Isabel and smiled. "There you go. We've been invited to a house party, as beloved guests, and we've got two weeks to enjoy every bit of it."

Isabel had a look in her eye, almost like a general assembling the troops and putting each person, each detail, into place.

"Are you okay?" I asked.

"For a man who doesn't communicate much, my father is making himself loud and clear this time." She shuddered as if resetting herself. "No matter. You are right. I've got two weeks to enjoy this. Let the fun begin."

Chapter 8

Sandwiches, tea, cake, and a warm fire soon revived us, and we went in search of the Green Room. We found our way back to the front hall, peeking in every open doorway and cracking those that were shut. Halfway up the stairs, Isabel stopped to study a headless mannequin dressed in burgundy silk.

"This is what we'll be wearing." She reached up and ran her finger around the inside of the dress's delicate lace neck. "I think it's genuine. Look at the stitching and the silk ribbon pulling it together. It's all hand sewn, and you can see the disintegration here at the edges. Circa 1810, I'd say. Within a couple years of this, they quit using ribbon or tapes for their dress closures."

"Show-off." I laughed.

"I'll let you wax long on the house's wiring later." She smirked in reply and moved on.

The last steps landed us in a broad portrait gallery running each direction along the entire front of the house. It was capped at the ends with the sweeping bays I'd seen from outside. Large paned windows lined the exterior wall to let in light. The gray was clearing to blue outside.

The opposite and interior wall was colored a deep, almost blood red and was filled with paintings and lined with bookcases and display tables.

"Look at all this." I ran my finger along the case's lead trim. It was warm to the touch. I bent and looked up into the case to find a small row of lights wired beneath.

"Get up." Isabel tapped my back.

"The lighting is mounted in a tiny tape strip, not discrete bulbs. I've never seen a strip that small or this application."

Isabel tapped my back again before walking on. I stood and studied the cases. They were filled with gloves, small books, tiny silver brushes, pillboxes—little personal treasures. It looked as if someone had dumped out the contents of the bedside tables and dresser drawers and arranged them for display. What was once personal and intimate felt oddly sterile and detached from use, if not meaning, in these cases with their small lights.

I thought back to my mom—the things she loved. The things that had meaning because she loved them. Her Austen books, now resting in a box on my bookshelf; her sterling silver pillbox tucked away in a shoe box in my closet. She had loved that tiny treasure, kept it close and polished it with the edge of her nightgown when the silver oxidized.

Isabel backtracked to me. "I'm sure all this came with the house. They probably had boxes of junk in the attic. One owner for all those years? Can you imagine what it must have been like, or how hard it'd be to let all this go?" She turned around slowly to take in the grandeur of the house.

"I doubt they had a choice." My focus remained on the glass cases. "Makes you realize how deep the loss went. When industrialization came along, all this was a relic of the past." I glanced to her.

She looked doubtful that I knew what I was talking about. "Junior year. The Industrial Revolution and the rise of automation."

She conceded with a nod and walked ahead again.

I called after her in a half whisper. "Can you imagine what this place must cost to run, not to mention the five full years of renovation?"

"I know what Daddy paid for two weeks." She faced me and continued by walking backwards. I raised a brow and received a wagged finger in response. "Uh-uh ... You don't want to know."

"You're probably right. Hey ... Come see this." I stopped in front of a small velvet-lined and gold-latched book. It looked like a little handbag, a lady's evening clutch, but it was a book.

Isabel materialized beside me. "It's the Book of Common Prayer. They carried those to church on Sundays." She pointed to the small book next to it. "And that's a hymnal. Often one lady carried one, another the other, and they shared."

"My mom used to have her own hymnal. It was as marked up as her Bible. She sang in the church choir for years. She said she felt closest to God in music."

"She did?"

I glanced up. It always surprised us both when there was a memory we didn't share.

"She stopped when I was young; I can only remember a few Sundays. She stood at the end of the first row, near the stairs to the altar, and after she couldn't sing at church any longer, she'd sing softly while I played the piano ... She left that hymnal to me. Some of them were the first songs I learned to play."

Isabel looped her arm through mine and squeezed it. "Where is it now?"

"Home. With all the other music books I haven't touched in

years." I caught sight of the small brass sign on the door next to us. "Didn't Gertrude say the Green Room?"

"In Austen's day they often named rooms this way." Isabel opened the door and stepped inside while I glanced back to the glass-encased hymnal. Something about it struck me as sad and lost.

"Come see this," Isabel called.

I leaned against the doorjamb and took in our room. By nature and inclination, I'm a hard sciences girl, raised by an electrician, and—although I love a special Saturday visit to Nordstrom's makeup counter and I did once spend an entire paycheck on a pair of shoes—I'm not usually drawn to fluff and frill. But this room, all twenty by thirty feet of it, took my breath away. It transported me through time, into time, and told a story. The colors were rich and varied like the notes from the hymnal I'd just left in the gallery.

First and foremost, the room was green. My favorite color. Again, I was struck by its abundance here and its absence in my life. Austin, Texas, had not been green lately, and suddenly it felt more than "not green"—it felt dry and barren. Here I found it in shades I didn't know existed and in textures I'd never touched. Green draped every soft surface.

The two full-size beds were covered in pillowy moss-toned duvets and draped in an avocado patterned silk held at the top by carved wood finials and gold detailing. The colors contrasted yet complemented each other. A small sofa sat beneath the central double window, covered in white with a spray of kelly-green flowers and a profusion of pillows. The desk chair, another armchair, and the curtains were upholstered in fabrics covering the spectrum from citrus to forest, with textures that made me want to rub them against my cheek. And the rug...I kicked off my shoes. It was thick and soft. My toes sank within the teal and gray swirls that covered the floor's surface area.

As for hard surfaces, they were reserved to a writing desk set in front of the smaller side window, two large wardrobes on either sidewall near its respective bed, and the twelve inches of wood floor bordering the rug.

I turned my attention to the walls. They were papered in a cream color with laurel-colored vines running up every few inches. I ran a finger along a vine. It was slightly bumpy.

"Could these be hand painted? It's three-dimensional."

"Sure, lots of papers are, especially the really expensive ones." Isabel dropped her handbag on one of the beds. "It feels a little too haute couture, doesn't it? Modern meets Regency meets Limitless Funds."

"Stop." I flapped a hand to soften the command. "You're used to this stuff, but it's the most exquisite room I've ever seen. Don't tell me this doesn't floor you. You can't have seen anything like this often—ceilings this high, the fabrics, the furniture. Look at those carvings."

Isabel tipped her head back. "Plaster." She then caught my expression and held her hands up in surrender. "What? They are. Plaster moldings applied to the ceiling. That's how it's done."

"Please. Let me enjoy this."

"You *are* getting into it."

"It's surprising me too." I lifted a shoulder. "Maybe because it's all so different. It feels like nothing I could imagine. What in my world approaches this?" I walked to the window and grabbed a section of the curtains. "Come feel this. It's so heavy. I bet there's more than fifty pounds of fabric here."

"Do not weigh the drapery." Isabel laughed as she headed to a large standing wardrobe.

I opened the door to the bathroom and ogled again. Here historical accuracy ended. It was all white marble with two porcelain freestanding sinks and a huge claw-footed soaking tub. The fixtures were curved and arched like the necks of swans and their slight warm coloring let me know they were finished in polished nickel rather than chrome, including the heated towel rack mounted outside the shower. But it was the sense of air and light that captivated me most. Sunlight shot through tree limbs and dappled the marble in subtle color. It was so much softer than the bright white glare of a Texan sun. It felt like music. Brahms' Lullaby compared to Def Leppard. And . . .

"Isabel, get in here. The floor is warm; the marble floor is heated. You've got to come feel this."

She came in and didn't comment, but I could tell . . . She liked the floor as much as I did. Her lips were pressed tight. She was trying not to smile.

"Oh, let it out."

She giggled and clasped her hands together. "This is so awesome. The pictures were gorgeous, but I didn't expect this."

A few minutes later I crawled under the desk to plug in my adapter and insert cables for both my computer and my phone. "I wish I didn't have to do this. It feels like I'm betraying the house." I backed out and sat on the carpet, pressing my hands into the soft wool. "What do you want to do now?"

Isabel was curled on her bed tapping on her phone. "Give me just a second to e-mail my father, then we'll dress up."

"What?"

Isabel didn't reply. "There." She dropped her phone onto the bed and stood. "Come on. I checked both wardrobes, and since these dresses are shorter, this wardrobe must be mine." She bent out of sight on the other side of her bed. "The bottom drawers are full of underclothes. They've even got boots and silk slippers." She pulled up one champagne-colored shoe with a pink bow on the toe. It looked like an icing rose atop a birthday cake. "I sent in all our sizes. They even asked color preferences."

I pushed off the floor and opened my own wardrobe. "So everything here is tailored to fit me? In a week?"

"Actually, they had a month—I knew you'd say yes." Isabel tossed out the sentence with light flippancy, then froze. She faced me. "I *wanted* you to say yes, Mary. I didn't *know* you would, but I hoped. That's why I called your dad." She pointed back to my wardrobe. "Pick one. Did you notice the palette?"

I turned back to my wardrobe. All the dresses had that same high empire waist of the mannequin halfway up the stairs. Some were thick and heavy, wool for winter. Others were light. Cotton for warmer weather. And some, just a few, were organdy and lace or silk, with intricate flowers or swirling designs embroidered on the bodices and hems. And all were warm colors—browns, purples, oranges, dark yellows.

"Thank you. All my best colors." I pulled one out and draped it across my bed. "Can you imagine peeking into the room to find this lying across the bed? Maybe Lizzy has just stepped into the bathroom and you missed her, right before the Netherfield ball."

"Or Emma has pulled out one of her good gowns to go to the Coles' party. After all, she'll lead the dance. She takes special care in hopes it might be with Mr. Churchill, but of course, little does she know . . ." Isabel raised her brows as if keeping back a salacious secret.

"Or maybe we've just missed . . ." I searched my newly gained repertoire of knowledge. "Anne going to check on little Charles, because this is Mary's room and she's wearing this dress to dinner at the Musgroves', terrible mom that she is."

"Well done." Isabel's grin lit her whole face. "You're deep into *Persuasion* now." She pulled down a dress, a light summer sky blue, from her own wardrobe. "Come feel this."

It was made of thin wool and felt heavenly soft, like cashmere.

"These aren't cheap." I picked up the one I'd pulled down, a dark-brown silk with red and rose flowers embroidered along the edges. There was a narrow matching ribbon circling each sleeve. It looked rare and special and long enough to fit my five-nine frame. "Not cheap at all. Look at this detail . . . This one's definitely the loveliest." I held the dress at my chest.

Isabel stepped to me and dropped the gold chain around my neck over the dress's collar. The stone's gold and maple tones glowed atop the brown silk. "The color matches your eyes and it's beautiful with your amber."

I reached up and fingered the necklace my father had given me for my college graduation—a beautiful chunk of polished and radiant amber hanging from a delicate gold chain. It was the only piece of jewelry I always wore. He loved that *amber* meant "electron" in Greek. It was to remind me of him, of our work each and every summer, and, in many ways, to signal my bright future. Dad was optimistic like that. It also meant "beaming sun." I liked that definition best; it felt hopeful. And after Nathan's recent gift of the unpolished rubbing stone, it now reminded me of him too. "You know—"

"*Electron* from ancient Greek. Electricity. Energy. Light." Isabel smiled and recited words I'd probably told her a thousand times. I appreciated that she understood its importance to me and never made fun of the gift, just the fact that I constantly defined it for her.

"Nathan, that guy at work, gave me a piece of amber the other day. It's about the size of a small egg, unpolished, and you rub it to relieve stress."

Isabel held the blue dress to her body and crossed to the full-length standing mirror. "That was nice of him. I haven't heard his name in a while; I thought nothing was happening there."

"Nothing is. He saw it in a shop, I guess."

She turned back to me. "Put on the brown. You'll be beautiful in it."

Her lack of interest surprised me. She was constantly trying to set me up, console me after bad dates, or celebrate with me after great ones. I laid the dress on my bed to untie the laces.

"We're not wearing them outside our room, right? Gertrude said dressing begins tomorrow."

"We're just having a little fun." Isabel slipped on the blue dress.

The brown one dropped over my head and cascaded in a wave of silk to my feet. "Will you fix the back?"

I felt Isabel first work the eye hooks, then pull the ribbon at the neck tight. "No wonder we have our own Sonia," she said. "If you came here alone, you'd never get yourself into these."

"No one would come alone. That'd be embarrassing, wouldn't it?" I twisted to catch her eye; after all, she was the expert.

"You'd be surprised. True escapism is not something people tend to do in groups. Like many addictions, it can be kept hidden."

My back arched as she pulled and the bodice cinched into place. I did the same for her, and then we walked together to the standing mirror.

It was like stepping into a fairy tale. Better actually. The dress was formfitting, flattering, and the silk caught the light and shimmered. It danced around my hips, and the weight of the embroidery allowed for a good swish at the ankles. I gently twisted to enjoy its movement.

"Let's do your hair. I'll play Sonia and 'arrange' it for you." Isabel pulled me into the bathroom and pushed me onto the small stool in front of the vanity. In minutes she had my hair piled high, twisted and secured with bobby pins. She even pulled a ribbon off the neck of another dress to weave through the coils.

I moved my head from side to side. "Whoa . . . Where'd you learn how to do this?"

"YouTube."

A firm, and loud, knock silenced us.

"Miss Dwyer? Miss Davies?"

I froze.

"Yes?" Isabel managed a normal tone. She caught my eye in the mirror. "Oops . . . I rang the bell. I thought more tea might be nice." She narrowed her eyes at something she saw in mine. "It's why it's there, Mary. It's no big deal."

"May I help you?" Sonia called again.

"Never mind. I completely forgot I pulled the cord. We're fine."

"Thank you," I added to Isabel's call.

I almost wilted with relief. I did not want Sonia to open the door. First, summoning her felt wrong. Second, as much as I loved the feel of this silk and thought I might enjoy dipping a toe into Austen's world, the appearance of a witness terrified me.

True escapism is hidden.

Sonia called again. "Very well. If you are interested, drinks will be served soon in the front parlor. Or you can meet everyone at dinner this evening."

"We'll be right down." Isabel owned the full reply this time.

"That's it . . . What if she'd walked in? We look ridiculous." I stood and yanked at the dress's neck. "Get me out of this."

"Slow down. Sit. There's a knot." Isabel worked at the ribbon, then used it to pull me back down. "And it's not silly, Mary. This is a big deal to me."

I dropped to the stool and watched her in the mirror. She kept her eyes on the knot.

"You're right," I acknowledged. "But actually dressing like this is harder than I thought. I feel exposed somehow. Like in costume, I'm not actually covered, I'm naked."

"Stop squirming or you'll feel more exposed than that. You'll feel 'humiliations galore.'" She cast a sideways smile into the mirror. She knew Austen, but we both knew *The Princess Bride*.

She paused and watched me. "Or shall I ring for Sonia again and get some help?"

Chapter 9

Within ten minutes, Isabel turned the key in the lock and we headed to the stairs. I hesitated. What if Sonia came to "freshen" our room? Dresses and loose ribbons littered the floor like confetti.

While Isabel led the way down the gallery to the front stairs, fully set on what was ahead, my mind remained fixed behind us—first by my wonder of this experience, then by my reaction. I couldn't deny that when Sonia knocked on the door, I had felt fear and—Isabel wasn't wrong—humiliation. Dressing up felt weak and frivolous—like a part of my armor was being stripped away. Rather than the "ultimate escape," it felt like an augmented reality. And I had two weeks of this to look forward to. Would it get easier? Worse?

Isabel must have felt me stall behind her. She stopped and studied me. Again, I felt exposed.

"I was willing to take the risk. Are you?"

My expression must have conveyed confusion, for she twirled a finger at me, circling me from head to toe.

"I need you here, Mary, but it was a risk to ask you. What you must think of all this . . . And you can't deny it; it's all over your face."

She continued down the stairs. I took a deep breath and ran my hand down the front of my khakis to smooth the wrinkles. Slim beige pants, a deep purple sweater, and ballet flats for me. Twenty-first-century simplicity at its best.

Isabel, on the other hand, was dressed in a bright multicolored blouse and an A-line skirt that swirled about her knees with each step. She skipped down the stairs. The skirt bounced in ripples of black.

I caught up to her on the marbled floor. I stood in a black square, she in a white. "Hey . . . I'm sorry. But you have to cut me some slack. You just said you knew I'd have trouble with this; you can't get angry now because you were right. Besides, I'm here. I'm all in."

"Are you?"

I felt myself nod.

Isabel smiled. She believed me. "Okay then . . . Do I look okay?"

"I love the blouse."

"I found it on sale, then had it tapered further. It's not too tight?"

"Not at all." I felt a pinch above my ear and pulled a bobby pin from my hair. "How many of these are in here?"

She batted at my hand. "Stop pulling them out. You look gorgeous." Her tone lifted, and I recalled her first question.

"You too; you look beautiful."

"Thank you." She gave me a slow smile at odds with the quick repeat her fingers tapped against her thigh.

"You're going to be fine, Isabel."

I expected a "parlor" to be small, wood-lined, and intimate. And this room was paneled, but it was huge. First glance revealed four furniture groupings and plenty of carpeted space between. The small band of guests stood gathered around a fireplace so deep and tall, I could have stood within it.

Isabel immediately entered the scene. I heard "Good evening, I'm Isabel Dwyer" in her signature notes as I scanned the room from the doorway.

There was an elderly couple, at least eighty, and I knew they must be the Muellers. Mrs. Mueller sat next to the fireplace and watched, an amused expression on her face, as her husband took one of Isabel's hands in both his own.

The Swiss family Gertrude had mentioned stood nearby. The wife was tall, only a little shorter than me, blond and delicate. The husband looked two, no, three times her size—six-foot-sixish, muscular and thick. Boxing huge? Soccer huge? Do soccer players get that large?

Presently he was discussing something very serious with his daughter, a tiny girl, blond like her mom. Gertrude had mentioned an eight-year-old, but this girl looked about six. Her obvious concentration and distress led me to believe her father was delivering a serious reprimand. Then she popped something into her mouth and smiled.

"*Est-ce délicieux?*"

She nodded. "Not bad at all, Papa, but not my favorite."

Isabel called me over. "Mary, this is Mr. Mueller. He and Mrs. Mueller are here from—"

"Herman and Helene, please," Mr. Mueller cut in. "We are from Salzburg." His chest swelled and broadened.

"*The Sound of Music*," I blurted.

Helene laughed. "You would be surprised how often we hear that."

"It was not real; they do not get it right."

"He is talking about the movie," Helene clarified.

Herman thrust a finger straight at me. It was an aggressive gesture, but the arthritic bend at the second knuckle softened any insult. "They changed all the names to make them American sounding. They were not Americans and they did not carry their suitcases over the Alps while singing. They boarded a train to Italy. It was all scheduled and planned and dangerous enough without all that hiking, chasing, and whistle blowing."

"Herman," his wife said.

He waved her off. "There was no need to change the truth. They did it for the Americans; they do not understand." He turned back to me. "But they still sing. That is true."

"Who still sings?" I looked back to Helene.

Herman shifted into my line of sight. "The Von Trapps."

"Aren't they all..."

"They are dead, yes, but the great-grandchildren, Werner's grandchildren. Another lie. They named him Kurt in the movie. They still sing. They make recordings and tour. They came to the *Altstadt* music hall last year. The Von Trapp Family Singers."

"We saw them in concert," Helene added, then addressed me directly. "Where are you and your friend from?"

"We're from Austin, Texas. I work as an electrical and design engineer for a technology company, but Isabel here is an Austen scholar. This trip is part of the research for her dissertation."

Helene brightened. "Gertrude mentioned her. I consider it very lucky to have her here. I have loved Jane Austen all my life, but I have never studied her. I only know her stories, but your friend will know what our characters should do and say."

"Our characters?" I tapped Isabel's arm.

"You didn't read that part? It was on the website. You get to pick a character."

"But Gertrude said we didn't—"

Isabel flicked her fingers at me, breaking contact. "No matter. I picked Emma Woodhouse from *Emma*. We can be in the same story. What about Harriet Smith or Jane Fairfax?"

I schooled my expression.

"Well then, what about Eleanor Tilney from *Northanger Abbey*? You liked that book." She added a pointed inflection to her words.

"If I get to choose, I'll guess I'll pick a heroine too. What about Catherine Morland from *Northanger Abbey*? And if you still want to be in the same story, you can be Isabella Thorpe."

Isabella, as I'd stated the other night, was beautiful and charming. But her other attributes hung between us now—she was also a cunning and manipulative gold digger who relished adoration and flattery.

Isabel matched my flat expression. She glanced to the Muellers, then shot her gaze back to me.

"I've already chosen Emma."

"I choose Catherine." I nodded to the Muellers, as if their witnessing the decision made it final.

I liked Catherine Morland. She was young, naïve, got carried away with Gothic romances, and made some pretty poor assumptions, but she was also honest, kind, intelligent, and eager to get things right—and she wasn't the sidekick. From page one, with her plain tomboyish beginnings, I cheered this unlikely heroine on as she grew, learned to think for herself, question, and take ownership of her own story.

Helene looked between us. I sensed she caught our swirling

undercurrents. They were so tangible I almost raised my hand to swipe them away.

She cleared her throat. "I have chosen Mrs. Jennings from *Sense and Sensibility*. Isn't she fun?" Her words landed like a white flag between us. "And because I have long since married off my own children, I have little to do but . . ." She slipped a piece of paper from her pocket and read, "'project romance upon all.' Also I have a knack for the 'quick discovery of attachments.'"

Isabel scrunched her face. "Austen's description didn't deter you? She has some fine qualities but is also marked as *vulgar* immediately."

"Isabel." I squeezed her forearm. She was annoyed with me, not Helene. She was angry that I had balked at dressing up and about something else I had noticed. Her eyes had hardened right after she'd dropped my necklace upon the dress. Isabel was ticked with me on multiple levels.

She shirked away from my grip as I addressed Helene. "I loved Mrs. Jennings. She enjoyed her daughters and life and had fun, and in the end was an incredibly practical woman."

"I thought so too. Good common sense." Helene's words held hesitancy now.

"And you, Herman?" I said.

Isabel stood silent.

Herman looked confused, and his eyes clouded with worry. "I . . . I don't remember. I haven't read any of the novels. I don't want to disappoint Helene. This means so much to her."

Helene stood and looped her hand through the crook of her husband's arm. He laid his hand over hers. I could see it whiten as he pressed hers close. No words were spoken, but by looks alone, I sensed he could never disappoint his wife. He took a breath. "She said I could play . . ."

Helene supplied the name. "Sir Walter Elliot from *Persuasion.*"

"She said it was okay I hadn't read the story. Is that right?" he asked Isabel.

Helene and Herman both looked at her and waited. Isabel's eyes flashed an entire conversation but her lips remained pressed together, before she remembered her manners and offered a flat smile.

"Are you discussing characters?" The blond joined us. "I'm Sylvia Lotte. I chose *Pride and Prejudice*'s Jane Bennet, and Aaron—he hasn't read the books either, Herman—will play Mr. Bingley." She waved her daughter over and held her so she faced Helene. "And did I hear you say Mrs. Jennings? You and Clara will have fun. There aren't many young girls in Austen, so she will be styled as a young Margaret Dashwood from *Sense and Sensibility* as well."

"You come sit with me, 'Margaret.'" Helene returned to the love seat and patted the silk cushion beside her. Clara looked to her mom, who gave a quick, eager nod, then sat beside Helene, feet swinging a couple inches above the floor. "We will have great fun together," Helene whispered to her.

Clara grinned. "Mama says I don't have to be Margaret in our room, and I can play my iPad there too."

Helene looped an arm around Clara and squeezed.

I stepped away as they talked on about characters, dress, and activities. Sylvia was keeping up with Isabel. They batted facts, impressions, and Austen trivia back and forth like players in a tennis match.

Clara came over to me and lifted a small plate.

"For me?"

"Duncan is passing these around. I tried one."

"Thank you." I selected a small corner of toast spread with brown. "I'm Mary, by the way."

"You're not going to like that." Isabel's voice, so close, startled me.

I popped the bite into my mouth and widened my eyes.

"See? A country pâté. You should see your face."

I wiped my face free of any expression. From the set of her mouth, Isabel was apparently still irritated with me. "I know you better than you know yourself, Mary. You hate stuff like that." She looked down to Clara. "Are there other things you can go and find?"

Clara shoved her plate at me and skipped away.

"I'm sorry if I upset you. Can we call a truce?"

Isabel shook off my apology.

I gestured to the table. "You needn't have sent Clara hunting for food. There's plenty here."

"Gives her something to do." Isabel picked up a cheese square. "Have you ever noticed how silly adults sound when talking to kids? My nanny used to do that. It's embarrassing. But kids Clara's age are the absolute worst. They want to be treated like adults, like you could actually be friends with them, and yet they demand almost as much attention as a toddler." She turned and surveyed our compatriots. "I hope she doesn't ruin this."

"She's eight, Isabel. She can't ruin anything. Besides, Austen had plenty of small kids in her books."

"No, Sylvia was right." Her *right* ended with a hard *t*. "Other than Fanny's sister in *Mansfield Park* and Catherine Morland's barely mentioned sisters, there's only one real girl and a few boys by name; none got any page time." Isabel leaned closer. "But if she doesn't ruin it, *he's* sure to." She sent a smile Herman's direction.

"He's lovely," I whispered back.

"He's completely unaware. Probably Alzheimer's." Isabel mumbled the words.

"Isabel." Again I whispered her name, but she didn't hear. She'd turned away and, without missing a beat, replied to another of Herman's concerns.

I studied the plate Clara had left in my hands. There was one pâté-laden toast point left. I put the whole thing into my mouth and chewed.

Clara returned with another plate. This one carried four cheese puffs.

"Duncan has these now and Papa said we'd like them. Mama said I could only take four."

"I hope you don't mind; I just ate the last pâté. I think I liked it. What did you think?"

"It was not my favorite."

I smiled; she wrinkled her nose.

"That's what I'm supposed to say if I don't like something."

"Very polite. And to be honest it wasn't mine either."

After a round of more personal introductions, I decided that I liked Sylvia and Aaron Lotte, and I adored Clara. I was about to ask her what we should eat next when she tugged her dad's sleeve.

"Now?"

"Fine." He crouched to address her eye to eye. "You may go, but you must meet us back here in one half hour. Do you understand? Where is your watch?"

"One half hour." She clasped her wrist and nodded at each word. Then she skipped away.

I looked at Aaron.

"Gertrude said she should act as if the house is hers and

assures me there is nothing off limits. So, naturally, Clara wishes to test the theory."

"Naturally." I smiled—and excused myself as well.

Clara had almost made her escape with me only a few steps behind when Gertrude walked into the room. Rather than the waxed coat and bright-pink boots of earlier, she was now dressed in a black sheath dress with diamonds in her ears. They sparkled in the candlelight. Her gray hair fell like platinum, smooth and sleek, to just above her shoulders. She glowed—as if part of the room and the experience.

After a few words to Clara, who spun on her Mary Jane heel and rejoined her parents, Gertrude turned to me.

"Good evening, Miss Davies. I'm so glad you made it down before dinner. Did you and Miss Dwyer rest?"

"Please call me Mary, and not exactly . . . The room is magnificent."

"Thank you. The Green Room is very special. The desk in that room was a gift to the family in 1815." Her gaze drifted up, perhaps envisioning it and enjoying the memory. She then looked around the room and called, "Everyone, please, dinner is served."

The "experience" was to begin tomorrow, but I could feel the pieces dropping into place. We had chosen our characters and now we processed to dinner.

Herman held his arm for Isabel.

Aaron shot him a glance, then followed his lead and lifted both of his in a stately and stiff fashion—one at a ninety-degree angle, one at a low forty-five. Sylvia and Clara grinned and latched on.

Helene grabbed for my hand in delight and pulled me beside her. "Herman will be fine. He is already having fun and as he relaxes he won't get so fretful. He does like to make people feel important." She nodded to her husband's back. "It's his gift."

Despite how close her words hit the mark, her face was so kind and open I was sure she hadn't heard Isabel's comments. I squeezed her hand in unspoken thanks.

Herman and Isabel led our small retinue. Even from a few steps behind, I could tell Isabel was relishing his attention. She tucked close to the older man and her head bobbed up and down as if she, like our driver upon entering Bath, couldn't hold in all she had to share. Herman was listening and nodding with equal vigor.

We made a wide variety of noises as we crossed the marble hallway—the tap of high heels, the squish of a driving loafer, the thud of an oxford, and the soft shuffle of a couple pairs of ballet flats. I wondered if tomorrow we'd hear only a masculine heel strike and a whisper of soft silk slippers.

The dining room was long and narrow. A rectangular table, capable of seating at least twenty, stood centered beneath two impressive chandeliers. Light bounced everywhere and refracted to reveal the full spectrum off the crystals and the glasses below. It appeared as if thousands of tiny rainbows had been tossed into the room.

It felt like magic. White linen place mats allowed the light to bounce off the table's red-black mahogany, adding warmth to the cool light display. Clara stopped so abruptly I bumped into her.

I laid a hand on her shoulder. "Me too, kiddo, and look at that table. There are no lines. It's one piece."

Gertrude heard me. "It is. When they renovated this room it could not be easily moved, so they built a crate around it. Then they suspended it by a pulley system to finish the floor underneath it. The family's history has that it came in through the windows before they finished the stone and glass work in 1767." She gestured to several small tables nestled in the two bay windows. "I've seated us together this evening, but the individual tables will be set in the morning for breakfast."

I walked down the table's right side as Clara followed Isabel down the left.

"Thank you, Herman." Isabel ignored Clara and scooted her chair closer to her clear admirer. If possible, Herman's chest swelled further.

"Herman told me this is an anniversary trip." Isabel leaned forward to address Helene, on his opposite side.

"It is long overdue. Our first trip in over twenty years." He matched Isabel's posture, blocking the view to his wife.

"We are celebrating our sixtieth anniversary this month." Helene addressed the entire table.

Herman turned from Isabel to Helene. He looked at her again with such devotion that I understood her indulgence as he gave time to Isabel. In my world, I'd call it flirting—regardless of the inappropriate age difference—and so would Isabel. In his, I suspected, he would call it chivalry. And Helene was right; it was a gift.

"Let us toast to your anniversary." Aaron raised his champagne glass. "That is truly something worthy."

"Helene always wanted to come to the English countryside and most especially to Bath . . . We've saved twenty years for a trip, and this is what she chose." He leaned to Isabel. "Like you, these stories have been very important to my wife."

He then looked around the table and seemed surprised by

what was before him. We held our glasses high. Herman reached for his so quickly he almost toppled it.

Helene helped him right it, and he joined us. "We celebrate my beautiful bride."

In that toast and flowing from Herman's obvious warmth, the disparate groups in the parlor became one. Conversation flowed smoothly throughout an endive salad, a light fish course, and a main course of beef tenderloin, before the discussion turned to tomorrow and the roles we were to play.

"It was not a hard choice for me. I have always loved Elizabeth Bennet," Helene said, "but my time for her has passed. At my age, I am more suited to Mrs. Bennet or Lady Catherine de Burgh. But either would give us all a headache. But Mrs. Jennings, as you said, dear . . ." She looked to me. "She enjoys life and has fun."

Helene's very nature contradicted any comparison to the sour and dour Lady Catherine of *Pride and Prejudice*.

"Jane Bennet was easy for me too. I've never been called quiet or demure, and I've wondered what's so alluring about those qualities." Sylvia winked at Aaron.

He raised a brow. "I find nothing alluring about them at all. Ice and fire, dear." The raised brow became a wink and his wife turned crimson.

"What about . . ."

"And . . ."

The names and stories flew faster than I could catch them. Isabel sat in the center of it all and visibly relaxed, but having read all the books in a week, I was soon lost in the myriad ancillary characters.

"And you, Mary? How did you choose Catherine Morland?" Gertrude's soft question reached me through the cacophony.

"I . . ."

Isabel lifted her chin. "I'm not sure she's right for you. We'll discuss it tonight. You might have more fun joining with Clara and Helene."

Clara grinned at me. "Mama says I'm Margaret from *Sense and Senseless.*"

"*Sense and Sensibility.*" Isabel's correction fell harsh and heavy.

Clara bit her lip and frowned at her lemon tart.

The conversation continued, but Clara did not raise her head again and I did not speak. I suspected we struggled with the same weight. I laid down my fork. She pushed her tart away, untouched.

"Clara," Sylvia scolded from across the table. "Don't push your food. We eat what we are served."

"I won't," Clara whispered and scowled at the dessert.

"Children." Isabel's voice lifted with her eye roll. "You'd think she'd love this. When I was young I used to believe there were two separate compartments in the stomach, one for dessert alone and nothing else could fill it. In fact, Daddy used to tell me that . . ."

Isabel's words drifted away from me as I watched Clara. She was losing the fight against tears.

"Youth does not excuse my daughter's behavior."

Isabel and Sylvia squared off. They knew it; I knew it. I looked around and suspected everyone caught the tremor of battle. Aaron watched his daughter.

"As I said . . . Children." Isabel dismissed the conversation and returned to her own dessert.

Sylvia focused on hers as well. Clara was the only victim. She had struggled for Isabel's attention all night and now she had it—and her mother's. Her lip trembled and she caught it between her teeth.

I stretched my leg out under the table and kicked her foot. She looked up. "Hi." It was all I could think to whisper, but it seemed to work.

"Hi." The single word released the poor lip. She wiped her hand across her nose and slid the plate back in front of her. Sylvia sent her a brusque nod.

"Gertrude, whom do I see about reserving horses for tomorrow? Clara started riding lessons last year, and I think she'd enjoy riding here." Sylvia's chipper voice sent a clear message: Clara was forgiven. Horses were her reward.

Gertrude, now standing, gestured for us to adjourn to the parlor. "The path is marked to the west of the house, and you'll find the staff ready to assist with riding, fishing, lawn games, and walks throughout the property. Or you may tell me the time you'd like to ride and I'll notify the stables."

"We could go for a ride together." I met my new eight-year-old friend at the end of the table. "You could teach me. I've never been on a horse."

"If you can do that, I'll think you have magic in your little finger." Isabel walked behind us and spoke in the high-pitched tone she hated.

Clara and I both halted: Clara at the comment, me at the tone. Isabel bent to face her. "Mary is afraid of horses. She doesn't like animals whose heads are at the level of her own. Isn't she silly?"

"I am not afraid of them. I've just never had any interest in riding."

Isabel continued. "When I was your age I won local events. I had trophies all over my room. I'm not sure Mary knows what a pommel is." She offered a trilling laugh and led Clara into the hallway. Her heels clicked a steady tap across the marble.

I watched them go.

"Are you coming?" Aaron paused. As his eyes shifted from me to his daughter and Isabel, I plastered on a quick smile and fell into step beside him. "Thank you for being kind to Clara. This trip might be hard on her. I am afraid we misunderstood the formality when we booked our reservation."

I, too, watched Clara trail Isabel across the room. "Please don't let us make it that way. Ignore us if you need to."

Aaron's eyes narrowed at Isabel, then he directed his gaze back to me. We agreed—there was no ignoring Isabel.

We took the final step into the parlor. It had been transformed. The furniture was now situated into one large cluster centered on the fireplace. It was a wonderful subtle signal that we constituted one party now. Family members. Beloved guests.

The side tables were fully laden with coffee and teas and a variety of small desserts. Sonia picked up a cup to pour coffee for Isabel.

Isabel flicked her finger to me. "She'll drink that. Could you pour me a cup of tea? Preferably mint?"

"Certainly." Sonia handed me the cup and prepared Isabel's tea.

"Thank you." Isabel looked around the room. "I expected more guests to be here. There must be more rooms. It's such a large house."

"There are eight more guest rooms, but this isn't our busy time. The house is full most weeks in summer, from June into September, and then the Stanleys either come for Christmas or rent the house for a private party in December."

"Are they all costumed parties?"

Sonia shook her head. "We book out several of these in the high season, but parties that book the entire house may choose anything they wish. We had a two-week costumed party last fall that required us to shut off all amenities invented post 1820. We did everything by candlelight and had to spread druggets under the dining room table."

Isabel understood. I did not.

Sonia smiled at me. "Huge drop cloths—as they requested we not use the vacuum. It was that or sweep the carpet each day, which was what we had to do anyway in every other room."

I nudged Isabel. "Don't even think about it. This is authentic enough." I imagined poor Sonia sweeping carpets and Clara missing her iPad—and me, my Wi-Fi.

Chapter 10

When the Muellers started peppering Isabel with more questions, I drifted away to wander the house. I didn't want to stand by and witness any more cold comments or implied disdain.

I suspected it was my fault. The Isabella Thorpe comparison had hit its mark on Friday, and I'd gotten annoyed and followed it up today. It was unkind of me. But when she suggested Emma's sycophants for me rather than a real character, a leading lady, I felt again all the reasons I'd refused the invitation in the first place.

Even so, I hadn't been wrong in the comparison—and tonight proved it. Isabella Thorpe was coy, charming, and often manipulative. Isabel could be all those things. Both women also had shades of kindness, loyalty, and vulnerability—even brokenness. They were certainly both fighters. When backed into those painful places, they came out swinging.

I wondered, as I crossed through the front hall, if I needed to offer another apology to put us back on an even keel.

Braithwaite House was laid out along a central hallway on the first floor, stretching from the front door to a large set of paneled windows at the back. Small side hallways led me to the smaller, more intimate rooms such as the Day Room, the library, and what I suspected was a gentleman's sitting room. It was all brown and deep red, with horses pursuing foxes across the upholstered armchairs.

I passed from room to room through a web of connecting doors. I also came across many with closed doors. Isabel and I had opened a few that afternoon, but nighttime made the trespassing feel more intrusive—I left them shut and headed back to the front stairs.

The upstairs was designed along the long gallery at the front of the house with two main hallways dividing it toward the back like a squared-off U. I suspected the guest rooms were on the outer sections of the U, allowing each to have an exterior wall and lots of windows. Those facing the sides of the house would enjoy views of the hedgerow maze on one side and the terraced gardens on the other. But guests in the back rooms would get the best views of all. I walked to the end of one of the hallways and could make out the formal gardens in the deepening gray. There were rows upon rows of rosebushes and sculpted hedges. I envied guests who visited during the high season, as Sonia had called it.

At the end of the gallery I found a flight of narrow stairs. The door was painted the same color as the wall and when shut would make the passage invisible. At the moment it was cracked open and very inviting. I looked up and down. The stairs were lit by the same Edison vintage bulbs I used in my living room. I loved the look of the exposed filament and the yellow to orange light they produced—and I loved the mystery of a set of secret stairs.

I wandered down and soon found myself in a long, narrow hallway. Cupboards lined its entire expanse. There were at least fifty small doors, unmarked, on each side.

I opened one. Linens and lightbulbs. Another, china. The next, silver. I shut the cupboard and turned around, finally recognizing there might be limits to "nothing is off limits."

"Mary? Are you lost too?" Clara had entered by a door I hadn't noticed.

"Hey . . . I'm not lost. I'm . . ." *Being rude and rummaging through their closets.* "Are you lost?"

"Daddy finally said I could explore." Clara opened a cupboard. "This one has lots of glasses in it." She shut it and moved on to another. "I'm lost on purpose. Gertrude said I could go anywhere and even gave me a torch, but it's not working." She rattled the offending flashlight.

"May I see it?"

She handed it to me, and I led her to the hallway's end, where we found a broad window ledge. She scooted onto it. Her legs dangled, and the heels of her Mary Janes tapped the wall.

I unscrewed her flashlight and dropped the batteries into my hand. "How is it you speak English with hardly any accent?"

"Momma is American, like you, but she sounds different. Daddy is from France, but he went to college in the States. That's where they met."

The batteries looked fine. I tapped my phone and shot its light down her flashlight's barrel. There was oxidation on the coils. "Give me a second . . . Besides English, how many languages do you speak?"

"I can't count Italian yet. I just started this term." She counted on her fingers. "English, German, and French. We learn them all in school."

"Only those?" I lifted a brow and she smiled. She was missing the teeth on either side of her front two. "Wait till you see this." I pulled at the hem of my camisole and used it to rub the coil until it shone. I replaced the batteries and handed it back to her. "Now try."

Clara pushed the button, and bright-white light hit me in the eyes. "You made it work. Thank you." She hopped down and hugged me at the waist.

"Do you want to see something else cool?"

She nodded and I dashed back to the third cupboard on the left. It wasn't what I expected. I opened another, but they all looked the same and I couldn't remember. I opened silver, cleaning products, candles, and china before I found it. "Lightbulbs."

I grabbed a lightbulb and walked back to her, pulling two of my homemade "rings" from my elaborate hairdo and loosening a slew of bobby pins in the process. I pulled a third piece of wire from my back pocket. "Can I borrow your flashlight again?"

She handed it to me without question. I dropped out the batteries, unraveled the wire ponytail holders, and attached one from the battery to the lightbulb. Then I pulled out my key and attached it to the lightbulb with another wire. "Watch this." The final one completed the circuit. The lightbulb glowed.

"Can I try?"

At my nod, she reached, then paused.

"The current isn't strong enough to hurt you. I promise."

She made the connection, and her smile was brighter than the bulb.

"Can I show my parents?"

"Of course, but I'm not sure running through the house with a lightbulb is a great idea. How about I carry it and come with you?"

We disconnected our project, and she grabbed my hand to drag me from the hallway.

"I can't wait to see their faces."

I let myself be pulled. "I can't wait to explain what we've been up to."

A half hour and countless questions later, I found my way back to the Green Room. Isabel was already curled in bed.

I plopped onto mine and relayed the adventure—wandering the house, opening dark cupboards, finding Clara, making a light-bulb glow, and the embarrassment of explaining the entire story to her parents, including how I'd fixed the flashlight.

Sylvia had shuddered good-naturedly at the thought of what her daughter might do next if left unsupervised or, worse, met me in another abandoned hallway. She had a lot of questions and concerns. But Aaron, in a soft voice with a quiet smile, declared it a very good scientific experiment.

His contradiction had not pleased Sylvia, which I thought might amuse Isabel.

She was not amused. By the end she had sat up straight and swung her legs off the bed. "You didn't."

"It was easy. A simple circuit. No big deal. Tomorrow I might teach her—"

"It's not the circuit, Mary. It's the fact that you dug around in the pantry, a private, off-limits-to-guests kind of space, and started making your little projects. You're a guest here, not the resident electrician." She slapped her hand over her eyes.

I pulled back. "I . . . I'm sorry."

We sat, knees almost touching in the small space between our beds.

"No." She dragged her hands down her face, pulling her cheeks with the gesture. "That wasn't fair. I shouldn't have said that." She arched her back and pressed her fingers into the inner corners of each eye. Only then did I notice she'd been crying.

I tapped her knee. "I am sorry, Isabel. I won't embarrass you again."

"No . . . It's not you. I was horrid tonight. I felt horrid. It's . . . How can a place I've never been bring up memories? Daddy used to take me on business trips after we moved to Texas. He'd get furious when I acted like a kid. I was eight. What did he expect?"

She took a deep breath and dropped her voice low with a hint of southern drawl. "'With decorum.'" She let her father's two words rest between us before continuing. "I clearly didn't have any, because he quit taking me and hired Mrs. Trumbull. Remember how she smelled like onions? And her voice . . . Anyway, after hearing from Gertrude about the interview thing and—he's in my head tonight."

I caught the *and* in her statement. "You talked to him today, didn't you?"

"He replied to my e-mail." She shrugged. "It usually takes days to get him to reply to anything."

"And?"

Isabel's father, distant at best, had declared his job done when she graduated college. But I often wondered if he had ever thought raising and loving Isabel was his job. He never attended any school events, wasn't around for birthdays, even missed high school graduation. In August, right before we parted ways for college, Isabel and I came home from the movies to find a Honda CRV in her driveway. Mrs. Trumbull handed her the keys with a note: *Happy Graduation. It's a three-hour drive to Dallas. Work hard at SMU. Dad.* He didn't even pretend he might make it to her college graduation.

Isabel didn't reply. Instead she reached for her phone, tapped it, and handed it to me.

Isabel. Your petulant e-mail was not appreciated. I expected a thank-you rather than a temper tantrum. Five years is ample time to finish your doctorate and move on. If this trip is what you need, as you have claimed, just thank me. Do not pout. Consider it my gift to you, but if you continue to behave like a child, you may consider it my last gift.

This reply is also to inform you that Abby and I were married yesterday. As you set yourself against her from day one, your attendance was not desired.

Please e-mail when you reach the States. I want to hear of your progress. If you wish to meet us for Christmas this year, I expect you to be more respectful to Abby.

No signature line. Certainly no ending endearment.

I pushed off my bed and dropped next to her. "Yesterday? You're thinking that's why he sent you here. He couldn't have written that, Isabel. Maybe Abby planned the timing and wrote the note."

"He wrote it. I know Malcolm Dwyer." Her head rested on my shoulder. "I hate him, Mary."

"You just think you do." I drew my arm around her.

"I hate me." She took a deep, shuddering breath and then, without another word, headed into the bathroom.

I crawled back onto my own bed and reached for my phone. Now I missed *my* dad. My screen saver was a picture of his latest gizmo, the Skittle dispenser.

Your little projects. I loved those projects—loved the time my dad and I spent planning and creating them, and the fact that, in our ways, we both still built them. What was Golightly, after all, other than a gizmo I dreamt up and wanted more than anything to create?

I tapped his face to text him.

> Arrived safe and sound. The house is beyond belief. Thanks for bullying me into coming. I miss you.

I received an immediate reply.

> Bully? Who me? Father knows best, right? You couldn't turn down a trip like that. Please take lots of pictures. Is Isabel dancing on her toes like she did when we gave her that movie?

I'd forgotten "that movie." Dad and Mom gave Isabel the four-DVD commemorative set of the BBC 1995 *Pride and Prejudice* for Christmas when we were fifteen. She had just given that huge report in English class and they were so proud of her. She took it home and watched one each night in succession for weeks on end. She called them her bedtime stories.

I glanced to the bathroom, realizing that, even then, they understood what I had failed to see. I tapped my phone and lied to my dad . . .

> She's having the time of her life. Couldn't be better. I forgot to tell you I paid the invoice for sponsorship at the ball park. Ballard Sign Shop will print and hang the signs.

When a reply didn't come, I checked my phone. Four bars of Wi-Fi . . .

Sorry you're still worrying about the business. I got
three new clients and should hear back on the concert
hall proposal you submitted soon. Go have fun. Sorry to
bother you.

I closed my eyes. I'd always liked helping Dad. The boys were much older and had been gone so long—it often felt like the two of us. Only occasionally did I see it from his side.

Sorry I mentioned it, Dad. And hey, I texted you. Have a great
day. I love you.

Isabel and I passed in silence, she coming out of the bathroom as I went into it. She kept her eyes trained on the carpet. When I climbed into bed a few minutes later, she reached up and switched off the light.

"Thank you for saying yes. I thought he was being so generous, offering to pay for a friend. He just wanted to appease his guilt, if he ever has any."

I twisted in the dark to face her. "I'm sorry, Isabel."

We were quiet for a few minutes.

"Doesn't this remind you of when we used to camp in your backyard with that lantern your dad made us?"

It didn't surprise me that her thoughts shifted to my dad. It was my dad who cooked us burgers on Thursday nights as far back as I could remember and popped popcorn during Sunday evening movies. He had made Isabel almost as many gizmos as he'd made me.

"How is he?" Her voice was barely above a whisper.

"You know him . . . Behind in his billing and allowing customers to pay what they want. After Mrs. Harris paid him a chicken for rewiring her chandelier last month, I standardized some of his pricing for him. Not that he's going to tell clients about it."

"Mrs. Harris is rich. She should pay double."

"But apparently she roasts an extraordinary chicken."

"She probably wants to show off her culinary skills. Didn't her husband die a few years ago?"

"If that's her goal, poor Mrs. Harris." I snuggled deeper into the pillow. "Despite enjoying the chicken, he'll never notice her, not like that."

"He'll always love your mom, but he's a relational guy. He needs people. I can see him marrying again."

I twisted onto my back. I could just make out the ceiling's plaster detailing in the dark. "I don't think he'd risk it. How could he? Watching her struggle for so long . . . It was too hard."

"No one should be alone. I don't think we're wired for it." She offered nothing more. Moments later a faint "Are you happy?" drifted toward me.

"Not now. I'm feeling a little alone over here." I answered with bravado, but it came out flat. I rushed to cover the anxiety her observation had left. "Let's see . . . Even though Golightly is dead, I'm still employed. Fall is coming, so running is getting easier. Dad's business, despite chickens and undercharging, is back in the black and he's good. He seems content. And I–" I stopped as Nathan and his impending departure flashed through my mind. "I'm fine."

"Any word from Brian?"

Brian. A nice guy Isabel set me up with months ago–a few laughs, a few dates, then silence.

I punched the pillow to soften it in the center. "I know you thought he'd call again, but he never did."

"Did you call him? . . . Never mind, I know the answer. You were too good for him. Hopeless romantic that you are."

I smiled into the darkness. As much as I resisted it at times, it was nice when someone understood. Isabel and I often joked about this hidden aspect of my personality. Looking at what we did, how we dressed and even spoke, one would think Isabel the romantic. Yet she was oddly pragmatic about love and relationships, almost clinical. Me, on the other hand? No one but Isabel and my dad knew, but I cried at rom-coms, adored Broadway ballads, and really did believe in true love—fairy-tale-knight-in-shining-armor love. But I suspected it only existed in actual fairy tales.

"Nathan never asked me out either, despite the rubbing stone."

"Who? Oh . . . You mentioned him earlier. I never thought much of him."

"He's a good guy." Her sharp tone stiffened my spine. "Moira said I was the one who pushed him away. Maybe it was self-protection. There are some guys who you just know if you fell for them you'd go too deep and never make it back."

"So you don't end up a puddle?"

"Something like that."

Isabel turned to me. "He wasn't all that, not how you described him. If you'd dated him, you'd have been disappointed."

"Okay . . . And you? Other than the e-mail, are you happy?"

It was time to shift the conversation. Besides, Isabel had only asked the question so that she could answer it. At each sleepover, late in the night, she'd whisper it in the dark. *Are you happy?* was her litmus test to prove all was well in her world. And I'm sure tonight felt like a good time to take a measurement.

"Tonight didn't change anything. It's the same story, just a different chapter. But I'm getting the message. He wants me . . ." She fell silent before adding on a slow exhale, "Off and away."

I sat up. "Don't quote that book. Don't think about that book."

She had violated our fifteen-year-old rule.

"Had to. The writing is on the wall. Or in the e-mail. Get going, Isabel. Get it done, Isabel. Go. Go. Go."

Dr. Seuss's *Oh, the Places You'll Go!*

Isabel's dad gave her a copy for her eighth-grade graduation gift. We opened it together, we read it together, and apparently, unlike the book's other ten-million-copies-sold recipients, we hated it together. While reading it, Isabel could hear only her dad's voice pushing her up and out. And I could only see my life's story spread before me on the book's single dark page. I remember those words, that description, and the fact that it was truly the only dark page smack in the center of a razzle-dazzle rainbow-colored book.

You can get so confused that you'll start in to race . . . Headed, I fear, toward a most useless place. The Waiting Place . . .

Mom was deep into a couple bad years at that time, and waiting was what we were doing. Scott was at college, and Dan and Curt had long since graduated—had their own lives and wives. It was Dad and Mom and me . . . And we three waited, probably Mom most of all.

Reading that book was the first day I realized I was powerless and alone. I hated that page and that feeling. It crept into me in the dark, suffocated me and terrified me. But I found I could avoid that feeling of helplessness too . . . It didn't exist in math or even in science. Answers could be found and they were solid. You could rely on them, stand on them—no agency, luck, or grace required.

I shifted my gaze from the black ceiling to out the window. There was a yellow glow across the clouds. The moon was up there somewhere. It cast new shadows across the room. I heard Isabel tuck deeper within her covers. I did the same.

"Good night, Mary."

"Good night, Isabel."

Within minutes, she fell asleep. I did not.

Chapter 11

I climbed out of bed to find the moon outside the window. It hovered half in and half out of the clouds. In the charcoal gray, I could see the land slope down then rise into a hill in the distance. There was a tree line at its base. I suspected the stream flowed there—as the water would encourage the tree growth. I turned back and looked across the room.

Eleven o'clock in England was only five o'clock back home. And despite the fact that I hadn't slept in thirty-five hours, I was still wide awake. I grabbed my Kindle from the table and tapped to *Persuasion*—my last Austen novel.

There was nothing "bright and sparkling" about this one. It was subdued, almost melancholy. Heroine Anne Elliot, perhaps my favorite of the Austen women I'd encountered, waited as circumstances and her world closed in around her. She helped where she could, she got tossed about with little care—and she waited. There was no other word for it.

But if Anne's story ended like Austen's others, I knew she wouldn't stay there. She'd get her glorious end, most likely with that handsome Captain Wentworth who kept popping up in memory and now in person. But something told me that, as in real life, it might not be so easy this time.

"Captain Wentworth is not very gallant by you, Anne, though he was so attentive to me. Henrietta asked him what he thought of you, when they went away; and he said, You were so altered he should not have known you again."

I tapped off the Kindle and let my head bump back against the bed's headboard. Poor Anne. I could only imagine the hope, the anticipation, and then the anguish of that moment while Mary had her sport. Austen really had a thing against Marys.

I'd met Mary Bennet first. Then came Mary Crawford from *Mansfield Park*. She initially misled me. She had all the wit and vivacity of a Lizzy Bennet, but it took me time to catch on. She had none of the wisdom—no discretion. And she got no happy ending. And now Mary Elliot . . . We Marys weren't a kind and gentle lot. We didn't grow. We didn't change. We didn't get redeemed.

I threw back the covers, grabbed a sweatshirt to pull over my pajamas, and slipped into my ballet flats. Gertrude's graciousness had welcomed me to the house, and the camaraderie at dinner had made it feel like a home. I decided to wander—again.

I found my way to the Day Room. The dying fire threw off a weak warm light, and I dropped into my same blue-and-green armchair to watch the embers glow.

Soft treble notes captured me. G-sharp. B-flat. The tune changed, and a Debussy song drifted to me through a cracked door I hadn't noted earlier. I cracked it further, but at the squeak the piano silenced.

Gertrude spotted me before I saw her. "Did I wake you? Or are you not tired?"

I stepped into the room. It was about the same size as the Day Room, but painted a soft salmon. There was a tiny fireplace, almost a miniature one, with a lit gas fire; a baby grand piano; and two chairs, only two chairs.

"This is lovely."

"It was the Music Room." Gertrude looked around as if seeing it for the first time. "Still is, I suppose. There used to be a harp sitting where the chairs are and a cello propped in that corner, but both were of little value. I think the Stanleys disposed of them." She nodded to one of the chairs. It was plush, floral, and of a larger scale than the set in the Day Room. "Please join me."

"I'm not disturbing you?"

"Not at all." Gertrude resumed her song. "This is your home for the next two weeks."

"'Clair de Lune.'" In reply to her quick glance, I said, "I started playing the piano when I was ten. That was one of the earliest I learned."

Gertrude looked comfortable seated at the piano bench in a cardigan sweater and soft shoes. Her pants flowed around her legs like wide yoga pants. She finished the last stanza, stood, and gestured to the stool.

"I don't play anymore. I haven't touched a piano in years."

"If you played 'Clair de Lune' at ten, then you were talented. Jane Austen would call you 'accomplished.'" She tossed me a wry smile.

We'd met only hours before, but there was something about Gertrude I understood. It was almost as if I were looking at my mom, or at myself. She stepped back. I could not step forward.

"It's a piano." The unspoken *only* floated between us.

I stepped forward and sat down. I didn't even need to adjust the bench. We were the same height.

I laid my hands on the keyboard. Fists tight. Knuckles white and strong. I had to force each finger to spread wide. I hadn't seen them this open in years. It surprised me how far they stretched. My breath felt shallow, like it did when I stood on the high dive at the pool. Isabel always came up the ladder after me. Without her behind me, I would retreat.

Close your eyes and jump.

I tested the tone. It was rich and true, and the keys held a perfect strike. I warmed my fingers and my memory with a series of slow, heavy scales, and then "Brahms' Lullaby" emerged without summoning. It was light. It danced.

My past swept through me on the notes—lessons from Mrs. Danvers next door; playing for Mom; recitals with Mom and Dad sitting in the front row bursting with pride; more playing for Mom when she was weak, and listening was better than talking, better than sleeping, and the only thing that brought a smile.

Another memory struck, and I heard the discordant note that accompanied it. I'd planned to audition for the piano part in our high school's spring musical. Voice auditions came first, though, and Isabel won the lead role. When it came time for instrumentals, piano had been scratched from the sign-up sheet. Word was that Isabel had insisted that the music teacher, Mr. Lennox, play. *Anyone else would make me too nervous,* she had said. We were close then, but that's when I noticed the few sharp notes in our friendship that never vanished.

I pressed on, letting that memory and others wash over me. Isabel and I had pushed and pulled for years. Iron sharpening iron? We were safe in each other, but never quite. Maybe that's what held us together. Neither of us would have trusted the other had it come too easy.

The song ended and so did the memories.

"You're very good. Why did you stop playing?"

I rested my hands in my lap. "Music is memory."

Gertrude's eyes flickered from mine to the fireplace. "I play *to* remember."

"And I stopped to forget." I ran my hand over the mahogany top. "It's a beautiful instrument."

"I've always thought so." She returned her attention to me. "If you choose to remember more, please feel welcome to practice anytime. There is also a grand piano in the ballroom. You must try it. The acoustics are powerful in there. When the house isn't occupied, I practice there. This is more the equivalent of the housekeeper's room."

The curl of her lips indicated a joke, but she didn't explain it. She pointed to the ceiling. "The servants' quarters on the third floor were converted into three full-living suites during the renovation. I live in one, but I couldn't bring myself to go up tonight. Not yet."

I looked up as if, like Superman, I could see through the walls and peer into her home, and suddenly I knew.

"This was *your* family's home, wasn't it? Two hundred forty-four years in your family?" I cringed as I sank into the chair next to her. I hadn't needed to calculate the years and throw them at her.

"Hard to believe we held it that long." She slipped off her shoe, tucked a foot underneath her, and curled tighter into the chair, displacing any lingering formality between us. "The house never thrived after World War I. Few of the old homes did. Some families adapted, but Grandfather couldn't and Father didn't try. My eldest brother, Geoffrey, inherited in 2004. As I told you, the Stanleys bought it in 2009." She surveyed the room, but I suspected she couldn't see it through the past.

She dropped her gaze level with mine. "He was right to sell; he couldn't support it. But I had this crazy idea I could keep it up, pay the taxes, and even renovate it . . . I never checked my dream against reality."

"It'd be hard to do. I've never been to a place like this. I can imagine paying almost any price to stay." This room alone was worth staying for, with its soft light, rich walls, and ceiling moldings so pronounced they cast shadows.

"My brothers say I've paid too much." We sat silent for a moment before she continued. "Geoffrey thinks I'm stubborn, or crazy, but I find it hard to let go. If I go, who will remember?" Her spine stiffened just enough to roll her shoulders back. "The new owners have been very generous."

"But?" The word popped out before discretion could catch it.

"There are certain things they'd rather I not do, and I understand. It's their home now, and they must manage it as they see fit. And they have saved it. I am so grateful to see it restored. But not using my last name sits hard at times."

"Braithwaite House. Gertrude Braithwaite."

She raised her hand as if answering a roll call in elementary school. "The home is too old. Registered. A name change would've been needlessly consuming and confusing, so the house kept its name and I lost mine. The Stanleys would prefer that I not call out my connection to it."

"I shouldn't have asked."

"I'm glad you did." She studied me, and I got the impression that for her, as for me, the fact that we'd just met was irrelevant. "You're the first guest who has."

Chapter 12

In the hinterland between asleep and awake, music, books, and a world with swirling texture and color wove through me. Austen's books. Picnics and walks to town. Hymns, singing, and the feel of my old piano's sticky foot pedal. *The Giving Tree, Where the Sidewalk Ends, Alice in Wonderland . . . The Little Princess.* Beloved books full of whimsy, giving, mystery, fantasy, and magic. Colors and ideas I hadn't touched in years. The tree bent, offering another branch . . .

I opened one eye. The room was too bright for how tired I felt. I closed it, rolled over, and dug for a comfy spot under the pillow. Then it hit me. It was too bright, and too quiet. There was a hard quality to the silence. Something was wrong.

I sat up and scanned the room. The curtains were pulled back to reveal a cloudless sky. Abundant sunlight illuminated the mess. There were clothes strewn everywhere—not a dress or two, twenty. Isabel had pulled dresses from both wardrobes.

I sorted them by length and rehung them. I then threw Isabel's clothes into a few empty drawers at the bottom of the wardrobe closest to her bed and tossed the rest of her mess into her suitcase on the stand. I did the same with my clutter.

Once I could see the gray-green carpet again, and knew Sonia would be none the wiser, I grabbed a pair of jeans and a sweater and went in search of Isabel.

The gallery was empty. I stood and absorbed the complete stillness. Here the silence felt right. I wondered if I'd ever truly heard it before. The realization of how much noise filled my world only became apparent in its absence. Work and my small apartment always emitted the low-level hum of computers, AC units, and cars on the street. And at work there was always Moira's soft jazz, and at home the upstairs guy's Macklemore.

I sat on a cushioned chair outside the Blue Room and let the stillness sink in.

This deep quiet felt as if it had been growing and solidifying for years rather than moments or hours. I better understood Gertrude's love for the house, all it represented and why she couldn't let it go. I felt myself expand, breathe deep. I felt myself listening.

After returning to my room last night, I'd thought about the similarities and differences between Gertrude and me. *My brothers say I've paid too much.* I smiled at the thought that she, too, at least thirty years older than me, had brothers chirping in on her life and decisions. I'd adopted the mantra "easy come, easy go" from one of mine, though they'd say I took it to an extreme. They would never say I paid too much or held too tight.

I dropped against the chair's wood back and bounced up again as if it had burned me. That sensation struck again—the vacuum and absolute stillness before the charge, the precursor that signaled something was different, and unbalanced.

I loped down the stairs, checked the two front parlors, and made my way through the hall that ran past the dining room; the only noise was the soft tread of my ballet flats.

I pushed a swinging door at the end of another short, narrow hall, expecting to find the side door Gertrude mentioned—the one leading to the stables and fishing stream. Instead I landed in a long, exquisite kitchen. It was tiled from floor to ceiling in cream-colored subway tiles, with two porcelain farmhouse sinks, stainless steel counters, and a huge bright-red cooking range that lined almost one full wall. The room was dry and warm as if self-heated.

Sonia emerged from a side pantry dressed in a simple long black dress with a white apron laid over the front. "Good morning. Everyone's left breakfast already, but I can make you eggs or—"

"Please, no. I'm not hungry." I pointed to her dress. "It's begun then? I need to put on a dress?"

Sonia smiled. "It only feels awkward at first. You'd have felt better if you'd made breakfast. Helene is wearing a bright-yellow dress and is already in full character. She tried to tease poor 'Margaret Dashwood' about Duncan, who was serving sausages. Clara was too young to understand, but poor Duncan turned bright red and dropped a sausage. He was so embarrassed he refuses to serve table again. Helene also insisted we arrange a ball for tomorrow night."

"Wasn't there going to be dancing anyway?"

Sonia poured me a cup of coffee and slid it across the counter. "Yes, but part of the fun is letting a Mrs. Jennings direct the household."

"Okay then . . . To Mrs. Jennings." I raised my cup and took a sip. "I'll go find a dress. Save this for me?" I set down my coffee. A waver in the air above the stove caught my eye. "Did you know that's on?"

"An Aga is always on."

"What do you mean?" I stepped toward it. I could feel the heat hit me a full two feet from its bright-red doors. I crouched down and touched one of them.

Sonia laughed and crouched next to me. "It's made of enameled cast iron. Each chamber is calibrated to a different heat, so you move your dishes between them, adjusting how you cook rather than adjusting the oven to your cooking. There are no dials, no on and off switches. Gertrude sent me to a class a couple years ago, but Penelope is the cook. I just help out when needed. Water and boiled eggs, that sort of thing."

I tapped a finger to each bright-red door. I could feel differences in temperature. "How do you know they stay true?"

"Every now and then Gertrude puts in a thermometer to check them, but it's never needed. You'd have to ask her how it works. But I do know that because it never turns off, she has the heat set low in this end of the house. The Aga warms the kitchen and you can even feel the drier heat in the Gold and Blue Rooms above."

"It would be drier. Radiant heat keeps wood 11 percent drier than forced air, and in drywall, the percentage is higher. I can't quite remember . . ." I caught her look. "In my work, ambient moisture and temperature are important." I stood and leaned against the counter, adoring the stove and lamenting its impracticability in Texas. "Is it too hot in here in the summer?"

"It can get toasty."

"So what are the BTUs for the burners? Is it all—" I stopped at the small smile playing on her lips and felt my face flame. *You're not the resident electrician.* "I should go dress." I looked around the kitchen again. "I don't want to embarrass Isabel. Am I not supposed to be in here?"

"Don't think that at all. Gertrude was serious when she said there are no rules. And I figure even in Austen's day, an Emma had to come see the cook or Lizzy the housemaid. In one of those movies, they even got Elinor Dashwood outside Norland Park beating the rugs with the maid. You can dig around in any pantry you want and take all the lightbulbs you wish."

My jaw dropped. Sonia grinned again. The back door slammed shut and startled us both.

Gertrude crossed half the kitchen before she noticed us. "Good. You are awake."

Sonia and I stiffened. Gertrude stopped short. "That was abrupt. I simply meant . . . We have a problem."

"We do?"

"Breakfast with Miss Dwyer was . . . unusual." She glanced to Sonia, who gave a tiny commiserating nod. "I have just left her at the stables, and I think you should come with me. She appeared to not know anyone this morning, and her mannerisms, her speech . . . She concerns me."

"She's been styling herself as an Austen escapee for years. It's her thing, and finishing her dissertation is important. She calls this the 'ultimate escapist experience for the modern literate woman.' She's role-playing and she's really good at it. Trust me."

Gertrude's expression didn't change.

"Was it awkward? Do you want me to talk to her?" I pointed back toward the hallway. "I should change first."

"Could you do that after?"

I glanced to Sonia. She, too, held a tight, anxious expression.

"This is more than role-playing. Please?" Gertrude gestured to the back door.

She was dressed in dark blue, an apron tied at her waist and a small mobcap attached to her silver hair. Oddly, she looked like she fit the kitchen, the house, everything. I was the one out of place.

She led me across the gravel drive toward the path marked by a small black sign with gold lettering. *Stables, Spa, and Stream.* I shifted my gaze from her back to the sky. The day was glorious. Rain through the night had cleared all the gray and clouds away. The sky was bright blue—not a washed-out, bleached, Texas-sky blue, but the color I used to mark cool currents on my drafting charts, the one just lighter than Sharpie's royal blue. And the air was crisp. It felt like drinking a cold glass of milk after a long run. You could feel it moving through you, cooling and calming you from the inside.

"Is it always this gorgeous?"

Gertrude's shoes crunched at a faster cadence beside me. She was taking two steps to my one. I got the impression I was holding her back, so I picked up my pace.

"October is usually full of rain. Yet summer was dry this year and predictions for winter are much the same. So while these days are rare, my hope is that you will have a few of them."

At the path's first bend she spoke again. "I feel I've tattled on your friend. It wasn't that I was insulted that she didn't appear to remember me or the interviews when I mentioned them. If this were a real nineteenth-century house party, she would have no reason to talk with the staff outside her own maid. But it was the sense she didn't remember she'd met anyone at breakfast before. The Muellers loved it. Helene commented on the authenticity of her character, but that only seemed to upset her. Then Clara's questions almost frightened her. You could see it in her eyes. There is something very worrying about them."

At the path's next turn, the gravel crunch morphed to a mulch squish. It was beautifully maintained, not a wood chip falling

beyond the low stone border, and it was well positioned, with man-
icured areas allowing glimpses through the trees into the gardens
and fields along its edge. We rounded a corner, and the sight as we
passed out of the trees brought us to a halt.

There Isabel stood dressed in a soft blue dress—the thin wool
one with the white trim she'd tried on the day before. Her black
hair was piled high, spilling in curls down her neck. Her hair was
the same color as the horse with whom she was conversing.

"Hey, Isabel . . . Have you been riding?"

Isabel looked up. She scanned me from head to toe and
stepped away.

"I'm sorry. I know I should have dressed. I will." I closed the
distance between us. "But Gertrude was worried. Are you okay?"
A memory pricked me. "Isabel? You remember me, right?"

Her eyes morphed from blankness to confusion, then through
surprise and recognition, and settled on delight. Delight like I
hadn't seen since we discovered we both liked salsa on our eggs and
s'mores with the marshmallow burned almost to disintegration—
second-grade, new-best-friend delight.

"Mary. I hadn't expected to see you." She pulled me into a tight
hug, then pushed me away as abruptly. Her gaze trailed again
from the top of my head down to my ballet flats. "What are you
wearing? You look dreadful . . . Did you just arrive?" She waved
her question away. "Tell me later. Now we can ride." She looked
around as if searching for someone. "Grant, who is the groom here,
said he would take me riding. And while that's not inappropriate, I
wouldn't want to start talk. But now that you're here . . ."

She pulled my hand and stepped toward the stables. "I thought
we'd ride to town, but he says we cannot. It's no matter. This estate
covers over thirty acres. Come on . . . I can accept his invitation for

us both." Isabel spun back and drew me close, whisper-distance apart. "He's very kind, a perfect gentleman, and so handsome, but he's only a few years older than we are. Not like home."

"Home? Texas home or an imaginary home? Are we in character?" Something about her tone kept me quiet, calm, as if trying not to spook her. "Because also, I don't ride. You know that." I watched her, waiting for a crack in the charade.

I expected a half-knowing smile or a flash of annoyance; instead she clutched my hand.

"How is that possible? You'll love it. You simply can't have tried it and . . ." She stepped back to the horse and held his long head between both hands, lowering it to look in his eyes. "You aren't scary, are you, Tennyson? Tell her you're the dearest thing in the whole world." She reached for me again. "Pat him. He's sweet. You will love riding." She let Tennyson's head go, then grabbed his bridle with one hand and my hand with the other. She pulled us both toward the stable's open door.

I glanced back to Gertrude, then I tugged at Isabel and dropped my voice to a whisper. "This isn't funny. Can you stop for a sec and talk to me?"

Her eyes went wide with confusion, almost a look of panic.

"Isabel?"

"Why . . . What?" Her voice wobbled. I felt a shadow draw near and twisted toward it. A man emerged behind her. His presence startled me, but pleased her. "Here is Grant. If you hurry and change, we can set off."

"Stop it, Isabel. I'm not riding with you." Fear cracked my voice. "Give me a second to catch up. We don't need to be all Regency for two weeks straight. Please don't take it that far; it won't be any fun."

She shook her head. Black curls bounced about her face. "Why are you yelling? I only wanted you to join me. I was trying to do something nice and fun and–" She took off, running up the path.

I started to follow when a firm hand clamped down on my arm. I looked from the hand to the man. He was tall, made taller by his rigid stance. Clean-shaven, short hair. Military short. He wore a khaki shirt that matched his hazel eyes. He held me so close I could see flecks of gold in them. I tried to step away.

"I'm sorry I startled you, but may I talk to you?" He nodded up the path. "She won't go far."

"I need to go talk to her." I looked to my arm. He still held it within his hand. "Who are you?"

"Grant Chessman." His focus was not on me, but above my head. I followed his line of sight to Isabel's retreat. Gertrude followed at a fast walk. "Your friend is hurt."

"She's playing some weird game. I just need to talk to her."

The memory solidified.

"Didn't you see her eyes? She's not playing at anything." Grant dropped his hand the exact moment I stopped struggling. "Serve in combat and you learn who's afraid, who's faking, who's lying. Work with animals and you see the same emotions. Some will deny the pain and fear, some will push it down, and some will run." He tilted his head back to where Isabel had disappeared. "Miss Dwyer has run to safety. Please be careful with her."

He hadn't meant up the path and to the house—but that's where I needed to go. I took off before he could say more and caught up to Gertrude on the path. She gestured to Isabel in front of us, and I raced on. Upon reaching her, I stretched out to grab her arm, then stopped before contact. We needed privacy. She stiffened as I matched her stride, but would not look at me. So side by side and in silence, we walked around to the house's front door and proceeded straight up the stairs to our room.

She opened the door and flung herself on her bed. I shut it and leaned against it, watching her. "Can you tell me what's going on? You have Gertrude worried. Me too now."

"Why would she worry about me? I have barely spoken to the woman. And why should you worry?" Isabel sat up. "Did you have to be so dreadful? I just wanted to go for a ride, and you embarrassed me in front of Grant. We're here to have a lovely time and enjoy ourselves. This will be the last party of the season and then we'll be back home where it is dark and cold and I . . . Can't we enjoy ourselves?"

"Texas is never dark or cold."

Isabel's face fell and paled. She took a deep breath and seemed at a loss for how to reply.

I held up a hand to stop her. "You're right. We are here to enjoy ourselves." I pointed to my wardrobe. "Will you please choose a dress for me? I'll be right back." I palmed my phone and headed into the bathroom. I locked the door behind me.

Dad answered on the second ring. "Hey, dar—"

"I'm sorry I woke you, but do you remember that spring break when Isabel's dad didn't come home and she stayed with us?"

I heard a scratching noise. I envisioned him rubbing his face to wake up. "How could I forget? What's going on?"

"She's like that again. She's doing that pretending or dissociative thing the doctor talked about. This is beyond role play, Dad. It's like she really believes we're at a Regency house party."

"What happened?" Dad's voice was strong and clear. He was sitting up now.

"Everything was fine yesterday. She was so excited . . . Well, she got a little upset because her dad set up all these interviews and—" My breath caught. "He got married yesterday. Her dad married some young girlfriend and sent Isabel a horrid e-mail. It was cruel, Dad. I couldn't believe he wrote it, but she assured me it was real."

"She should have been taken from that man years ago."

Dad always contended that Malcolm Dwyer wasn't just indifferent to his daughter, his neglect was abusive. One spring break Malcolm had approved his nanny's request for vacation but then had not returned home to Isabel. She came home from school to a locked house, broke in through a window, and we only found her three days later when I went to empty her mailbox and pick up the newspapers in the driveway. She recognized me, but neither of my parents. Dad, because he was listed as the school's emergency and medical contact, was able to take her to the doctor. He never told me the full extent of what was said, but the result was we brought Isabel home to our house.

"What do I do now?"

"Back then, Dr. Milton said rest and safety. It took a few days, but she was fine. Does she know you?"

"It took a second, but she does."

"That happened last time too. She recognized you almost immediately. It took her almost a day for your mom and me, then after three days she was fine."

"Do I need to take her somewhere? A doctor? Or I wonder if we should hop a flight home. But you should see her with the horses—she's confused, but she was happy. Before I upset her, that's what struck me. Remember how happy she was that week? It's like her protective coating is gone again."

"Then she feels safe there. Don't take her anywhere and don't upset her. Let me call Dr. Milton and I'll get back to you. Do what we did before—stay close and reassure her."

"Do I need to call her father?"

"You can. He didn't come fifteen years ago; I doubt he'll do different now. I'd throttle that man if I could."

Dad's conviction soothed my fear. "Call me back?"

"Of course, Peanut. You can do this."

I nodded as if he could see me.

"I'll call as soon as I reach Dr. Milton. Text or call if you need me."

"I will. Thanks, Dad."

I tapped off the phone and exited the bathroom. Isabel stood next to my bed holding up a plum-colored dress. She was grinning.

"This one."

Chapter 13

Isabel was Emma. Lady Bountiful at her best. And maybe I was Catherine from *Northanger Abbey* as I'd insisted the day before—naïve and completely out of my element.

Within an hour Isabel had me dressed and my hair pulled up in a matching fashion—a high bun with tendrils framing my face. It looked better on a head full of curls rather than one with straight brown hair, but I had to admit it was soft and pretty. And some deep place within me got a kick out of the transformation.

"Are we ready?" I heard my nerves coming to the surface.

"Not yet." She pulled a black ribbon from another dress and tucked it into my hair. "You look beautiful."

Her compliment surprised me. It wasn't the words so much as the delivery. Gone were all the sharp edges. In their place, I found *glee*—there wasn't another word. It was bubbly anticipation—it was glee.

"Thank you."

Isabel clapped her hands together. "I am so glad you are here. What shall we do now?"

Isabel rarely asked me what to do or where to go. Isabel led.

"Didn't you want to go riding?" I thought back to spring break fifteen years ago. We watched her favorite movies, played her favorite games, ate her favorite foods. And she came back.

"You said you don't ride."

"But you love it. You've been riding for about twenty years and, honestly, you're happiest on a horse. Riding is better than Austen for you."

"Austen?"

I felt my lips part and pressed them shut. They made a soft guppy noise. "Never mind. We can talk about her later." I opened the door and waved Isabel through.

We walked together down the path, but she skipped ahead at the last bend when the horses came into view. "Tennyson, you're still here." She called back to me. "Come meet Tennyson now. I'll ride him, and Grant said he would saddle another horse named Lady Grey for you. He said she is very gentle. He is going to ride Lord Byron. I hope he's here and we haven't missed him."

Isabel walked inside. "Grant? We've come back. May we ride?" No one was there.

She walked back to me and stepped close. "I had so wanted to do this. There are few things I feel I can do, really do, to be on my own."

"We could go for a walk. We could . . ." I tried to think of the things Austen ladies did. They walked, painted, drew, drank tea, visited the poor, flirted with officers . . .

I noted movement and turned.

"Hello again." A deep voice reached us before the man emerged from shadow. It was the same man who'd held my arm, rigid and stiff. Yet it wasn't at all. Grant's stance was relaxed, his smile broad.

The sharp lines of his face seemed soft and inviting. He looked at Isabel. "How are you?"

Isabel blushed.

Grant faced me. "When Miss Dwyer was here earlier, I assured her she didn't need a chaperone, if you'd rather not ride."

Still the color of roses and cream, Isabel drew me close. "That's not possible, Mary."

"I'll ride, but I haven't before. I've never even been on a horse."

He held up a finger for us to wait, then disappeared into the stables.

"He's handsome, isn't he?" Isabel whispered.

"Very," I agreed.

Grant reemerged, walking a large gray horse. "This is Lady Grey. Clara has just finished a ride with her." He looked to Isabel. "Are you planning to ride sidesaddle?"

"Of course."

I almost laughed at the shock-tinged horror that skittered across her expression and its implications for me.

"Not me?" I ventured. "I think I've read it's dangerous."

"You'll be fine." Grant handed us both riding helmets.

He helped Isabel fasten hers under her chin. I struggled with mine and clicked the fastener just as he turned to assist me. Amused was the best way to describe his eyes. He then held his hand out to me and led me to a small flight of stairs. Lady Grey stood next to them.

"It can be challenging, but I modified the saddle, and Clara was perfectly at ease this morning."

"Clara has been taking riding lessons," I reminded him.

"Clara is eight years old," Grant reminded me.

"Good point."

He positioned me in the saddle.

"I'm just supposed to balance here?"

"I've lengthened this pommel and added one here for greater support." He swung my right leg over and around the second pommel. "As I said, Lady Grey is gentle and knows what she's doing. I trust her. But . . ." He paused until my eyes met his. "If you must fall, fall this way." He patted my dangling shins and smiled without any humor.

"Got it. Fall toward my feet. Not my head."

He lifted Isabel to her saddle without any instructions, but then again, Isabel had been riding horses for years.

As we ambled out of the pen, I called to Grant. "You made these changes yourself?"

"Ladies love riding sidesaddle on these vacations, but few have ever done it before. I spent some downtime on my last deployment working out improvements. It helps my grandfather." He twisted in the saddle. "Then when Gertrude mentioned a young girl was coming, I felt we needed more safety measures."

"I'll be sure to thank Clara."

Grant's chuckle was deep and genuine. Isabel darted her eyes between us.

After a few moments of awkward silence, I spoke again. "Did you say your grandfather lives here?"

"Yes, and he's lived here his whole life. I used to come here for summer vacation as a kid. My grandfather—you'll meet him somewhere on the grounds—has been head gardener here for over fifty years." He twisted the other way to address Isabel. "You said you were interested in the gardens. If you want to learn about them, you need to talk to him. I'll introduce you later."

She said nothing in reply but gave an almost shy-looking nod.

Grant turned back to me. "I'm staying with him while on leave."

"Oh..."

Flirt with military officers ... Napoleon was on the edge of every Austen story. Britain was at war and soldiers populated her scenes. And, unlike the Marys, Austen liked her soldiers.

"You're part of all this too. Fighting the French, are you?"

Grant burst out laughing. "Lieutenant Grant Chessman at your service. Real name. Real officer. On real leave from the real British army." Lady Grey, as if needing to be near Lord Byron, brought me beside him. "But it was a natural assumption. Gertrude has the house staff dress for these parties, but they do keep their real names, real life stories too. It can get confusing. But I'm not on staff, and Granddad steers clear of it all." He glanced to Isabel again. "Are you all right, Miss Dwyer?"

"Yes. I'm fine. Thank you."

We walked on. I asked a few questions about house parties in hopes that Isabel would chime in. I wanted to draw her out. It didn't work.

She said nothing more during the entire ride. So as we looped back along the path, I decided to find out all I could about this Grant Chessman, who made Isabel blush at first meeting and left her speechless now.

He was on leave for six months, having just returned from two deployments to places unknown and classified, was staying with his grandfather and helping him through the winter, and appeared very adept at soothing horses and nervous women. I liked him.

When we reached the stables, Grant helped us both down.

"Thank you, Grant." I patted Lady Grey. "Isabel? I think Gertrude is expecting us for lunch."

"I wanted to meet . . ." She stepped to Grant. "I thought you might introduce me to your grandfather."

"I'd be happy to. He's beyond the terraced gardens. We can go after lunch or . . ." He looked back at the horse. "If you feel comfortable coming with me alone, we can ride there now."

Isabel raised her arms for assistance. It was a definitive answer. "Mary, will you tell Gertrude I'll be along shortly?"

I looked at Grant.

"I'll take care of her."

I nodded and headed up the path. I knew he would and—more importantly—Isabel did too.

Chapter 14

I walked to the house alone and, rather than walk to the front, headed straight to the kitchen door I'd exited earlier.

The kitchen was a bustling enterprise. Two enameled stockpots sat on the Aga; a short elderly woman, who reminded me of my maternal grandmother, was putting away dishes; and Sonia stood at the counter cutting a selection of cheeses and meats. Six full platters lay before her.

"Is Isabel okay?"

"Yes. She is deep in character." As soon as the words left my mouth, I realized I could leave it there. They didn't know Isabel; there was no reason to expose her. "Is this lunch?"

"Cheese, cucumbers and other vegetables, and a variety of cold meats. We even have a lovely salad of boiled eggs. Our nineteenth-century version of egg mayonnaise. And a pudding for dessert." Sonia wagged a finger to the Aga. "It's in the blue pot."

"There's a brick on it."

"Sticky toffee pudding is sealed in a tin inside, then submerged in boiling water. The brick keeps the top on." Sonia poked her knife toward the door. "Head into the dining room. Everyone just came in. You haven't seen them all yet."

I entered the dining room and found everyone seated. Helene, sitting at the end of the table, flapped a hand at me. She was now dressed in beige with a red wool shawl pulled tight around her. It puddled in her lap.

I stalled, unsure where to sit.

"Come in, my dear. Have you been out with the young men? I met that handsome Grant at the stables." Helene pointed her fork at an open chair to her left, then cast her gaze behind me. "Where is your pretty friend?"

"She is off with that handsome Grant from the stables. They went to meet his grandfather."

"Oh, this is fun. He'll have to join us for dancing. I hear he's in the military." Helene's eyes lit. "Do you think he dances?"

"I have no idea." As I walked to my seat, I noted everyone was halfway through a salad of greens and what looked like pears. "I'm late. I'm sorry."

"Not at all. I'm Mr. Bingley from Netherfield Park. We missed each other at breakfast this morning." Aaron popped up and pulled out my chair.

"I . . ." I felt myself heat. It was time. "I'm Catherine Morland from some small village, I can't remember the name, but I'm happy to be here and sorry I missed breakfast. Emma and I went riding."

Mr. Bingley sat again. "Capital. Miss Bennet"—he gestured to Sylvia—"assured me that a love of the outdoors was part of Mr. Bingley's charm. Glad to hear you feel the same and have already been out and about this morning."

"That was the movie, darling. In the book, it just says Bingley is an idle fellow who has more books than he'll ever look into," Sylvia called from across the table.

"I think I prefer the movie description. No one has ever called me idle."

Sylvia laughed. "True."

Sonia and Duncan passed around the platters while the table indulged in stories—all made up—of exploits on horses, duels with swords, or drawing room happenings that never happened.

By the sticky toffee pudding we were toasting our adventures, making up new ones, gossiping about the accomplishments of local young ladies, discussing the dangers of war with cannon fire, and sharing our hopes for the upcoming social season.

Isabel joined us as we finished dessert. She seemed flustered at first that she had missed the meal, but Sonia quickly seated her and brought a plate. Her face soon lost its pinched expression.

Watching her, I realized that no one would notice anything was different. She spoke with her slight British tones and inflections. She sat at the table with ease, as if in command of the room. She added to the conversation here and there and sat with a certain degree of formality. She was Emma.

Helene soon brought up dancing, and the advantages to having military men nearby. If Isabel caught that "Mrs. Jennings" was teasing her and planning a great romance, she didn't let on.

"It's very nice to have him stationed here. If offered, I don't think an invitation to dine and dance would be rejected."

Isabel enjoyed herself until the conversation turned to gossip again and Sylvia started making up names. Then her eyes widened and her face paled.

"Miss Thistlebum has thirty thousand a year, but her betrothed is a rake."

Helene joined in. "Yes, but Miss Mopflop has an estate in Devonshire and her betrothed is a rattle. That's far worse."

"Is it? I'd think sexual indiscretions far more damaging than silly talk," Sylvia shot back.

"I suppose it depends on how much silly talk is foisted upon one," Aaron added on a dry note that made me smile.

"Who is this Miss Mopflop and why are we talking of her?" Herman punctuated his inquiry with a few fist taps on the tabletop. He looked as anxious as Isabel.

Helene smiled and reached for his hand. "It's pretend, dear. We are making up names."

"But aren't we already making up names? Why do we need more of them? It's too much."

She shifted to him more fully. "You are right. You are playing Sir Walter. Remember, we talked about him this morning."

We caught the hint and Aaron steered the conversation back to Austen. Helene took it a step further and gently focused our comments on Sir Walter and his friends and family from *Persuasion*. Herman soon looked more comfortable and so did Isabel.

Lunch wound down and we broke apart for quieter activities. The Muellers excused themselves to rest. Clara, with a yawn of her own, expressed an interest in returning to her room as well— "One show, Mama?" Sylvia acquiesced and joined her. Only Aaron was not to be "idle." Grant had promised him shooting.

I walked to the end of the table and looped my arm through Isabel's. I led her from the room and toward the stairs. I didn't want to talk to her in front of the others.

When we reached the Green Room, she curled against her headboard and hugged her knees tight.

I sat next to her. "Was lunch confusing?"

"How do you know everyone so well? Miss Mopflop? Miss Thistlebum? I had no idea what to say."

"I could tell that bothered you. Jane Bennet was just being playful. Sir Walter didn't understand either."

"So they weren't real?"

"No. You'll have to dismiss a lot of what people say here. They are having fun, playing roles at a party. There might be a lot you won't understand."

I wasn't sure if this was the right thing to do, but this wasn't as contained an atmosphere as fifteen years ago. That week we never left the house. My parents controlled all the variables. Here I was alone and lost. I peeked at my phone. No message from my dad or Dr. Milton.

"Oh ... There's that noise again. I heard it this morning." Isabel swept her hand around the room.

"It's your phone." I slid it from the bedside table and held it out to her. She shied away and crawled off the bed, then crossed to my side of the room and opened my wardrobe. "After we change, what shall we do this afternoon?"

"Everyone is resting." I tossed her now silent phone onto her bed. "Except Mr. Bingley. He's off shooting with Grant."

That piqued her interest. "Could we walk out with them?"

"I suppose . . . But I don't think they are walking the fields. There's a clay shooting range beyond the stable." I pushed off the bed and stood beside her. "How's this? We'll spend some time here doing whatever ladies are supposed to do in the afternoon, then we'll join the bowls game Mrs. Jennings plans to set up on the south lawn." I couldn't stop my smile—how often did one get to say that sentence? "Mr. Bingley, and maybe Grant, plans to meet everyone there."

"May we change first? I'm covered in dirt, and you have mud on your hem. Try this one." She pulled out a dark-green dress, then crossed the room to her own wardrobe. "It really is embarrassing to be so disheveled. I once knew a girl who walked three miles in the mud. It covered her dress six inches deep. She wasn't fit to be seen . . ."

As we dressed, Isabel told story after story of awkward situations and happenings. Most I recognized as from Austen. The ones from *Emma* she told in the first person. They were more definite, like real memories. The game of "blunder" with Mr. Churchill seemed to have actually happened to her and caused her real embarrassment. There were also a few stories I did not recognize, and I concluded they must have come from the movies, for they all involved the same sets of names.

The stories slowed as Isabel became increasingly agitated over my hairdressing skills. She had already fixed mine. It had fallen out during our ride, so I'd fashioned a ponytail and fastened it with my own electrical wire. She had taken the ponytail, twisted it high, and looped it around itself. Once again, I was amazed and secretly in awe of the transformation.

"Sit still or I won't get it to stay." I pulled a bobby pin from my lips and anchored it into her curls.

"Ouch," Isabel yelped as a section flopped over her eyes.

"It's too heavy. How do you have so much hair? I don't know how you get it all piled up." I needed a new approach. My approach. I reached across the dressing table.

"What are you doing?"

"Securing it with something that will work." I grabbed an eight-inch length of black electrical wire, wrapped it around the bun, tucked in a few loose strands, wrapped again, and stepped back. "There. See? We could have accomplished that an hour ago—and the wire matches your hair color so you can't even see it."

"What is this stuff?"

I watched through the mirror as Isabel rolled another piece of wire around her finger, unrolled it, and rolled it again.

"It's electrical wire." I paused to gauge her reaction. I wasn't sure about the rules . . . Was I to gently remind her of the present? Avoid it at all costs?

Fascinated, she continued to twist the wire. I continued. "My dad used to bring me home spare clippings from jobs. Everything in our house, growing up, revolved around electricity." I paused again. She said nothing. "You'd like my dad. He gave me this too." I lifted my necklace in another gentle reminder of who we were and what we knew about each other. I almost expected the usual litany. *Of course, Mary. Amber means "electron" in ancient Greek. It's all about electricity.*

Instead she turned it over in her fingers, inspecting every detail. "What's on the back?"

I resisted the urge to pull it away. We never talked about the back, and most days I forgot about it. "Dad soldered my mom's Saint Cecilia medallion to the frame. She is the patron saint of music."

I hadn't wanted my dad to solder that to the stone. He did it right after my mom died, and rather than a blessing, it felt like an indictment. It reminded me of my push-pull relationship with the piano, which mirrored my relationship with my mom. A never-ending cycle of yearning-delight-fear-distance. How could you love something, invest in it, as you saw it slipping away?

Inches away I could see Isabel's focus cloud. "I don't remember my mother."

I wasn't sure if this was real or pretend. Emma didn't remember her mother either. "I know."

Isabel let the necklace drop. The gold medallion against my

skin was now warm from her fingers. Her hand fluttered at her neck. She looked around the room as if searching for something safe and familiar.

"Let's go for a walk." My own brightness surprised me.

Her face cleared. "I need to get my boots. Can we go back down to the stables? Grant mentioned another horse that should be back by now. He's bigger than Tennyson. He was pulling that Mrs. Jennings and Sir Walter around in a gig all morning."

Isabel sank to the desk chair and pulled on the brown leather boots she'd worn riding. I heard a snap and a sigh as I did the same from across the room.

"I broke the lace and I don't have another." She crossed toward the bell pull–again. Clearly she didn't remember our conversation.

"Don't. That's more work for Sonia. She'll have to come up here, then go back down to find a shoelace. I'll go find her."

Isabel stood. "But you are less ready than I am. I will find her and meet you in the drawing room."

"That's the Day Room, right?"

"Yes, isn't that odd? Day Room. That's what Gertrude called it this morning." Isabel left the room.

I dropped to the bed and tapped my phone. There was a text from Dad.

Dr. Milton will call you soon. He agrees with keeping her there. He wants to talk with a few colleagues as to timing and next steps. More soon.

I was on my own.

Chapter 15

Fifteen years ago, I had simply watched movies and sat beside Isabel. I knew something was wrong, that was obvious. But I also trusted my parents, and they assured me she needed rest and comfort and she'd be fine.

I hadn't been in charge. I hadn't been responsible. I'd simply watched fun movies and eaten macaroni and cheese and pizza for three days straight.

Now... I sat up, swiped at my eyes, and reached for my other boot. It was time for a walk. Sunshine. Fresh air. Peace. One step at a time.

A phone rang. I grabbed for mine, but it wasn't ringing. I reached across to Isabel's bed and tapped accept before I glanced at the screen.

TCG. "Oh... Oops." I almost tapped it off, then realized I'd said the words aloud. I recovered with a quick "Isabel Dwyer's phone."

"Isabel?" an oddly familiar voice replied. "Is Isabel there?"

"She isn't right now. May I have her call you back?" As soon as I said the words, my heart dropped and I shot to standing. I recognized that voice. "Nathan?"

"Who is this?"

"Mary Davies. From WATT."

Time stopped—at least on my end. It seemed to take a beat on his end too, because he rushed on after an inordinately long pause.

"I'm sorry, Mary. I thought I called someone . . . You did just say . . . I . . . Did you say you have Isabel Dwyer's phone? Or did I call you?"

I imagined him pulling his phone away from his ear and staring at it—his brow furrowing and his top lip dragging through his teeth like they did whenever he concentrated. I could practically hear the questions spinning through his brain. *Did I call Mary? Did I call Isabel? Why is she answering Isabel's phone?*

And if I wasn't sure laughter would tip to tears, I would have laughed at the absurdity of it all—at every single aspect of my life.

"You called Isabel's phone. We're on vacation together."

"You're in England with Isabel Dwyer? How do you even know her?"

I countered with a "How do you?" then cringed. My tone was aggressive, defensive, and hurt—all conveyed clearly in three little words. "Sorry . . . We're friends. Best friends since second grade, I guess. How do you know her?"

"We . . . have a bunch of mutual friends. She left me a voice mail, and I was just calling her back . . . Did you know I knew her? Why didn't you say something? Did you think— Why didn't you tell me you knew we both . . ."

Nathan sounded as flustered as I felt.

"Me? No one told me anything." My tone wasn't defensive or hurt now—only aggressive. The pieces fell into place. Six months of pieces fell into place and got capped off with last night's *Who? I never thought much of him.* Isabel knew exactly who. "You're dating

Isabel." The realization came, not as a lightbulb, but as a slow dawning. "I wish you had told me, Nathan. Isabel . . . She never said a word. How long have you two been dating?"

"It's not like that. I met her with a couple friends in March and we exchanged numbers. She called me."

Seven months. After he'd started working at WATT. After we'd met. After I'd told Isabel all about him. I closed my eyes. My face flamed. "She gave you her number. She called you . . . She knew who you were." I saw the scene, felt it too. "I'll tell her you called." I lowered the phone from my ear.

"Wait; don't hang up."

I pulled it back. "It's okay, Nathan. I'll tell her you called, but it's going to be a few days before I do, before she can call you back." I pressed my thumb and pointer finger into the corners of my eyes. Questions and answers, so many answers, flooded my brain. It hurt. Each and every question and the story I was imagining simultaneously overwhelmed and tore apart something inside me.

"Wha—"

I cut him off. I couldn't listen. I couldn't breathe. "I can't deal with this right now. She'll call you, I promise, but not for a while because I can't reach her, I can't tell her you called, and I don't know what to do and I'm alone over here and—" Tears filled my throat and burst beyond my fingers. I tapped off the phone and tossed it on her bed.

It rang. *TCG.* I clicked decline.

My phone rang.

Nathan Hillam. I tapped decline. It rang again. I tapped again. It rang again. I tapped accept but couldn't speak.

"Don't hang up."

I scrubbed at my eyes and held the phone away from me for

several deep breaths. I refused to let him hear the tears. Finally a breath came out without a shudder. "What do you need?"

"I need to talk to you or listen to you. Tell me what's going on."

"I can't, Nathan. I feel like an idiot right now and there's nothing you can do."

"What do you mean you can't reach Isabel? You just said you were with her."

"I am. I mean . . . I can't explain."

"Try." His voice was calm.

"You always say that." The tears were evident in my voice. I pressed my lips shut. But he stayed silent. And I soon found myself, despite everything and a steady flow of tears, telling him what had happened only hours before and how that aligned with fifteen years ago.

"Can you bring her home?"

I shook my head, then realized he couldn't see it. "I just got a text from my dad. He's talking to her doctor. I'll get more details, but right now they say no . . . She's happy here. Her expression is clear—like there aren't any shadows or pain, if that makes sense, and before, that's how she was at our house. There's a man here, Grant, who works with the horses, and he saw it too. He's been in combat; he wasn't comparing Isabel to a horse." I flopped back onto the bed.

"How can I help?"

A snort escaped. I sat up and swiped at my eyes again—now he would know how messy all this crying really was. But if something was going to hurt even more, it was hearing that question. It was quintessentially Nathan.

In the months I'd known him, I'd heard him ask it countless times, and he meant it too. Nathan was hardwired to help. He explained things again and again until someone at work understood; he once held a thirty-pound compressor for an hour while Benson worked to reconfigure a sensor he'd designed; he'd brought boxes of Starbucks coffee to our staff meetings since day one; he even helped Peter deliver mail after we'd played musical cubicles for the third time in as many months.

"I have no idea . . . I don't know what to do."

"What if I came to help you?"

I felt the blood drain from my face and was surprised that I could actually feel it. It wasn't merely an expression. My skin felt cool. It felt blue.

"Mary?"

"You and Isabel are that close? You'd fly here for her? I didn't realize." My voice broke. My heart broke. I tried to cover it with a cough. "I mean I can ask her, but she won't—"

"I didn't ask Isabel. I asked you." He took a breath and rushed on as if afraid I'd interrupt. "I'm asking if *you* want me there, for you, not for Isabel. I mean for Isabel too, but mostly for you."

I stayed silent.

"I'm finished here at WATT and I don't start a new engagement for a couple weeks. I was planning to take the time off and you wouldn't believe how many airline miles I've accrued. It wouldn't cost me much."

I smiled. I'd only heard him nervous once. It was one of the few Friday nights he had come out with us. Moira had grilled him all night. He never joined us again.

"Isabel's dad paid for everything, and it's expensive. I don't know about a room here, or even one in Bath."

"I can handle it."

I couldn't reply. The idea of facing him . . . Facing them together . . . He couldn't be coming for me . . . It had to be Isabel . . .

A clicking sound brought me back to the conversation.

"I found a flight for this evening that lands at Heathrow tomorrow morning. E-mail me anything I need to know and where to find you once I land."

"Stop." I sucked a huge breath. I wondered how long I'd been holding it without realizing it. There didn't seem to be enough air in the room now to fill my lungs.

There are some guys who you just know if you fell for them you'd go too deep and never make it back.

Nathan could not come—I wouldn't survive it.

"You can't do this. I'll tell her you called, and as soon as she can, she'll call you back."

"It's done. Send me the e-mail. And, Mary?" Nathan paused. "I'll see you tomorrow."

A knock on the door finally moved me. I had no idea how long I'd been lying there, stunned and numb.

At my fairly incoherent reply, Gertrude poked her head in. "I wanted to see if everything was okay."

I struggled to sit up. My whole body felt beaten and heavy. "Everything is not okay."

She sank beside me. She looped her arm around my shoulders and that's all it took. I couldn't remember the last time anyone had held me like that; I couldn't remember ever needing it. And I couldn't help myself. I leaned into her and cried—sloppy, messy, once-upon-a-broken-heart cried. I felt her brush the hair from my forehead and tuck it behind my ear. She didn't say a word.

After a few minutes I straightened my back and pressed the back of my hand under my nose. "I'm sorry. I hardly even know you."

"Sometimes it takes a lifetime to know someone. Other times, only a few minutes." She gave me a last squeeze, then sat straight. I felt the loss of her support as she shifted on the edge of the bed to face me. She pulled a tissue from her pocket and handed it to me. "How is Isabel?"

I blew my nose. "This has happened before. The doctor will call me later, but as of now I'm to keep her safe and relaxed here. Do you mind? She's clearly in her element here, and I doubt the others will notice. They think she's playing at Emma. And she's really good at that."

The tears started again.

"You must stay. I just saw her downstairs with Sonia. She does seem content." Gertrude tilted her head. "Which fits. For the most part, Emma was content."

"I should get down there. I'm supposed to take care of her." I pushed to stand, didn't make it, and flopped back on the bed. "I just found out she's been lying to me about something, something that was really important to me, and it hurts."

"I'm sorry."

"I feel bottomed out. That's it. Bottomed out." I flopped a hand toward the floor. "I'm squished down there and ... How do you get up from that?" I sucked in maximum air again. "I should go. Isabel is meeting me in the Day Room and she's my job right now. But once she's well ..." I forced myself to standing and smoothed my dress's skirt. The hem almost met my soft kid leather boots. "I can't do this, any of it, anymore."

Tears started again, but this time they were slow, so slow I could feel each wind its way down my cheek. One. Two. Three.

Gertrude stood in front of me and held one hand to my cheek. "You're going to be okay."

"Promise?"

Gertrude nodded. I nodded. We looked like bobble heads. And although she didn't know me, it felt as if she did, and I believed her.

I slid my phone into my pocket and we walked down the stairs in silence. With one last consoling nod, Gertrude left me outside the Day Room door. I decided not to confront Isabel. It would do no good. It could wait.

I pushed open the door, and my best intentions died at "There you are." She leapt from the chair. "I've been waiting for you. Sonia had a lace right away. What have you been doing?"

"Nothing. Let's go." I turned and walked back down the hall and out the front door. The gravel shifted beneath my boots. I heard softer, faster crunches behind me before Isabel tugged at my arm.

"Slow down. I can't keep up if you walk that fast."

I stopped. My hands dropped to my sides.

Isabel kept her hand on me. I resisted the urge to shake her off. "Mary, what's wrong? Why have you been crying?"

"I . . ." I pressed my palms against my eyes. I refused to cry in front of her. "Why didn't you tell me you were dating Nathan Hillam? Last night you acted as if you didn't remember him. You actually said you didn't think much of him—from my description, not from meeting him. But you've been dating him. You gave him your number. You pursued him and you can't tell me you didn't. He just called. You've been listening to me and lying to me for over six months."

"Who? Who is Nathan Hill—Hillsby?"

"Don't do that." I ground out the words, then stopped. Fear and something even more vulnerable shuddered through her.

It took a few breaths, but I calmed my voice. "Nathan Hillam. The consultant at WATT. The man you met last March. You call him TCG." Isabel's blank face drained my anger. I was too tired. "Don't think about it. We'll talk later. Let's just walk and enjoy the day." I started again at a slower pace.

"No." Isabel clutched at me again. She pulled me to a stop so forcefully, I slipped on the pebbles. "I'm sorry, Mary. I've made you angry somehow and I'm very sorry. You must tell me."

I tilted my head down the path. She walked with me.

"Let's just walk," I said. "Austen women walk. We can talk about it someday, but not now."

We crossed from the drive to the path down to the stables and the stream.

"But if you don't tell me, how can I make it right?"

Her words, her pleading tone, almost stopped me again. I concentrated on forward motion. "You can't right now. I'm not so much angry as hurt. More hurt than you can possibly understand, but I'm also worried for you and that makes it all worse."

I led us to the stables. Right or wrong, I hoped to leave her with Grant.

"Whatever I've done, Mary, I'm sorry. Please forgive me."

I wiggled away. "Can we not talk about it anymore? I shouldn't have said anything."

"Then I'll wait."

I felt my forward motion falter. When Isabel was in the wrong, and knew it, she asked for forgiveness, begged for it, and didn't let up until it was granted. She badgered you until she felt better. She never waited for you to catch up.

I stared at her. "Thank you."

Chapter 16

I'm so nervous. Do I look all right?" Isabel pirouetted around the bathroom in a soft pink gown, this one silk with intricate green beading sewn along the hem.

"You look beautiful."

I felt calm now. My plan had worked. Grant had been at the stables and visibly happy to see her. I'd left her with him and a horse named Goliath—and the offer of a gig ride.

Isabel had lit up before grabbing my wrist. "Should we take turns? It is not strictly appropriate, but I have always wanted to ride in one. Can we?"

"You'd feel comfortable with Grant alone?"

"Of course." She glanced to the man in question. "Don't you?"

I looked to Grant. He smiled. I looked back to Isabel. Her face was eager and open, without strain or anxiety.

"I'll take care of her, Catherine." Grant winked. I almost corrected him, then remembered who I was. Catherine Morland. *Northanger Abbey.*

"You two go and take your time. I'll go for a walk."

Four hours later, and probably twice the number of miles, we met back in our room to dress for dinner, Isabel acting like a girl in love. I shoved bobby pins into my hair.

She stopped and swatted at my hand. "It won't stay like that. You have to twist . . . Here, let me."

I watched through the mirror as she removed the pins. The afternoon had given color to my cheeks, and even my eyes felt bright. Nathan had always questioned why I ran on a treadmill, and after a day outside I questioned it myself.

Nathan was coming to Braithwaite House. I glanced at my watch. Seventeen hours. Would Isabel recognize him? What would she say? When she did remember, would she laugh it off? Maybe with an *I never realized* or a *You know me; I'm terrible with names* or worst of all a *You couldn't have really cared about him.* Or maybe she wouldn't say any of those things, maybe I was being unjust and it was all a horrid miscommunication or an innocent mistake or . . .

I willed my thoughts to stop tumbling toward every scenario simultaneously. All would be clear soon enough. Nathan had e-mailed his flights, and I had replied with the link to the Braithwaite House website.

We would all have confrontation and clarity soon.

Isabel pulled me into a hug from behind, pinning my arms to my sides. "You don't look happy. Please know, again, that I'm sorry for whatever I did to hurt you."

I bit my lip. The twinge of pain acted as an antidote for impending tears.

"Let's get this up." Isabel addressed me through the mirror as she slid the brush from my hand. She brushed my hair in long, gentle strokes, much as my mother had when I was little. Much as she herself had done for our eighth-grade Turnabout Dance.

I hadn't wanted to go. Dad, Mom, and I were pretty low that year, but Isabel and Dad insisted. And Isabel made sure I felt beautiful. She found me a deep-red dress at the mall, did my makeup, and brushed my hair "one hundred times for shine." It had flowed down my back in one silky chestnut wave.

We had fun that night—amazing, laugh-out-loud, best-friend, silly-girl fun. I also got my first kiss from Billy Lungreen as we left the gym. Then Isabel spent the night and we relived every moment until we watched the sunrise.

"You have lovely hair." Her soft compliment brought me back to the present. She gently twisted it up and put in the bobby pins I couldn't make work. "You look exquisite."

I thought nothing more could surprise me, but Isabel did. Or maybe Isabel-as-Emma did. Whatever it was, this was new.

She pulled a strand of my hair from the bun and, twirling her finger, curled it to drape down the side of my face. "Perfect."

With few words—because I couldn't find any—we left the room. Again she surprised me by stepping back, gesturing to me to take the lead down the stairs and into the parlor.

At the threshold I stopped so abruptly she tripped into me.

Gertrude, standing at the doorway, tapped her fan against my arm. "Don't gape, dear, it's rude." She gestured into the room. "Please come in. We've been waiting for you both."

Herman crossed the floor, gunning straight for Isabel. He enveloped her hand within both of his own. "I have been waiting for you tonight. Come sit with"—he paused to search for the name, then with a tremulous smile found an answer—"my wife by the fire. It's so chilly since the wind changed."

Isabel let Herman pull her away, while I stood in awe. The lamps had been cleared. Huge silver candelabras sat on tables and cast a gorgeous yellow glow over everything. Even the furniture was different. The large armchairs had been replaced by delicate pieces with needlepoint cushions and graceful scrolling woodwork. The thick rug was gone too. The room glowed with wood, light, and warmth—and that was only the room.

The people . . . The men were dressed in pants so tight and smooth they must have been made of silk; socks white beyond bleaching; and linen shirts that stood stiff but looked so thin you could see them billow with air and movement. Their coats were velvet. They reflected light. And their neck bows . . . They were beautiful in their stiff, odd perfection.

The women were even more stunning. Helene and Sylvia were dressed in the same high-waisted style Isabel and I wore, but having more cleavage, they filled them far better. Sylvia looked ethereal in pale-yellow silk with matching gloves. Her fair skin and hair completed the picture of a delicate yellow rose. I had imagined Jane Bennet to look just that way. No wonder Sylvia had cast herself and her husband in those roles.

"What do you think?" Gertrude cut into my thoughts.

"It's a fairyland. You could almost believe it's real and we're in the stories."

"Isabel's thesis is accurate." Gertrude's gaze followed mine across the room. "It's a most extraordinary and purposeful form of escape. Watching guests, it's clear some find the dressing and role play more than relaxing, they find it liberating. In playing others, they find themselves. Austen was even astute enough to put that in a book; have you read *Mansfield Park*? There's a play smack in the center of the book, and only there do the characters reveal their true selves and motivations."

I thought of Isabel and what I saw within her, a transparency

I hadn't seen in years. I thought of myself and the fact that I, who hadn't cried in—I couldn't think of the last time—had leaned against Gertrude and sobbed that very afternoon. "It feels a little dangerous, doesn't it?"

"Can be, I think. Not all guests take it so far. Most find an escape from their lives and a new perspective, something any vacation can provide."

An escape... "That holds a certain allure."

"For a time." Gertrude's voice was heavy. She handed me a champagne flute, and we offered a silent toast. It felt more like commiseration than celebration.

Clara came across the room then, her steps slow and unsure, looking adorable in a pink dress, hemmed mid-calf. Her eyes were fixed on Isabel. I knew that look—it was adoration. I'd seen it on many faces over the years, starting with Missy Reneker in the second grade. Everyone adored Isabel.

Isabel and Herman had drifted back our direction. She was within reach. I took a step and clamped Isabel's wrist to pull her close. Putting my lips close to her ear, I murmured, "Here comes Margaret Dashwood. Please be kind to her."

Isabel pulled back only far enough to look me in the eyes. Hers asked, *Why wouldn't I be kind?*

I turned back to Gertrude. She was watching Clara as well. "She heard Isabel would be dressed in pink tonight. Her matching one is no mistake. Sonia made that happen."

Clara stopped a few steps from Isabel. She stopped because Isabel, with open arms, cut the distance between them. She wrapped Clara in a hug, then led her to the small love seat. They sat head-to-head as if sharing a delicious secret. Clara beamed and, oddly, so did Isabel.

I almost commented to Gertrude, then realized it would do no good. No one here knew the real Isabel or that she disliked children. And I didn't want to draw attention to what was really happening. Dr. Milton had called me during my walk. If Isabel felt safe, he wanted me to watch her. He was willing to give her four days. If she wasn't fully cognizant by then, I was to hop a flight home or take her to a local hospital. In the meantime, the doctor and I were to talk every day, as many times a day as I needed.

Clara's father, our Mr. Bingley, caught my attention next. He stood selecting appetizers from Duncan's tray. Ripples of fabric pulled tight across his chest.

"How could you possibly have a coat and pants—"

"Breeches." Gertrude corrected me with a tap of her fan.

I nodded. "Breeches. Where did you ever find a pair to fit him?"

"Custom-made. Guests send in their measurements and we make sure we have all they need. Isabel sent in yours." She glanced toward my feet. "A good approximation."

I, too, noted that my dresses hit at the top of my feet rather than breaking on the slipper as the others' dresses did. "Isabel always thinks I'm shorter or she's taller than either of us really is."

"It was our Sir Walter Elliot who was the most challenging to attire this evening. We had the clothes, but he wanted very crisp linen. Poor Sonia couldn't get that collar high enough for his taste. I think she used an entire spray canister of starch."

"Poor Sir Walter. No one will notice. His wife steals the show."

Helene was dressed in white silk with plumes of lace all around her. She looked like a cream puff from her white hair to the white slippered feet that peeked from beneath her dress's hem. A glittery cream puff—Helene was covered in diamonds. They were in her hair, across her neck, draping from both wrists, and covering her white-gloved fingers. A large diamond dropped down the front of her gown and with each breath became lost in her cleavage. I laughed as she waved to Clara just to make the diamonds on her wrists rattle and sparkle. She spoke loudly and held all the vulgar enthusiasm that made Mrs. Jennings such a delightful character.

"That was the most fun." Gertrude raised her glass toward Helene. "I brought her our selection of paste jewelry and she chose every single piece. She is wearing them all tonight."

"Good for her."

Herman noticed we were watching them and jumped up. He took tiny stuttered steps toward us. Either that was how he expected Regency men to walk or the floor was so highly polished as to be slippery.

He pulled me into a one-armed hug. I squished against him. "Aren't we having a marvelous time? I have never seen her look more radiant." He pointed to his wife, then repositioned me by pulling at my shoulders.

Once he was satisfied I was centered in front of him and paying close attention, he moved both his hands to his chest and patted it lightly. "I'm . . . Sir . . ." He looked back to his wife, who was not paying attention.

I supplied the name. "Sir Walter Elliot."

"That's right. Helene said he had a tie just like this. It is important to have it stand, not to wilt. I have seen pictures of my grandfather. I am sure he must have worn a tie like this too. It is hard to tell in the very old pictures. They are grainy and I only have the one. Untied, this strip of linen reaches to my knees. And—"

Helene joined us and laid a hand on his arm. He gave a soft sigh.

"You are the picture of beauty and health tonight," she said to me.

Herman patted his chest again. "I did not say this, but it is true. That was very wrong. Here I am talking about my own tie and I have not done the compliments of the evening." He pulled my hand to his lips, and with a wink he kissed it.

"I didn't feel neglected." I twirled for them both. The deep-brown dress with its accents of red and rose billowed slightly as the weight of the embroidery kept the hem close to my slippers. As I spun, I noted all the other dresses glittering like pale gems in the candlelight, and I felt dark, dramatic—almost mysterious.

"And you . . ." I stopped daydreaming and regained my equilibrium. I tapped the jewels on Helene's wrist. "You are very glamorous."

"Why not?" She flourished her wrist. "Mrs. Jennings was rich, after all. Perhaps not this wealthy, but who's to know? Here, have one." She pulled off a huge bracelet circled in paste gems. If real, each diamond would have been at least ten carats.

"I don't think Catherine Morland had any money." I laughed as she fastened it on my wrist.

"It does not matter. Every girl needs a little diamond glitter." She then patted her husband's chest. "And my dear husband is a perfect Sir Walter, do you not think?"

"Did he look as dashing in his vest and neckcloth?" Herman stepped away before receiving an answer. He preened in the mirror above the mantelpiece and fluffed his neckcloth. He then ran his hands in slow, measured strokes down his chest.

"He's a wonderful Sir Walter," I agreed. "I'm reading that one right now. Austen's description of him struck me; something about vanity being the beginning and the end of Sir Walter's character. I liked the way she phrased that."

Helene and I watched her husband for a long moment.

"Is he playing that up on purpose?" I whispered.

Helene shook her head and took a sip of her champagne. "That's what makes it so enjoyable."

Chapter 17

I started the evening angry and anxious. I ended it as close to content as I'd felt in . . . I couldn't cast back to a time. Even Fridays out with work friends never felt so relaxed. After dinner, Gertrude led us to the ballroom merely to show us what was in store for the next evening. Mrs. Jennings had wanted a mere dance; Gertrude was planning a ball.

Isabel's eyes brightened when she spied the grand piano in the corner. "One song. Can you play us one song, Mary?"

I looked at her. After the incident in high school, we had never talked about the piano again. It was as if we both knew it was a line we didn't dare cross—our friendship wouldn't survive.

As I walked to the piano I wondered if Nathan was now another such a line. If we would survive, not him, but the lie of him. I glanced down at my watch. Fourteen hours.

I selected a piece and began, not as adeptly as I would have liked. My fingers felt stiff and clumsy on the keys. Isabel turned the pages for me.

"I shouldn't be doing this. This isn't what these people paid for."

"Hush. No one who has the pleasure of listening to you could find anything wanting."

I compressed a smile. I only recognized Mr. Darcy's line because it had involved a piano and I could relate to Lizzy in that scene. She knew full well the deficiencies in her playing, but like me, she hadn't taken the time to practice. I focused on the music in front of me and imagined that's what this was—a practice session.

At the last note I glanced up. Everyone had gathered near. Helene began to clap.

"Play another and we shall dance."

Isabel sprang into action and led an impromptu lesson in nineteenth-century country dances, and I warmed to the music.

During my third piece, Isabel determined her pupils were ready to step out on their own. They paired up and she found herself without a partner. With a sigh she lowered herself onto the bench beside me and resumed turning the pages.

I almost felt sorry for her. Until halfway through "Turner's Waltz," when Grant arrived. I heard her gasp before I caught sight of him. He was stunning. There was no other way to say it. He was dressed in Regency-style regimentals. At least, I assumed the British army didn't still wear such tall hats and bright-blue coats. He removed his hat and shot me a wry glance as he led Isabel from the bench beside me to the floor.

I returned to the music and was soon swept away by Turner, Haydn, Mozart, and an Irish jig. Lost within music I hadn't played in the two years since my mom had died and hadn't felt for years before that.

I added a final flourish to the jig, sending Clara into giggling fits while Aaron and Grant stomped and swung the women around like Texans in a bar dance. The Muellers confined themselves to clapping and an occasional foot tap—not because they were surly, but because they were exhausted. And Gertrude stood on the edge of it all with a small smile and bright eyes.

Yes, the music worked its magic, as did the people—Gertrude's emerald-green silk with pearls woven through her silver hair; Helene's diamonds dancing in the candlelight; my own wrist looking equally dazzling; the Lottes dancing, mesmerized by each other; and Isabel and Grant, dancing a final and closing waltz as Sonia and Duncan snuffed the candles in the ballroom.

After the others went upstairs, Gertrude and I sat back down and discussed the next day's plans over a cup of hot cocoa. She brought me to the Blue Room to lay out Nathan's clothes together.

When she flipped on the light, I gasped. "I wish we could've stayed here. I love this room."

It was slightly smaller than ours, with blue toile wallpaper and matching curtains. Not frilly curtains, straight ones with clean lines and right angles. The area rug was bright blue woven with navy. It was thick and chunky as if made from the ropes that rigged ships. It was a man's room, a sailor's room, clean, neat, and comfortable. An imposing wood-framed bed sat in the center of the interior wall, a wardrobe filled one corner, and an armchair and ottoman another.

"I'm glad you like it. It was my brother Geoffrey's room. The Green Room was mine."

"It's so comfortable. Not that ours isn't exquisite, it's just that . . . I have three brothers. I guess I'm more used to this." I ran my fingers down the drapery, then remembered Isabel's admonishment: *Do not weigh the draperies.* "Do the rooms look like they did when you were a child?"

Gertrude scoffed. "Back then the wallpaper was peeling, the paint around the windows disintegrating. The lead frames had warped at least a century earlier, and right up in that corner there was a leak that dripped nine months of the year. Geoffrey used my blue sand pail to catch it until we were teenagers. Then he mounted a catching system made from a canvas tarp and garden tubing. It was all a mess. I don't remember a time it wasn't . . . Wait here."

She returned moments later with a rolling portable wardrobe. She unzipped the canvas side and began withdrawing coats.

"Not that one." I scrunched my nose at the coat she laid on the bed. "I promise you it's too large. He's more narrow, and taller. Do you have anything slimmer?"

She looked like she wanted to laugh, but instead she pulled out three more coats.

"These two." I laid aside a dark green and a bright blue.

She then pulled out shirts, neckties, and three pairs of breeches. "Too small? Too big?"

I shrugged. "How would I know?"

"I have no idea." That time she did laugh.

⁂

. . . A company of clever, well-informed people who have a great deal of conversation.

The line from *Persuasion* came to me on a shaft of morning sunlight. I recalled the enchantment of the previous evening, then let it drift away as I watched the sunbeams strike our room's many shades of green.

I stretched and glanced to Isabel's bed. She was gone—again. I took a deep breath. Day two. I reached for my phone to send a quick text to Dr. Milton when another thought hit me.

Nathan. I calculated the time. Five hours.

I pulled a dress from my wardrobe, this time a rich cream one with blue detailing. The fabric was sumptuous, a soft thin wool, and it fit. It dropped long enough to reach my toes, and the front pleats made me look like I had cleavage. I twisted my ponytail into a bun and secured it with the stretch of electrical wire I'd used on Isabel's hair the night before. I even dabbed on blush and mascara.

Showtime.

I stepped into the gallery. Then I felt it—a shock of pure energy. It was noiseless. There was no change in pressure or sound. It simply felt like a charge reverberating through and around me, like when the guys in the lab set off experiments to see if my hair stood on end when I walked in the door.

I looked down the stairs and there he was, right below me, looking around but not up. Four hours early.

I closed my eyes, thankful for a moment to allow the heat in my face to cool. I shifted my weight to step back when a chuckle reached me.

"Look at you." The words were soft, almost flirtatious. I backed away further.

I took a deep breath and stepped forward. "You're early."

"There was a seat on an earlier flight out of Dallas."

I leaned over the railing. "Stop grinning like that. Wait till you see what you have to wear."

Nathan looked good. He always did. That perfect mix of hipster prep—jeans and Chacos, thin oxford-cut shirts and worn belts, and a touch of Texan thrown in—hair cowboy messy. It was cut short, allowing for only minor ruffling, and, like now for instance, he was often five o'clock scruffy. Thin and fit, lanky and mobile—his body moved with the same facile energy that moved his mind. And he was good at his job. That appealed to me—competence always did.

I stopped cataloguing him as he climbed the stairs; my litany of his attributes felt like a good-bye. He was dating Isabel. And as he neared, her descriptors filled my mind. *TCG. A little boring, but really nice . . . Does something financial for work . . . Quiet . . . Hair you want to run your fingers through, if it was a little longer . . .*

Okay, that last one fit.

"So you're TCG."

Nathan's step hitched. He stepped up the final stair and stood facing me. He'd walked the entire way in silence. "I take it you've heard of me."

I shrugged. "She said TCG worked as a finance consultant and was . . ." I stalled, embarrassed. I never used Isabel's nicknames. They were descriptive, informative, often brutal, and always private. He'd only learned his—or thought he had—by accident.

I shook my head in apology. "It doesn't matter what she said. I never made the connection. The surprise was on me." I bit my lip to stop anything more from coming out. I sounded hurt, surly, and immature. I wanted to be more than that.

"Is she okay?"

"Yes." I felt the tension between us release with the clarity of why he was here. "For all this craziness, when you see her you'll agree. She is safe and well, wherever she is up here." I tapped my temple. "But if she's not back in the twenty-first century in two more days, I'm flying her home, and then I don't know."

I felt Nathan's hand slide down my arm and clasp my own. I watched our hands bound together for a moment before remembering who and what he was—Isabel's.

I turned away, pulling my hand from his, and headed back toward the Blue Room. "Gertrude, the manager, is gone this morning, but she and I discussed everything and she'll formally check you in later. Follow me and I'll show you your room."

I glanced back. He hadn't moved. His face was shadowed, as if something dark or unpleasant had passed by.

"She's good, Nathan. I promise."

He registered my reassurance with a look of surprise.

"This is it. The Blue Room." I tapped the brass plate centered on his door. "We're in the next room. It's green." I twisted the knob and swung the door wide. "Welcome to Regency England."

Nathan followed me into the room. He scanned it thoroughly, then picked up a pair of socks from the bed and dangled them in front of me. "You're kidding, right?"

"Silk stockings." I reached for them. "Real silk. I'm not sure cotton could get this white. Aren't they nice? And you use this garter thingy to keep them up."

"*Nice* wasn't the word that came to mind." He looked back to the bed. "I wear all this? At once?"

"Yes." I opened the wardrobe where Gertrude and I had hung the other clothes. "There are two more outfits in here, and more stockings and stuff in these lower drawers. I recommend you wear your own underwear or boxers or whatever . . ." I felt my cheeks warm. "But you can do what you want."

"Good to know."

"I had to guess your sizes."

He held up the blue coat. "You did great."

"And . . ." My words toppled over his, but standing there made my heart race, my body heat, and my skin itch in the wool dress. "If you know any Austen, it all goes easier. The guests here are really nice, but they throw around names and quotations like WATT throws acronyms. We all have characters. I e-mailed you that, but if you haven't chosen one, you could be Willoughby from *Sense and Sensibility* because we have two characters from that book, Margaret Dashwood and Mrs. Jennings, or that guy from *Persuasion* . . ."

"Captain Wentworth?"

"The other one; the younger Walter Elliot. We've already got an old Sir Walter, so that might be fun."

Nathan closed the distance between us. His face was a disconcerting few inches from my own. "Are you mad at me? What have I done?"

"I– No. Why?"

"Those are terrible men, Mary. I'm a little worried you put me in their camp. Couldn't you pick Darcy or Knightley or Ferrars? Edward, not Robert."

"Not Knightley. I mean . . ." No way would I suggest a Mr. Knightley to pair with our Emma. "Hey, you know your Austen."

"I've told you. English major. Three sisters. Those movies were like background noise growing up." He laughed at my scowl. "I take it engineers aren't required to take nineteenth-century literary criticism. But . . ."

He paused to capture my attention and placed a finger under my chin to keep it up. I'd been looking somewhere near his Adam's apple. I changed my focal point.

"You *are* mad." He moved the finger to rest between my eyebrows. I felt the tension I held there.

"I feel like a fool." My face flamed as I backed away.

"Mary–" He stepped toward me. His eyes held a look of pity— and that made everything worse.

"You don't owe me anything." I backpedaled to the door at a faster rate than he advanced. "You change and then we'll go find Isabel."

His outstretched hand dropped with his nod.

I stepped into the gallery and shut the door behind me.

Chapter 18

Nathan finally stepped from his room. I'd spent the time pacing and was certain that in a half hour I had worn down the carpet more than the previous 258 years.

Military style, I turned on my heel at the gallery's end to find him watching me. He had chosen the green coat rather than the blue, and I'd been right; it suited him. But he was clutching the waistband of his pants—breeches—in one fist. The pants sagged within his death grip, and I could tell they itched. He fidgeted as if trying to keep the fabric from touching his skin too long.

"You look good." I walked back toward him as far as the stairs, then headed down.

"Hang on. You can't just walk away."

I paused. He had both highly-polished-black-leather-shod feet firmly planted.

"Can we take a second here? These are going to fall down." He pulled the waistband out a good eight inches from his body.

I came back and pushed his shoulder to shift him around. "Hold these up." I handed him his coattails as I caught at the back of his breeches. "There's a cord like a shoelace back here and . . ." I pulled it and tied a tight bow. "There. All better?"

He faced me and put two fingers under the waistband. "Perfect. Now this." He flapped at his necktie. "Is this right? It was super long."

"Almost." I stepped close and undid his pathetic knot. "Mr. Mueller told me he had to wrap it around three times . . . Here . . . Then . . . Another bow." I finished and pulled it tight as well. "You smell like bubble gum."

He lowered his face to mine. We'd never stood so close.

"I'm allergic to mint. Do you want a piece?" Before I could think of an answer, he raised his hand, paused for a second, then threaded his fingers through my hair. My eyes almost slid shut at his touch.

He pulled away my black ring of electrical wire, and my hair toppled about my shoulders. "Sorry. It was falling out."

I grabbed it. This time, more embarrassed than ever. "I couldn't find a real hair band."

He lifted a section of hair and gave it a light tug. "Despite your dress, I'm glad you haven't forgotten who you are. Though I must say . . . Something is different about you."

"What?"

"I can't put my finger on it yet, but give me time."

I nodded and led the way to the stairs.

Give me time . . . Time. Our timing was off. How many times had I read that line? Or heard it in movies? Time was never neutral and often felt dangerous. Either we think we have all the time in the world, or time moves too fast or too slow; a shock can stop time; fear or impending pain can slow it. Time never simply *is* . . . And no matter how much you want to hang on to it, time runs out.

I glanced back to Nathan. Our timing was off or it had run out. I had none to give him—so I let him go.

"Time to get you to Isabel." I wondered if he could wake her. Was she Sleeping Beauty waiting for her Prince Charming? The thought drove me faster. "She's probably at the stables. It's becoming her favorite place."

I pressed my lips together to keep from adding, *And Grant her favorite guy.*

"Hey . . . You're doing it again. Slow down."

I felt my shawl lift as I raced down the last few stairs. I halted when I reached the hall's white-and-black marble. Nathan stood right behind me.

He had pulled my shawl off and was fanning it out. He then moved close, flipped it over my head, and settled it on my shoulders. "This was falling off too." He looked down at me without stepping back.

"Thank you." I stepped away first and led the way to the front door, down the front steps, and across the gravel drive. I darted my eyes everywhere but at him.

"It's really beautiful here, don't you think? I love these trees, and the air has this tactile damp feeling, but not today, or yesterday, which I think is unusual. I thought we were going to get more rain, but Gertrude, she's the manager, says it's been dry and is expected to generally remain so, which must be unusual with all this green. But we know dry back home and this really doesn't feel dry." I heard myself prattling and stopped.

I tilted my head toward the path. Shadow met us at the copse of trees covering the hillside down to the stream and stables.

"It reminds me of the Pacific Northwest." Nathan caught up and walked next to me. "Does everyone always dress up here?"

"Sonia—she's the maid—explained that the other night. Costumed parties dominate the summer months, the high season. But there are only two costumed stays offered in the fall, the last week in September and this two-week stretch to Halloween. Then the Stanleys, the owners, keep the house for themselves all through the holidays. And..." I took a breath; it rattled on the exhale. "The house doesn't fill in the fall. It's kind of the time for the staff to wrap up all the details of the busy summer before the Stanleys come. That's why the Lottes—they're the family from Geneva—chose this week. They didn't want Clara, their eight-year-old, to feel uncomfortable. She already speaks three or four languages, and she adores Isabel. The other couple, the Muellers, chose it because I guess it's a little cheaper now than in the high season. They're from Salzburg. They're about eighty, and don't mention the Von Trapps. Well...Do. Herman likes to talk about them."

I risked a peek. My head reached right above Nathan's shoulders. It would probably tuck beneath his chin. I dropped my eyes—our hands were at the same level.

He glanced over. I glanced away.

We rounded the last bend to find an empty stable. The door to the dark-green building was shut, and the silence held a hard, empty quality. I peeked inside. Three horses. No humans.

"I didn't tell her you were coming...I'm sorry."

"Mary, I didn't come to—"

"Good morning, Miss Davies."

I spun as Duncan came from around the corner dressed in khakis, work boots, and a plaid shirt. He carried small needle-nose clippers.

"Duncan." I practically shouted his name. "Good to see you... Has our resident Emma gone riding?"

"She and Grant left about an hour ago. He took a picnic, so I expect they'll be gone awhile." Duncan's face split into a slow smile. "She didn't balk about no chaperone today, and he looked very pleased to—"

"Duncan, this is Isabel's boyfriend from the States. Nathan Hillam. Nathan, this is Duncan. He's interning here this summer while getting his veterinarian degree."

Duncan blanched. "I—"

"All good." Nathan cut him off. He narrowed his eyes my direction, then pumped Duncan's hand in greeting. "It's nice to meet you, Duncan. Those look like they're for fishing?" He gestured to the clippers.

"I was tying flies. Do you want to see—"

Nathan had already passed him.

Duncan followed Nathan. I followed Duncan. We rounded the stables and found a door on the other side. I stepped through.

Fishing rods lined the walls, and small bins of feathery flies lined the counter. There was a desk covered in brightly colored foam sheets, fluff, and more feathers. It looked like a kindergarten craft table. Rubber pants hung from hooks, boots stacked in rows beneath them.

"This is amazing. My grandfather tied all his own flies." Nathan pointed to the table. "Can we fish?" He directed his question to me.

Duncan answered. "Let me get you set up. You won't need waders; you can stay on the bank. There's a spot just downstream that has a good caddisfly hatch this time of the morning."

I leaned against the wall and watched while the two of them chatted like old friends and grabbed everything a fisherman needed. Nathan acted like a kid on Christmas Eve—all excitement and questions. Christmas Eve as most people think of it, that is— the holiday as it should be.

Nathan sent me a warm smile. It felt as if he'd read my thoughts and liked their direction. Then he turned back to Duncan like a puppy yapping at Duncan's heels. What kind of fish? . . . What's running? . . . Any rainbow? . . . What's hatching? . . . Dry fly? . . . Wet? . . . What do you tie? . . . Do you tie all your own flies? . . .

Once Duncan had everything sorted, Nathan stopped in front of me. "I'm sorry, Mary. Is there something you or we need to do? I didn't even think about Isabel."

"Don't you want to find her?"

"She's happy with Grant, right?" His gaze swept Duncan into the conversation too.

The younger man's face clouded in confusion. "She looked very happy this morning. She seemed pleased to see Grant and she loved the idea of a picnic. Not that anything would be amiss. Grant would never be—"

Nathan stepped to him and clapped a hand on his back. "I'm not worried about any of that. If she is safe and happy, I am too." His last sentence he directed to me. It felt like smoke—substantive enough to carry a message, but able to drift up and away before I caught it.

He wagged a finger at my dress. "It's not as if she can go too far."

"You're right," I conceded with a smile.

He and Duncan headed out the door. As Duncan strode ahead, Nathan paused to wait for me. He reached out and tugged my hand to hurry me along. And rather than let it go once we'd caught up, he twisted his fingers through mine and hung on.

I tried not to hold too tight. Then not too loose. Then chided myself for thinking about it at all. I then tried to enjoy the feel of my hand in his and the morning. All I really felt was confusion.

The sun refracted through the clouds. "Crepuscular rays—sunbeams." I gestured to the sky with my free hand.

Nathan smiled at me.

We walked on and I watched the sun and clouds dance above us. I felt myself relax. Everything was right with the world when sunbeams were present. My dad always called them "angel lights," and I'd believed him, until advanced physics proved they were merely parallel shafts of light passing through cloud and shadow. They only appeared to converge as if from some heavenly source. Regardless of the source or the explanation, they made the stream, the bank, the tops of the trees, everything, glow.

At the clearing, Nathan dropped his coat on the bench and met Duncan streamside. I hesitated, but Duncan waved me over too and held out a moss-green-colored rod.

"This one is for you. It's a five weight. Perfect for these trout." He then released the small fly attached to one of the rod's eyelets. "I rigged this with my Booby Hopper-Red. It's my own adaptation of the Red Squirrel Nymph, which is what you want right now. Mine sit high to give you more time on your cast."

I accepted the rod, holding it like a sword, as he spoke to Nathan. Nathan reached over and pressed down on the rod before I poked Duncan in the temple.

Duncan hadn't noticed. He was already focused on Nathan's rig.

"You . . . you've fished a lot . . . You've got my Hare Ear Dry Fly. It's a little twist on the more common Yellow Stone Dry. I named it for this patch of fur I added right here. Seems to work really well . . . And if you fish tomorrow, we'll get out a couple I'm tying right now."

"Right after breakfast?" Nathan prodded.

"Before."

Nathan laughed. "You're my kind of angler."

Duncan grinned. He looked back to me, then to Nathan again. "Right. You don't need me now. Come get me if you have any troubles."

He surveyed our supplies, then took off at almost a run. His brown hair stuck straight up and wagged in the breeze like cilia moving in water. For some odd reason, he reminded me of a young version of my dad, a young Albert Einstein.

Isabel was right; my dad was relational. So was Duncan. I turned back to Nathan. "You made his day."

Nathan looked up; surprise followed by delight moved through his eyes. "He made mine. He's a good kid."

"You know he's probably only ten years younger than you at most."

Nathan twisted to follow Duncan's retreating form. "His enthusiasm made him seem younger. Was I patronizing?"

"You're never patronizing. You're one of the most considerate men I've ever known."

Nathan stared at me.

I gave my attention to the bank beneath me. Rather than slope into the water, it cut a jagged descent to a foot below us. The water ran fast in the center of the stream, making little white bubbles and ripples as it passed over submerged rocks. Near the shore it moved more slowly, creating whorls and eddies in the current. Closest to the shore, right beneath me, the water sat like glass.

"That's where you want to cast first." He moved closer. "Right at the shoreline. It even digs in a little beneath you. Fish love to hide in those crannies. They get the bugs that drop from the land into the water, and if you start there you can work your way out without losing the chance for them. If you start out and come in, you'll spook any fish hiding close long before your fly gets to them."

I let the fly drop.

"Do you know what to do?"

I shook my head. "I used to fish with my mom, years ago, but only spinner rods for catfish or bass in a little lake near our house."

"This isn't too different. Watch." He pulled a bunch of line out of his reel and let it puddle at his feet. He then stepped back and bent his arm. His rod pointed straight up. "Pretend there's a clock resting on your shoulder, facing you. Up to midnight. Pause. Smooth to ten o'clock. Pause again to send the line out. Then drop the tip down to nine or eight." The fly shot twenty feet into the stream, taking all the line at his feet with it.

"Do it again. It's like you're cutting the wind with nothing at all." The fluidity of the motion was mesmerizing. He did it again, and again, and the line shot straight despite the breeze, at least thirty feet this time, to the far side of the stream. "Did you mean to do that?"

"Of course. I'm trying to impress you." He smiled. "That was one of my better casts. The next will probably be a disaster." He cast again. "It's all in the plane of your cast. That controls the loop of your line. You want to keep it straight. No loop is best."

He pulled the line in and let it lie at his feet, then cast once more.

"Amazing. The physics of it, the lines and angles... Once more."

He cast again, and with the most wonderful grin. "Now you try."

I did. It was a jerky motion that sent the fly two feet and plopped it in the water right along the shore.

"It's a good start."

"Liar." I pulled in the line as he had—and it caught on the hem of my dress.

"You're right." Nathan laughed, then swung his head in an exaggerated motion as if that was the only way to become serious once more. "Try again. Think of it like flicking paint off a paintbrush. Pretend you're Jackson Pollock."

"Well then . . ." I did exactly what he said and fared no better. But it didn't matter.

Nathan knelt and untangled the line from around my feet.

"I'm clearly not an artist."

"It takes time." He cast again.

After a few minutes, I reeled in my line and watched him.

He spared me only a glance. "My grandfather used to say that everything in the world could be solved at the cadence of a cast. Think about things, don't rush them, get a feel for them, live organically. Live life like you cast." He bent his arm again, and with fluid slow motion he shot the line straight across the pond into the slow-moving water near the far bank.

"All the stuff you've been trying to get me to do this past year?"

His brows met above his nose. I was tempted to press my finger there as he had done to me.

"I guess I have. I find work goes better when you ask for help and bring people into the process. And you do, don't get me wrong. I've never seen anyone more giving. But something hiccupped with Golightly." He returned to casting. "Please don't think I'm advocating the same approach Karen is taking."

"What? You're not promoting 'dialoguing' and 'collective creativity' and 'thought leadership'?" My voice felt as derisive as it sounded. "Karen wraps threats in buzzwords. There's not much else there, not for me at least."

Nathan didn't comment.

"That was inappropriate of me. I'm still angry about a lot of stuff she's doing."

Nathan looked at me. "Not at all. We aren't at WATT. In fact, WATT is no longer a client of mine. We are two friends talking about my fishing and your work." He winked.

"Yes, but you know a lot about my work."

"I also know you'll figure it out. You're good at your job, Mary."

I gestured to the rod, ready to change the subject. He was slowly pulling in the line. The fly fluttered across the surface of the water. "So you grew up doing this?"

"My grandparents had a place in northern Minnesota. It was a tiny cabin on a lake with no indoor plumbing, and it was heaven. I used to spend as much time there as I could during the summers. Granddad wasn't a talkative guy, but every now and then, after hours of silence, he'd reveal these great quiet truths. I should've written them down because I've forgotten most of them."

"What's one you remember?"

Nathan cast again. "He said that how people treat you is only 10 percent about you and 90 percent about them, so you need to be careful how you react and how you judge. You never know someone's story."

"Clearly a numbers guy. I like him."

"An engineer at 3M for forty-three years. Definitely a numbers guy." Nathan gave me more than a passing glance this time. "You would have loved him and he you."

A fish saved me from a reply. Nathan immediately yanked his rod tip up and started pulling line in with his free hand.

"How can I help?"

He tilted his head to the soft turf beside me. "Can you get that net over the side without ruining your dress?"

"It'd be my second. There was a muddy hem issue yesterday." I envisioned poor Sonia as I dropped my rod and grabbed the net. I pulled my skirt over my knees so as not to get it too dirty and knelt on the grass.

I scooped the net in a few times before emerging with an iridescent fish. It flipped and flopped, forcing me to wiggle the net to keep it inside.

"Here." Nathan pulled me and the net up. He patted his hands against the wet sides of the net, then unhooked the fish. "About a thirteen-inch brown trout; what a little beauty."

"Why'd you do that?"

"Fish are covered with a film. Dry hands will ruin it and hurt the fish, so you wet them in the water or on the net first." He held up his "little beauty."

"Now I feel bad; I didn't know they needed that viscous coating. I used to wipe it off as a kid."

"Ugh . . . Really?"

"We ate the fish," I whined, sounding like a five-year-old. "It hardly mattered."

"This one we'll release, if you don't mind." Nathan smiled and dipped his hands and the fish under the water. He pumped it beneath the surface like winding up a Matchbox car and let it go.

"Too small to eat anyway," I quipped, then retreated to the bench behind us. His pack of gum lay on top of his coat. I took a piece.

"Are you giving up?"

"I'm not very good at it and, you're right, this dress makes it awkward. I'll try it again someday, in my own clothes. Right now, I'd rather sit here and admire you while you fish."

As the words left my mouth, I realized that, like a true aficionado, I'd just appropriated an Austen line. Mr. Bingley's sister Caroline was a wonderful model for fawning adoration. She'd practically salivated over Darcy, and he was only writing a letter.

I sat and Nathan fished. The silence was light and lovely until I realized it wasn't silence at all. The stream gurgled, birds chirped, something called in the distance. It was downright noisy—and perfect. I closed my eyes to enjoy every sound . . . and then opened them to watch Nathan, like a good and proper Caroline Bingley. He still faced the river and cast with ease. But there was a rhythmic quality to his motions, as if he wasn't paying attention to what was in front of him. His shoulders lifted up then seemed to stiffen and broaden as they dropped back. I'd seen the gesture before. Nathan had made a decision.

"Mary?" He called and let my name linger in question, but he didn't turn.

"Yes."

"You know Isabel calls me TCG. She has nicknames for everyone. Have I heard about you?"

"I thought you knew." I closed my eyes. I felt almost swamped with relief that he didn't. But then . . . how fair was that? "SK."

I expected him to take time and converge the girl with the nickname. He didn't. "Will you translate it for me?"

"I can tell you when it started."

He slanted a look my way.

"When we were about ten, my mom took us to Dallas to the American Girl store and we each got to pick out a doll. Isabel's dad sent along the money to fund our expedition, so Mom said she could pick first. She chose Kit Kittredge."

"Who?"

"She's this spunky blonde from 1934, saves her family from the Depression and is a genuinely adorable heroine. Isabel beelined straight to her. She then spent the next hour cajoling me into picking Ruthie, Kit's best friend."

"Who you didn't want?"

I shrugged, which he couldn't see. "Not exactly. There was nothing wrong with Ruthie. She's quiet, cute, loyal, and all good things, but it was more complicated than that, at least it felt that way even then. Isabel and I . . . It doesn't matter. I bought Ruthie."

I envisioned Ruthie, with her long, dark hair and her fine coat of dust, sitting in her box at the top of the hallway closet. "She's probably a collector's item now. The company doesn't even make the sidekick dolls anymore."

I froze.

"That's it, isn't it? SK. Sidekick."

I shrugged again. This time he saw it. He turned back to the stream.

Einstein was right about the space-time continuum. Massive objects, or statements, or revelations, can cause a bending—a disruption. I sat in such a distortion now. I could physically feel him lining up WATT's Mary with Isabel's SK. I looked down the path—it seemed to tunnel away into the distance. Another distortion—that path hadn't seemed so long before. It wasn't a viable escape route.

"I'm sorry about your mom."

"What? . . . Oh . . . Thank you."

"You never told me. I mean *you* you. This is confusing, isn't it?"

I took a quick breath and shifted the conversation. "So how'd you meet Isabel?"

Nathan studied me. "Did you ever mention me to her? Not that you would, but . . . Did you?"

I begged my face not to flush and my eyes to stay steady. "When you started at WATT I must have. You kinda flipped my world, work world that is, a little upside down."

"I did, didn't I?" His mouth lifted in a half smile. "I think everyone was terrified of all those interviews and me shadowing everyone. Only Moira took it in stride."

"She would. But back to Isabel?" I wanted to know.

"We met at the Sahara Lounge last March. She was with Tiffany. Brad, her fiancé, and I have known each other for years." He faced me. "I told her what I did and where I worked that first night, Mary."

"I don't doubt that."

"You did. On the phone yesterday. You thought I'd been playing you."

I felt his focus fix on me; I looked up from my lap. I'd been shredding a dead leaf. "I didn't know what to think."

His focus returned to the water, and a soft "Welcome to my world" reached me.

I cast for a new topic. I was tired of Isabel standing between us, and I did believe him. It was one reason Isabel used nicknames. She liked to control information, variables. Control gave her security.

"The Sahara Lounge, huh? You like the blues." I smiled. Every new bit of information made me like him more.

"Blues, jazz, classical, rock . . . I like music. I've learned your friend does not like music."

Your friend. The words were sharp and punctuated. Distanced.

"No . . ." I couldn't help grinning. "Roger Taylor, Mick Taylor, James Taylor . . . For Isabel, there's only one Taylor. Miss Swift."

Nathan stared at me. "Whoa . . . Look at you, pulling out the unsung greats from Queen and the Rolling Stones—not to mention the artist behind one of the best songs ever."

"Which one?"

"'Your Smiling Face.'"

"Oh . . ." *Whenever I see your smiling face, I have to smile myself because I love you . . .*

"Great song, right?" Nathan's voice carried a light teasing note. He knew exactly what I was doing.

"Great song."

He gestured to my rod, which lay on the ground beside me. "You shouldn't give up so easily. Come try again."

I blew a bubble and popped it for the noise. It sounded like a small pellet gun. "I think this is a much more productive use of my time. Do you know the force it takes to blow a good bubble?"

This got him striding toward me. "Did you steal my gum?"

"You left the pack right here on your sumptuous green coat. It wasn't stealing."

"Please don't call it borrowing."

I popped another bubble. The air had changed between us. It felt like it did some days at WATT when the work was light and Nathan and I . . . We just had fun together. "I promise not to give it back."

"So . . . What does it take to blow a really good bubble?"

"I suspect anything over 1 psi is too aggressive. I'm playing with 10 to 15 kPa right now."

"You cannot judge that."

"Who says?"

"I do." He laid his rod on the ground next to the bench. His linen shirt billowed around the waist. He dropped next to me and I scooted a couple inches to give him room. "No, really, can you?"

"I'm not sure. I like to think I can." I glanced at him. He was so close I could see the lightest smattering of freckles across his cheek. "That small room off the lab can be pressurized, so the guys play around with it all the time. Sometimes they let me in on the fun. So . . . maybe my guess isn't without some foundation. But no, I can't really tell."

"Nice. But I'm not the jealous type."

"What?" I almost choked on the gum.

"You know all the lab guys adore you. You're the only one they bring their hard copies to, and they spend entire lunch breaks try-ing to figure out how to make your jewelry rise off your neck or create a decibel only you'll hear or something else that'll drive you crazy. They even freeze-dried some cookie you love."

"That was disgusting."

"I know. I was their guinea pig."

"I am so sorry. They're just goofy."

Nathan leaned back against the bench, arm crashing into mine, and laughed. "They're a bunch of brilliant physicists who respect you, trust you, and slightly adore you. Don't discount the power of the friendships you've built . . . But enough of WATT. Do I get a piece of my own gum?"

I handed him the pack and he joined me. No more words, just several very well-pressurized bubbles.

After several minutes and as many bubbles, he slid me a glance. Sunbeams caught his eyelashes and the stubble across his chin. It was darker in that little cleft in the center. His whole face became a contrast of light and dark while laughing eyes locked on mine. I also noticed the way the heat from his arm in the thinnest of linen shirts pressed into mine . . . I tucked the moment away.

"Why do you look so happy?"

In reply he drew his lips into a straight line and his face turned red. It reminded me of the couple times we bumped into each other climbing off the treadmills in the gym, or of myself, multiple times this morning.

"I'm not . . . Well, I am, but . . . I feel like I can see you better here. I'm enjoying this."

I felt something unfurl within me. I drew it tight again. "We should find Isabel."

"Not yet." He closed his eyes and lifted his face to the sun as I'd seen him do so often in Austin.

I did the same. The silence lay light until broken by a muffled sound, a clopping sound. Across the stream Tennyson came into view pulling a carriage. A bonnet . . . Grant . . .

"Hey." It felt as if cold water had been thrown at me. I shot off the bench and pointed. "It's Isabel. They're probably headed to the stables. We should go back."

"Why?"

I bit my lip. I couldn't articulate why—we just needed to leave. All my thoughts for the last twenty hours had been focused on this moment. Isabel seeing Nathan; Isabel seeing me with Nathan. Isabel waking up, running off into the sunset with him. Or Isabel facing us both and knowing I knew she'd lied and finally understanding that things couldn't be the same again. Isabel finally learning that some lines friends never crossed.

Without answering I picked up my rod and headed toward the path.

Nathan caught up within a few feet, his own rod in hand. "I'm serious, Mary. Why the rush? We were having fun."

I stopped and looked at him. "You wouldn't understand."

"Then tell me."

Then tell me. Nathan caught the flash of recognition in my eyes. He offered that same half smile. "We've been here before, I know, but this time, trust me. Please, Mary. Tell me." There was nothing professional about his look. It was intimate and compelling.

"You're Tall Consultant Guy. That's a nice thing."

His mouth tightened. I dropped my eyes.

"I'm Sidekick, and that doesn't feel so nice. I'm so tired. That's what you can't understand. I've wanted to walk away, and yes . . . I may have mentioned you more than once. Right now, I want her to know she hurt me and I want her to wake up, or come back, or whatever needs to happen to make this all okay. Then maybe I can be done and be okay too."

Nathan's fingers tangled within mine. He held tight and we started walking.

We stopped in unison when Isabel came into view. She stood patting Tennyson. The horse was free of the carriage now, and Grant was nowhere in sight. Isabel was dressed in a blue dress so pale it looked almost white. I glanced down. My cream felt dingy in comparison.

I glanced to Nathan. His eyes were fixed on Isabel and I felt myself falter.

Six months.

I took in what he saw: Isabel's matching bonnet was pushed back, and its black trim made her curls only glossier by comparison. She stood gently crooning. The high notes she used for young children were soft, coaxing, and endearing when directed at an enormous black horse.

I cleared my throat. This was not a moment in which I wanted to linger. "Isabel? Look who's come." My voice broke. Nathan squeezed my hand. I coughed to regain a normal tone. "Nathan came to visit yo—us."

Nathan smiled at me rather than Isabel. "Hey, Isabel." He walked to her and bent to kiss her cheek.

She stepped away before contact.

"Hello?" Her voice arced her greeting into a question.

"I . . . I'm sorry." Nathan shot me a startled look. He hadn't fully digested what was happening. Who could?

He took a steady breath and straightened. "That was forward of me, Miss Woodhouse, forgive me. It's lovely to see you again. We met long ago, in another city and on a much warmer day, at a concert." Nathan reached for her gloved hand this time. "You were with Miss . . . er . . . Tiffany, and you wore blue, not unlike today."

"I've never traveled, but I often wear blue." Her voice was cool and distant, as if she were really saying, *I don't know you, but I'll be polite.*

"Have you come to see Mary?" Isabel lifted her chin to me. It seemed that if I approved of Nathan, so could she.

Nathan stepped beside her. Both were now staring at me. He raised an assessing brow. "As a matter of fact, I have."

Chapter 19

A line came to me as we walked to the house. Tall, handsome Nathan walked between two Regency women, and we appeared "to uncommon advantage"—the "picturesque" was perfect.

Lizzy used that remark to skip away from Mr. Darcy and the fawning, competitive Bingley sisters. It was a light, playful comment. She was running away. I glanced to Nathan. I'd thought he had come for Isabel, but the fishing, his words, his looks had ignited something new in me: hope. I didn't want to step away from this walk, this group. In fact, I wanted more than that—I wanted to stay.

"Isn't that right?" Isabel looked across Nathan to me.

"Hmm?"

"We won't be here that long." She looked back to Nathan, who had been peppering her with questions the entire walk—all general, all polite, none concerning. "We need to head home next week."

I hoped Nathan wouldn't ask where home was. I'd tried that already, and it had brought a furrowed brow and a flit of panic.

"Did you ever tell Mary how we met?" He delivered the line perfectly—curious indifference.

Isabel's lips puckered. "I don't recall meeting you. Please forgive me."

"Not at all. I'm pleased you don't remember. It usually takes people a *third* introduction to remember me."

Nathan put an odd emphasis on *third*. Isabel threw me a quizzical glance. I threw it to Nathan. But rather than answer, he seemed pleased at something beyond Isabel and me. He compressed a smile and shoulder-bumped me.

As we entered the house, he pulled at my hand. Isabel didn't notice and stepped ahead.

"You didn't tell me your character."

"Catherine Morland from—"

"*Northanger Abbey.* She's no sidekick, Mary." Nathan stared at me as if I was yummy. There was no other word or feeling to describe it.

"I think it's the dress. Gives me courage."

His chuckle wasn't quite audible and it wasn't quite suggestive. It was something mysterious, quiet and intriguing. Before I could react, he pulled at my hand to catch up to Isabel.

We found everyone already seated for lunch. They'd heard of Nathan's arrival, so after well wishes and warm exclamations, we circled the table for introductions—real names, then fictional. When we reached Nathan, he stalled.

Helene tapped her finger on the dining room table. "Out with it. Introduce yourself, young man."

Nathan, who had just picked up his knife and fork, laid them down again. He glanced to me, then focused on Helene. He took a beat before replying. "Henry Tilney."

"Who? Who is that?" Herman tapped his wife's hand. "I have never heard of him."

Helene's eyes widened. She looked to me and smiled, and before she could answer Herman, Nathan did.

"He's the hero from *Northanger Abbey.* A clergyman, clumsy

at times with his delivery, but an all-around good guy." He glanced at me. "He's curious. Some might call him a conundrum, but he gets his girl in the end."

Helene clapped her hands together. "This is fun. I thought I'd have to winkle a romance out of you all, but this is blossoming splendidly. It's more than I could have hoped. Oh . . . Dancing will be such fun tonight."

I shook my head at Nathan. I didn't trust myself to speak.

After Sonia cleared dessert, everyone drifted away. Gertrude had printed a list of activities on linen paper, but the women chose to rest—and Clara wanted her iPad. Aaron slapped Nathan on the back with an invitation to go shooting.

Isabel looped her arm through mine. She tucked me close like a lifeline. "Will you come upstairs with me?"

"Of course." There was a concerning fragility about her voice and look.

Nathan caught it too. He hesitated outside Aaron's grasp.

"I'll find you later?" I asked him before leading Isabel to the stairs. Nathan nodded and followed Aaron.

"Do you feel okay? Shall we rest?"

"I'm so tired and heavy feeling." Isabel dropped to the bed and curled up.

I pulled out my phone to text Dr. Milton. "Do you have a head-ache? Chills? Fever?" I pressed my hand to her forehead.

She swatted at it. "You are such a worrier. Did I know this about you?"

I dropped next to her. "Probably not. You've never given me cause to worry before. Not like this."

"I'm fine. A nap will set me right . . . Sonia was looking for you earlier. She wanted to show you a center?"

The business center.

"If you nap, I'll go find her." I tucked my phone back into my pocket and grabbed my computer.

Isabel's eyes were already closed. "Mmm ... hmm ..." was her only reply.

I headed through the front gallery, now cool, as the sun had passed above the house and it lay in shadow. Down the stairs, I walked toward the back and the kitchen. It was bathed in light. I paused outside the ballroom.

A budding romance. It's more than I could have hoped. Oh ... Dancing will be such fun tonight.

Perhaps Mrs. Jennings was right.

"Do you want to see the business center? I'm headed there now." Sonia approached, carrying a multi-armed candelabra. She gripped the base in both hands. It wobbled within her grasp.

"I was just coming to find you. Can I help you with that?"

"If you could grab the candles tucked under my arm. They're slipping."

I pulled out eight candles tucked between her biceps and her body. "How did you get these in there?" I followed her down the hallway toward the kitchen.

"Everything is so far away in this house. You learn to carry as much as you can to limit the trips."

She backed into a side door and laid the silver on a broad, high worktable. "Here it is."

I rolled the candles off my makeshift laptop tray and onto the table. The business center was a fourteen-by-fourteen room, a little larger than the Green Room's bathroom. It felt like a butler's pantry that covered all the bases from the seventeenth century to the twenty-first.

In one corner sat a state-of-the-art scanner-printer-copier-fax machine. Above it resided the house's modem, router, amplifier, and bins for assorted cables. And a twenty-seven-inch plasma monitor and a thirteen-inch laptop stood on a narrow side table. In the center, at which we stood, sat a high worktable, four feet square with a polished wood top. The top was at least two inches thick and formed by woodcuts pressed together, like a fancy cutting board. It was oiled to a velvety finish. Cupboards lined three of the four walls, a paned window was centered on the fourth, and a single armchair with a small circular table beside it was tucked into a corner. It was a perfect little oasis.

"We use it for odd jobs like sewing, polishing silver, and ruling the modern world." She nodded to my computer. "May I quickly polish this silver, or is your work private?"

"Not at all. Please stay."

Sonia polished; I checked e-mails and wrote one to Dr. Milton. Sonia whittled the ends of new candles to place within the candelabra. I rewired two green lamps I found resting on the side table.

"Gertrude would die if she knew I had you working."

"Don't tell her. I love this stuff." I laid down the pliers as a knock drew our attention to the door.

Nathan peeked in. "I've been searching for you . . . Hey, Sonia."

"Hello, Mr. Hillam." Sonia fitted the last candle into place.

"Tilney now." He leaned across the table on his elbows to her. "You can call me Henry, but only in private. I wouldn't want Mrs. Jennings to hear you, because despite what you may hope, Sonia, we can't marry. I have to go back to America someday."

Sonia giggled, hoisted the candelabra high, and left us.

"You are such a flirt." I twisted the last wire and reseated the lamp's neck.

"As if you ever noticed." Nathan circled the table and climbed onto the stool next to me. He pulled the cord on the lamp I'd already fixed. On. Off. On. Off. "This is some room. What do you say we bring Isabel in here, show her all the tech, and wake her up? Turn on all the screens? Show her YouTube?"

"I don't think it works that way." I twisted the lamp's neck into place and continued to my real questions. "Did I really miss something? You flirted with me?"

"When I first arrived at WATT, yes. It was highly unprofessional, but I couldn't help myself. You never noticed. I figured you had a boyfriend. That was an easier blow to the ego than you didn't like me."

"Like you!" My exclamation surprised us both.

"You have resurrected my ego." Nathan's face split into a broad grin. "What was it then? Your focus was definitely elsewhere."

I almost quipped that he'd been too subtle, that it hadn't been my fault. But Moira closed my mouth before I opened it. *Everyone can see the way he looks at you. Why do you give him the Heisman every day?* Instead I offered him a clueless head shake—it was all I had.

Nathan laid a palm on my closed computer. "Do you have more work you need to do?"

"Just a couple e-mails I need to send. I was using the lamps to work out answers to a few of Benson's questions, but I can send them later." I placed the harp into its sockets and spun on the finial.

"Send them now. I'm in no rush." Nathan pushed away from the table and flopped into the armchair. He grabbed the book resting on its side table. "I'll wait for you." He twisted the book to see the spine. "Of course. *Pride and Prejudice.*"

"I think they have one in every room."

"And why not? It's a manual for life—setting right pride, prejudice, misconceptions, and self-illusions. Also some good fun. Right now I'm going to take my cue from Caroline Bingley and sit here and admire you while I pretend to read."

I blinked; he laughed.

"Well, go on . . . Get to work."

I opened my computer and got to work. Although I was focused on Benson's questions, I was also acutely aware of Nathan. He filled the room. I felt him lean back and I heard the book's spine creak upon opening.

The silence smoothed out until I came to a marketing question.

"Hey . . . TCG." I looked up and instantly regretted using Isabel's nickname.

Nathan's eyes remained fixed on the book, but they took on a hard quality, then within the same heartbeat, a hurt one. He cleared it as his gaze met mine.

"I . . . I have a marketing question for you."

"Shoot . . . But you must know what those letters mean."

"Tall Consultant Guy."

He dropped his head as if disappointed by my dishonesty. "I'm not an idiot, Mary, and by your expression, you know the truth too. TCG. Third. Choice. Guy."

"That's why you said that earlier. Third. How'd you find out? And if you knew . . . why'd you continue to go out with her? Why for six—" I left the question hanging, as I didn't know how to end it.

Nathan laid the book in his lap. "She was talking to Tiffany about someone being a first choice guy. Then I caught my picture with the initials on her contacts list one day. It wasn't hard to put it together. As for your other question, it was never serious. It was more to keep either of us from being odd man out with all the couples we knew. And she was persistent; she kept calling." He gestured to me. "I get why now. But why did I keep saying yes? I—" He folded his lips in. "Total honesty here? It was probably ego. An attempt to prove I was more. No one wants to be third choice, even if they couldn't care less about being any choice."

"I shouldn't have asked you to come." I rested my elbows on the table, head in hands. I recalled Nathan's stories from earlier. His grandfather was right. How people treat you is more about themselves than about you. Nathan and Isabel were more about Isabel, or even about Isabel and me, than anything else. Me and Nathan? I'd wanted help, I'd wanted to confront Isabel, I'd wanted . . . I looked up at him. Nathan. I'd wanted Nathan. And now he was here, smack between me and Isabel, and he was hurt and it was my fault. I'd made it about me. I raised my head. "I'm sorry."

"You didn't ask, remember? I kinda forced it on you."

"You did." I couldn't offer a smile. He gave me one anyway.

Nathan pushed out of the armchair and joined me at the table. He leaned against the side directly across from me and, elbows to table, our heads were about twelve inches apart.

"The minute I heard your voice . . . I didn't come for Isabel, Mary. I came for you. And her nickname doesn't hurt me. I couldn't care less about it—as long as you don't think of me like that."

Nathan narrowed his eyes. They held that intensity I'd questioned earlier, the one I'd hoped was for me, but wasn't sure about. This time I felt sure. This time I couldn't look away.

"I don't think of you like that."

Chapter 20

After dinner I stood at the edge of the ballroom again. The staff had hung a garland of greenery across the two mantels. Candles filled the room with light and warmth.

The night before, Isabel had pulled me to the piano so quickly I hadn't taken it in. Tonight I let my eyes trail through the entire room. The walls were paneled in a pale wood up to about fifteen feet. After two feet of layered and detailed molding, they continued for another ten. This upper section was painted an extraordinary gold color, layered with a green patina. In the candlelight it looked like oxidized copper. There were furniture arrangements tucked close to the two fireplaces, and the rest of the floor space was bare. No carpets covered the beautiful interlacing wood design that spread like octagons bisected and laid across the length of the room.

Along one wall the staff had laid out a selection of petit fours, chocolates, and cheeses on one table, and wines and crystal decanters of spirits on another. Coffee and tea sat on a third.

I watched Isabel twirl Clara. She was teaching her the steps to another Regency-era line dance, and Clara hung on her every word. There was no music, but it didn't matter. Isabel had been waiting for this moment all day.

When I had returned to our room after losing two games of bowls to Nathan and another we'd both lost to Aaron, I'd found Isabel fast asleep. I nudged her awake.

"Gertrude invited everyone to the front parlor early tonight for a welcome celebration for Nathan. Then there's to be dancing. Official stuff, not impromptu like last night. Do you want to get up now? It's probably time to dress."

"Oh . . . Yes . . . Did I sleep all afternoon?" She'd stretched and sat up against the headboard, then wrapped her arms around her knees. "Gertrude promised a proper party tonight. Do you think Nathan likes dancing?"

I paraphrased the next line for her—it was too easy. "And to be fond of dancing is a certain step towards falling in love?" I studied her. "With you?" I cringed at my need for clarification or reassurance, maybe both.

Rather than give me either, she gamboled off her bed and opened her wardrobe. "What are you wearing tonight?"

From there the conversation had turned to dresses and dancing. It didn't return to Nathan, and I didn't press further. At some point when she remembered, we would talk. Until then, it felt like recess and I wanted to play.

Now I watched Isabel spin Clara again. She caught my eye and smiled. I smiled back, but did not move from my place against the wall. She maneuvered the little girl my direction and stretched out to whisper to me, "I was right about the blue."

She had insisted I wear blue this evening. Standing in the bathroom, I'd shoved the dress back to her, saying, "It's your color. You like the way it makes your eyes pop. You even have a theory that it makes your teeth look whiter. And—" I couldn't stop myself. "Nathan knows blue is your color. I'll look silly in it."

She laughed and pushed the dress back into my hands. "No one can claim a whole color, Mary. That's ridiculous. You'll be the most glamorous woman at dinner tonight."

"But–" I stopped there. There was no kind way to say, *But you never let anyone outshine you.* And I didn't want to say it. If she was open to something new, I was too.

I plucked the skirt of my dress. It caught the light, billowed, and drifted back against my body. It had been gorgeous in the bathroom and was stunning here. The kind of dress Cinderella might wear–at the ball, not before. The small pearls and blue glass beads sewn into the bodice, circling the sleeves, and covering a full three inches of the hem shimmered like dark diamonds. Unlike Isabel's cream dress that floated about her, mine swished. It didn't just look beautiful. It sounded beautiful.

Nathan leaned against the wall next to me. I wondered if my dress and his coat had been commissioned for a couple–the colors paired perfectly.

"Are you playing wallflower?" He gently crashed against my shoulder. I swayed and stepped to keep my balance. "You look extraordinary tonight, by the way. You walked away earlier before I could tell you that."

"Thank you." I glanced over. "You're kinda cute yourself."

Across Nathan, my eyes landed on Helene. She sat only a few feet away and was clearly eavesdropping. She had the most implausibly innocent expression fixed upon her face. I bit my lip to keep from laughing.

Nathan noticed her too. "Mrs. Jennings." He pushed off the wall to stand before her. He offered me a sly smile, then turned again to Helene. "Mrs. Jennings, I have news that might inter-est you . . . I invited a friend to join us this evening. Lieutenant

Chessman is on leave and is an eligible handsome man." He cast his focus to Isabel and Clara. "I don't think any young lady here would be throwing herself away by consenting to a dance or two."

"You are a delight." Helene stood and tugged at Nathan's arm, bringing his head a foot lower and on level with her own. She kissed his cheek then wiped away the lipstick with her gloved fingers. She looked with purpose beyond us. "I feel our Emma should lead the first with him."

"My thoughts exactly." Nathan directed his three slow words to me.

"With whom will you dance?" Helene thwapped him with her fan.

"Miss Morland, if she'll have me." He offered us a neat bow, then added, "If you'll excuse me, I need to make sure Lieutenant Chessman knows his duty for this evening."

Helene patted the cushion next to her, and I joined her on the love seat. "Your young man is truly divine."

I laughed and started to protest, then stopped. Whether he was "my young man" or not, I wanted him to be. "Thank you. I think so too."

Helene sank against the cushions. Her face fell as if she'd remembered something exhausting or unpleasant.

"Mrs. Jennings?"

"Austen had it right." Helene rested her head against the back of the love seat. Her fluffy white hair squished against her head. "She focused on the promising young people because they had change and life ahead of them. The rest of us? It has passed us by." She cast her gaze out to the floor. "I feel that now. It's a joy to watch you, but I've fooled myself into thinking I'm not near the end of my story. It almost makes me wonder, what am I doing here?"

"You're celebrating your anniversary." I squeezed Helene's hand. Devoid of diamonds tonight, it rested in her lap. "Why don't you and Herman switch characters to the Gardiners from *Pride and Prejudice* or the Crofts from *Persuasion*?"

Helene's eyes widened as if I'd missed the point of anything she'd been thinking or saying. "Why?"

"Because you're right, Austen favors youth. But she has those two wonderful older couples, who love each other. Austen is very complimentary to them." I watched Herman join the group in the center. "They are what all we 'promising young people' hope to become."

"Thank you. That's a lovely compliment, and suggestion." Helene squeezed my hand. "You might want to take your own advice and change characters as well."

Before I could ask what she meant, she pointed to the central group. "Look at them." Nathan was now waltzing with Clara. "They are so eager, but Gertrude said the music won't begin for at least another half hour."

Isabel caught us staring and waved me to her. As I crossed the floor, she headed to the piano. I met her midway. "Will you come play for us? I heard the man practicing during lunch, and you are much more accomplished."

"Until he arrives." I dropped onto the bench and sorted the music. Someone had been practicing. New sheet music was stacked over what I had played the night before.

Isabel leaned over me. "I told Gertrude not to bother with that man. You are by far the superior pianist and you like playing." She bit her lip. "That was okay, right? You don't dance. You never do. I thought you'd enjoy playing tonight."

I don't dance? I never do?

"Why would you think I don't dance?"

Isabel's fingers fluttered at her neck. "But last night . . . I thought . . ."

"Don't worry about it. I'm happy to play." I looked to Nathan, who was dancing with Clara. The little girl kept stumbling over his feet every time he pulled her in.

I ran my hands over the piano—a Bösendorfer with curlicue decorations and detailing that signaled it was old, rare, and, by its condition, well loved, in the best sense. As much as I wanted to test the theory that dancing was a certain step to falling in love, playing this instrument was an honor.

I positioned my hands when another thought grabbed me. "Isabel, with whom are you going to dance?" *Emma* had taught me the significance of the first dance and partner. Mrs. Jennings had reminded me. Nathan had lined up Grant for her, but again . . . What was *she* thinking? Where would her instincts lead her?

"I had hoped Grant." She looked back to him just as his gaze met hers. "I thought he was going to ask me, but he didn't."

She walked toward him as if pulled.

And I began one of Mozart's Contradances.

"Another surprise." Nathan appeared beside me.

I kept my eyes on the music. "When I say 'now,' will you flip the page for me?"

"Of course." He dropped beside me. "I had no idea you played the piano, and certainly not like this."

"Now." I tossed him a thank-you smile and played on.

I glanced up and noted that Aaron and Sylvia had joined Grant and Isabel. Clara, too, as she danced between her parents. Isabel called directions, and the couples ducked under each other and stepped their circles. They laughed more when the steps worked than when they missed and muddled in the middle.

Herman and Helene joined for the first few, then, glancing up during my fourth piece, I saw them retreat to the love seat. They sat with tilted heads as if sharing unspoken opinions and secrets, a silent communication born of sixty years of marriage. The Crofts.

It was during my sixth piece, a waltz, that I noticed the couples dancing in more complete union. Isabel didn't call a single instruction. Her partner absorbed her attention. She was more than radiant—she glowed.

At the waltz's end, the Lottes called good night and gently pulled Clara off to bed. I shifted my fingers on the keyboard to begin "Brahms' Lullaby." It was the perfect denouement to the evening. It was the first song my mom ever asked me to learn, and eighteen years later it never failed to take me back to that feeling of awe and love.

A note of sadness swept through me. Something had been missing and its absence only felt with its return. Nature abhors a vacuum and will fill it—but you must create an opening. Music was that opening. It felt as if the universe was expanding right before me, in a ballroom in Bath, England.

And I was diminishing—as one should before the size and unending grandeur of the universe. It wasn't that I was smaller or less significant; it simply felt like I didn't need to fight for a place within it or for my own protection. I simply *was*, and that was enough.

I glanced up. Isabel and Grant were the last in the ballroom. Even the staff had disappeared. Isabel sent me a smile and a wave, then returned her attention to Grant, who held her arm on a rigid ninety-degree angle within his own, a perfect Regency gentleman or a modern military officer. The only flutter in his stiff facade came as he laid his other hand over hers. She tucked closer as he led her out of the room.

Where was Nathan? I'd felt him step away during the final waltz, but I'd thought he was in the room somewhere. I scanned corner to corner and felt my body wilt with the song's last notes.

"When I was really little, like two, I had a glow-in-the-dark mobile with animals that played that tune. Elephants. Giraffes. Lions. All twirling."

I twisted on the bench. "Where did you go?"

"I wanted to make myself scarce for a minute or two." A smile played on his lips. It tilted up at one corner as he dropped once more onto the bench next to me. "I didn't want to sit around talking to those two all night, and I doubt it would interest them either. I'd rather be with you, alone."

My delight came out in a burst of song.

He laughed aloud. "'Home on the Range'?"

"Happiest song ever, and every time I played it my dad crooned the vocals off key and at about ninety decibels—lawn mower loud."

"Sing me some?"

"No way." The lyrics filled my head, but I pressed my lips tight against their escape. *Where seldom is heard a discouraging word, and the skies are not cloudy all day . . .*

I switched songs in case he asked again, segueing into Scott Joplin's "The Entertainer."

"I haven't heard that in years."

I played on. "My mom and dad used to two-step in the living room to it . . . Or how about . . ." I switched again.

"'Somewhere over the Rainbow' . . . That one always made me sad, especially the Israel Kamakawiwo'ole version."

"Me too . . . Here." I shifted to that interpretation. At the last note I could remember, which landed us somewhere in the middle of the song, I dropped my hands into my lap. I wondered if he understood what I was trying to share. I barely did.

He took a deep breath and let it out slowly, eyes locked on mine. "I had no idea . . . Is there anything you don't do?" His question came out on a whisper.

"Cook."

"Ahh . . . Lucky for us, I do." Nathan smiled, then tapped a treble key. "How'd you learn to play?"

"When I was ten, my dad traded my babysitting skills for piano lessons with the woman next door. He wanted me occupied and she had a three-year-old terror." I tapped another key with one finger to create a complement to his note. "I can't smell Lysol and Febreze without being transported back to that tiny, hot house. Those first weeks were torture . . . Then one day, none of that mattered. I got it."

I trilled out a few more notes. "Music is math, and once you understand that . . . How can anyone not be in awe? It's the audible expression behind the laws of the universe. It feels like the only thing, apart from God, that lives outside time. Once released, it lives on and it can make you laugh and cry, rip you apart and heal you, all within a few discrete notes strung together. And while it follows rules, expression is limitless."

Nathan remained silent, and doubt crept in.

He turned to me, his face inches from my own. "I don't know if it's this place, or, as you suspect, the dress, or maybe it's that we're not at work, or perhaps it's this . . ." He flickered two fingers between an A and B at the top of the scale. "I feel like I'm seeing you for the first time, this fuller version of you. The best version of you."

"You've figured me out then?"

"Never, but I almost missed this. I almost missed you." He looked across the empty room toward the arched door Isabel and Grant had exited. He stood. "Dance with me?"

He tugged my hand to pull me with him, then led me a few steps behind the piano to within the open doorway to the patio.

"There's no music."

"Debatable."

Until I reached the threshold, I hadn't realized how stuffy the ballroom had become. But here, dry inside air mixed with the outside damp. I felt warm, but as the cool air touched my skin, suddenly chilled too.

Nathan twisted his hand within my own and, palm to palm, he pulled me close and wrapped his other arm around my waist. I looked down. I couldn't find where his blue coat ended and my dress began.

"Isabel said you never dance," he whispered.

"She said that to me too. She wasn't talking about me." I felt Nathan's head shift in an unasked question. "Anne Elliot from *Persuasion*. She plays the piano and doesn't dance."

"You'd think the role play, this getup, the stilted mannerisms, not to mention the fact that I'm saying words that should only be used in college essays, would be hard. But I'm finding it all very easy."

We stepped a full waltz rotation in silence. The breeze rustled my dress's hem. "Do you smell it?"

"What?" I felt his breath on my ear.

"Electricity." I heard the word and felt my face warm. I pulled an inch away. "I mean a storm. There's one nearby."

I'd been right during our walk to the stables; my head reached within that tender space between shoulder and chin.

"Is that your favorite smell?"

"I found a new one recently." I closed my eyes. I felt his head shift the minutest of degrees. The tiniest movement on my side and . . . I couldn't move. I smelled bubble gum and something fresh, like grass and sunshine, and I didn't want it to end. I closed my eyes and wished this moment was so significant, so weighted and so massive, that we could test Einstein's theory—bend time and freeze it.

Chapter 21

The best version of you...

The words, the feeling, and the anticipation of all it might mean played within my dreams.

We had danced, and sat by the dying fire in the Day Room to talk. Then, when the ashes grew cold and the room dark, he held my hand as we walked up the stairs and along the gallery. Outside the Green Room he'd laid a soft, lingering kiss at the edge of my jaw. Just off center enough to send chills up my spine.

"Until tomorrow, Miss Morland."

I must have leaned against the inside of our bedroom door for a half hour, savoring every memory and studying Isabel. She was tucked tight under her covers on her stomach. I could only see a mass of black curls against the white sheets. Would she wake soon? And how would everything change when she did?

I looked around the room. Isabel was gone, and once again I had not heard her wake or dress. One of the reasons I'd hesitated about this trip was my fear that our quarters would be too tight and confining. We didn't have enough space in our friendship for our adult selves, much less if we were stuck in a room together. Yet here we were, sharing that room, and I didn't even see her on waking. I no longer felt compressed or defined by her. We were divided by schedules, centuries, and the great distance between fact and fiction.

A brown wool dress lay across the foot of my bed with a note.

Good morning! Join us at the stables when you wake. I pulled this out for you. It's chillier outside this morning.

I set the dress aside and opened my wardrobe. There was a dress that had caught my eye the afternoon we arrived—a deep purple, a royal purple. I'd passed it over as too bold, but now I pulled it down and fingered the fabric. It had a slight bumpiness to the texture, probably a silk and cotton blend, with matching ribbons of velvet. It was the purple on purple that gave the dress impact. It wasn't frilly or frumpy. It had crisp pleats, right angles at the neckline, and fell in one-color splendor all the way to my toes.

I pulled my hair back in the same high bun Isabel had fashioned. This time I left no loose tendrils or curls. It felt dramatic and bold too. Soft leather boots and a black shawl, taken from the wardrobe's lower drawers, completed the outfit. I headed to the stables.

The gravel on the drive surrounding the house shifted and scraped under my feet. Rain had pattered the windows in the night and left the gravel moist and gripping and the grass glistening with drops in the morning light. But the air was dry. All the dampness had been pulled out with the rain, and the air was also cold, crisp. Each breath made a little puff of steam, and I almost turned back for a heavier dress or a jacket. Instead I tucked the shawl tighter around my shoulders and picked up my pace along the path.

"You're here." Duncan stood brushing Tennyson.

"Am I late?"

"They went for a walk. Isabel was keen to go, Nathan keen to stay, but she won in the end."

"I don't doubt it." I felt my buoyancy deflate with a slow leak.

Duncan pointed the brush down the path. "If you hurry you might catch them."

"It doesn't matter. Is anyone else around?"

"The Muellers are on a gig ride with Goliath. The Lottes are fishing on a north stretch of the stream, if you want to join them."

"I think I'd rather walk." I pointed down the path, the opposite direction he'd said Isabel had taken. "Will you tell Nathan I headed this way?"

I passed the spot where Nathan and I had fished. I walked to the stream and looked down into the cranny right by the bank. I wondered if any fish were hiding there today. Then I lifted the skirt of my dress and lengthened my stride . . . Time to walk. The path split. I headed down a small slope and, circling a hedgerow, ran into Gertrude.

"Good morning." She seemed surprised to see me. She was dressed in black pants, her bright-pink rubber boots, and a black sweater. "Forgive me for not being in dress. I was visiting Mr. Chessman and thought I wouldn't be seen."

I waved away her apology. "Grant?"

"His grandfather." She joined me. "He's been here longer than I have." She smiled. "If ever the world went sideways, a visit to his cottage always set it right—ever since I was a little girl. When I lose my patience with the Stanleys, I remember they let him keep his cottage and his salary, and I stop."

"Isabel met him yesterday."

"He mentioned that. He thinks his grandson is quite taken with her." Gertrude looked at me. "This is where these escapes can get dangerous." Her tone held a warning.

"I can imagine."

"Life often doesn't look the same. Can't look the same afterwards."

I wondered if Gertrude was talking about Isabel, me, or herself. It was hard to tell. "I'm beginning to think I don't want it to."

Gertrude pressed her fingers to her lips, as if she was trying to stop a smile or tears. I wasn't sure which.

"I need to get back to the house."

She went on up the path as I headed down. The realization of what I'd just said struck me. I didn't want life to return to what it had been. It wasn't just Isabel. It wasn't just Nathan—as much as he seemed to be smack in the middle of everything. It was about music, fear, voice, running away, and tucking close. It was about family and swirling emotions I couldn't name but felt in my heart as it pounded with each step. Everything was already different.

The path met up with the stream again. It was wider here and rushed faster. There was a log over it and a verdant sloping hill on the other side. I stepped onto the log and made it halfway across when it shifted beneath me.

The time-space continuum distorted. Space compressed. Time elongated. It took me three full sentences to fall.

1. That water will be freezing and, wow, it looks deep.
2. I'm going to ruin this dress.
3. This is really going to hurt.

The last sentence got my attention, and I twisted so that my shoulder and not my wrist crashed first. I landed in the icy water while thinking up sentence four.

4. *Oufff.*

I pulled myself upright but couldn't find solid ground on which to plant my feet. I slipped and landed smack on the stones. One ruined dress. One bruised shoulder. It reminded me of a scene I'd read in one of Austen's novels, but I couldn't place it and now wasn't the time to ponder. I reached forward to start my crawl to shore.

"Mary! What happened? . . . Wait." Grant sprinted across the log to get to my side of the stream. Without pausing he waded in and pulled me up and out.

Grant. Military. Captain Wentworth. *Persuasion.*

"I thought you went for a walk." I felt my teeth chatter. "I was just thinking I needed one of you."

He stood me on the ground and pulled the drenched shawl away. "One of me?"

"A Captain Wentworth to pull me out. Thank you."

Grant chuckled. "Right."

"I was trying to cross." I pointed to the hill. "I thought I'd get a good view up there."

"You would, and when you're warm and dry, there's a bridge about a quarter mile that way." He pointed farther downstream.

"I'll remember that."

He stepped close and rubbed my arms with both hands. We stood inches apart. There was something formal, strong, and almost sad about Grant. I hadn't gotten a good look previously or even had a good conversation. He and Isabel were always off and away. I'd heard she'd helped him check the fence line, feed the horses, even helped his father select plantings for spring.

He caught my stare, and a slow smile crept across his face, dispelling the sadness. He dropped his hands and patted at his sides, and his eyes widened as if surprised by something. "I took off my coat at the stables . . . I'm sorry. I don't have it to give to you."

"I retract my comment." I meant it as a joke, but my chattering teeth made him grimace rather than laugh. "I thought you were walking with Isabel and Nathan."

"I left them. I needed to get something done." Grant looked down the path as if figuring out the fastest way to get me back and dry, and yet he didn't take a step. He shifted his weight from foot to foot. "You and Isabel are best friends. You know her better than anyone."

Thinking back on the past six months and Nathan, I almost laughed. "Yes."

"I wanted to talk to you, to ask you . . ." He watched the water before shifting his gaze back to me. Then he nodded, crisp and decisive, the way I'd expect a soldier to do once a decision had been made. "My wife left me during my last deployment. The separation proved too hard for her; she said she wasn't cut out to be a soldier's wife and that no one could be expected to endure that fear. She had an affair, filed for divorce, and cleared out before I got home. I know she had her own issues, but–" He stopped abruptly and gripped the back of his neck.

"You're falling in love with Isabel."

"I don't even know her," he scoffed. It didn't fool either of us. "I don't want . . . I don't–"

"Want to get hurt again." It was my turn to shift my gaze to the water. "Believe me, I understand. And I don't blame you. Fear can make us do stupid things." I glanced to him. "I've got my own experience in losing someone you love, even letting them go first. It all hurts."

"Every day." His nail beds whitened with the pressure at his neck, then reddened with the release.

Twenty years had taught me that Isabel's pragmatism, almost disdain for love, was a cover. She wore boyfriends like fashions; they changed with the seasons and she attached a certain pride to that. She was shy to show what she really felt. She needed safety. In many ways, I'd done the same.

Yet with Grant, I'd seen more. I'd never seen her so in love, so free. So true to herself. Maybe that's where she went in these episodes. Maybe she, too, became her best self. I looked down at my sopping purple dress. It clung to my legs. Perhaps Isabel and I were more alike than I thought.

Grant's mouth lifted in a wry smile. "I should be talking to Isabel. Believe me, I would . . . I will . . . but . . ."

"No one can talk to her right now, not really."

He nodded. "Who is she, Mary? Who is the true Isabel?"

Oddly, it was Missy Reneker, not Isabel, who materialized in my memory. I could feel her hands push me off the lunch bench and the sticky linoleum beneath me as I landed.

Then came Isabel . . . I felt her strength, and even greater determination, as she held her breath to haul me up. I recalled the notebooks full of lists she carried around as she helped my dad plan every birthday party and even the rehearsal dinners for my brothers' weddings. I thought of her dad and the question she asked every Friday night, until we both knew it so well it no longer needed articulation: *If he's coming home, he'll be here by six o'clock. If not, can I spend the night?*

"I'm not speaking for Isabel. I have no idea what she feels, but I can tell you who she is."

"Okay." He drew the word out in invitation to continue.

"She is the bright, fun, and whimsical woman you see now—that's her without armor. In many ways, you have met the truest Isabel there is. Isabel with armor up can hide all that really well. But if she loves you, maybe it'll come down. She is loyal, fierce, and she can endure. She's tough. If you live for her, she can endure the separation of a deployment." I looked around at the stream, the hill, the path leading back to the house. "Considering where we are, you'll understand that allusion."

He raised a brow.

I smirked. "It's an idea from *Persuasion*. Anne Elliot says it, but don't think Isabel is your Anne Elliot. That'd be a mistake. She is not that compliant."

Grant laughed with a mixture of embarrassment and relief. "Even now, that's not an adjective I'd use to describe her." He then saw me, really saw me, and his face fell. "Forgive me. You're shivering. We must get you back."

He started down the path with such long strides I had to run to keep pace. We'd covered about a hundred yards before he stopped.

I heard it too—the clopping of horse hooves.

"I have a better idea. That's where my coat went. I took it off when setting up the gig."

The Muellers came into view. Goliath pulled them in a small carriage that had only two wheels, set side by side.

Grant smirked at me now. "By the way, that's Admiral and

Mrs. Croft approaching. Helene explained it to me this morning—she said you suggested a change of characters."

Herman pulled on Goliath's reins and stopped beside us. "What happened here?"

"Miss Morland," Grant said with wry formality, "decided to take a dip. Could you take her back to the house? She's shivering."

"Of course, and we come prepared. We have a blanket." Helene squished up against her husband. "Do let us have the pleasure of taking you home. There is excellent room for three."

Grant took the blanket she offered and led me to the back of the gig, where he lifted me onto the bench. "There wasn't room for three up there," he whispered. In a louder voice he called, "She's set back here. Walk on, Goliath."

We bounced away.

"Isn't this delightful?" Helene called. "Not that you are cold and wet, but that this is happening just as it is? I took your suggestion."

Before I could answer, Herman called, "Are you comfortable back there?"

"Very." I pulled the blanket around me and almost believed it to be true. I watched the sun shoot through the branches. I'd been so enamored with the green that I hadn't noticed—fall had taken many of the leaves. Time was marching on, and I wondered if the heat had broken at home.

"We took your advice," Helene said again. "Have you taken mine?" She twisted in her seat.

"I'm not sure what you mean."

"You chose poorly in Catherine Morland. She's a good sort of girl, and I know why you did it. Everything about her ached to be a heroine; she threw herself at it. Goodness, that girl was so lost in Gothic romances I had no humor for her for years." Helene was gripping the back of the seat to keep facing me. "But that's not you. It's not because you weren't born to it that you're not a heroine. It's that you've shunned it. Too much risk, too much fear."

"Are we talking about a new character?"

"We're talking about you, Mary. Your journey is nothing like Catherine's." She clutched her husband's arm. "Maybe I should go back to Mrs. Jennings. People at least believed her when she said stuff, even if she was wrong."

Herman made no reply.

She turned back to me. "I hope I haven't upset you, dear."

"Not at all." I was too confused to be upset. I turned to face the path behind us again. The stream was disappearing from view. Something was slipping away and I couldn't grasp it. I stretched up to see over the back of the seat. "So if not Catherine Morland, then who?"

"Anne Elliot from *Persuasion*, of course. She didn't think happiness could come her way either, but it did. She just had to stretch a little—and when she recognized it, hold it tight."

"Oh . . ." I faced backwards again.

After a few more hills, the Muellers were engrossed in their own conversation. I suspected they had forgotten me.

"So is it what you expected?" Herman said to his wife.

"It cost us so much . . . Somehow I feel I've been wasteful."

"Do not say that. What were we saving for? I'm not sure I'll be able to drive a gig on our seventieth anniversary."

"But we could have done something you—"

"Hush. I have enjoyed every moment with you. That is all I wanted. I . . . I can't remember all the names though. They get so jumbled in my head."

"It doesn't matter." Helene sighed. "None of that matters. You are still you and I love you. This is a game and I didn't expect it to show me how wonderful our normal life is. I'm beginning to miss it . . . When we leave here, let's ask the children to bring their families for Christmas."

"Are you afraid I will forget soon?" Herman offered a humorless chuckle.

"I'm afraid I already did. What we have . . . It's all I've ever wanted."

The gig stopped. I looked around and found myself at the stables rather than the house.

"Hello? What are you doing back there? You're soaked." Duncan reached for me.

Helene's hand flew to her mouth. "We forgot! Herman, we forgot poor Mary."

"Please don't worry. I was fine." A coat, holding a hint of citrus, dropped over my shoulders. I twisted to find Nathan close behind me. "Thank you."

"Your lips are blue," Isabel cried.

"I am a little cold."

"Come on. Let's get you to the house." Nathan drew me close and hurried me away from the group.

Before I knew it, we crunched across the gravel and the kitchen door swung open. Gertrude gestured us inside. "Grant called and said you got soaked. You need a hot bath."

"Th . . . That . . . sounds . . . lovely."

I slid Nathan's coat off, but he pulled it back over me. "Bring it to me after you're warm." He kissed my forehead. "I'll wait for you."

Chapter 22

If ever there was a time for a long bath, this was it. Buried in
bubbles, I let the morning wash over me. Lines from books
floated past with the ease with which I usually recalled theorems—
Ohm, Kirchhoff, and Pythagoras now stood beside the truths
espoused within *Persuasion*, *Pride and Prejudice*, and Clara's *Sense
and Senseless*.

We can all plague and punish one another. Elizabeth Bennet said
it to Caroline Bingley, who was trying to flirt with or "punish" Mr.
Darcy for some surly comment. That was true. We could all do
that to one another—protect ourselves by causing harm. *Intimate
as you are*, she said, *you must know how it is to be done.* It was a delicious wisp of spite.

Isabel liked Grant, and I could have ended it. The Nathan story
alone would have sent him running. Payback. But Nathan's grandfather had been right. That would have been about me, not her, and
I wanted to be more than that. I wanted more for me, and despite
everything, seeing her now as I did, I wanted more for her too.

Finally dressed in the brown wool Isabel had laid out for me,
I grabbed Nathan's coat, now dry from resting on the heated bathroom floor, and stepped into the gallery. I trailed my finger along

the glass cases. Books, fans, playing cards, gloves. Cases full of family history—Gertrude's family history. The prayer book carried
each Sunday by her grandmother, perhaps. A fan fluttered by an
aunt. They were mere objects now. The emotional value lost, the
connection lost, by being tucked away under light and glass.

It had struck me as sad to separate the people from their story.
But I had done the same. I recalled my Lanvin shoe box and my
mom's treasures I kept locked away inside it.

"What's wrong?"

I looked up to find Nathan sitting in the same chair I'd rested
in days before.

I shook my head. "I just thought of something I need to do
when I get home."

He stood, shrugged on his coat, and stretched out his hand.
Once mine was firmly within it, he tugged and we headed down
the stairs. "A special late morning tea is set up on the lawn. Sonia's
been darting up and down the stairs, afraid you would miss it."

"What have they got in store for us now?"

"If her excitement is any indication, it'll be over the top."

Nathan led me through the hallway toward the back of the
house rather than out the front door. We crossed the ballroom,
and in my mind I could hear the previous evening's music echoing
within its walls. We passed through the narrow glass door at the
end, and I could feel the notes of our beautiful silent dance.

"By the way, you were right. It doesn't work that way."

I glanced up at him. "What doesn't?"

"Gertrude popped the TV out of its hidden panel in the Day
Room. Isabel walked in, watched a moment of some odd show
with a girl with pink hair, then walked back out, no change in her
expression at all."

Day Three. Tomorrow I would have to get her home.

A huge white canvas caught my eye. "Over the top" was an understatement. Across the lawn, situated at the edge of the formal gardens, sat an elaborate picnic. It looked as if they'd moved an entire room out of the house and onto the lawn. There were two of the canvas shades held high on tall wood poles. On the rug laid beneath them sat a table filled with tiered silver trays and two tea services. Chairs were arranged in groupings, and at the edge of the scene stood large wicker bins. I saw the handles of badminton rackets and what I thought was a cricket bat sticking out. The bowls were scattered across their court, a small patch of lawn leveled and cut close like a putting green.

"How did they do all this?"

"When you went up for your bath, I watched from a window."

I yanked at his hand.

"Not you. This. I watched this. They've been carrying all this out for the past hour . . . Come on."

"There she is." Helene noticed us first and stepped off the carpet to envelop me in a tight hug. She looped her arm through mine and pulled me close. She smelled of baby powder and roses. "I wondered where you were. I was afraid your adventure was too taxing."

I met Gertrude at the table. "Thank you for sending Sonia up with the tea. It was wonderful to find it sitting on the desk."

"I can't imagine how cold you were." Gertrude looked to the house. "The last time I fell in that stream I was sixteen. My brothers pushed me."

I followed her gaze and studied the house as well. The back was even more impressive than the front. The front was straight—one austere expanse of stone from end to end softened only by the semicircular bays on the corners. The back, however, had two wings flanking each end of the house at ninety-degree angles. Glass windows filled the center section across both floors, and the wings were capped in their own bay windows, also two stories high.

I looked back to Gertrude. Her face had paled and fallen. She threw me a tremulous smile. "They're all gone now." The china rattled as she set down the teapot. She clenched her hands, released them, then reached to hand me a cup.

Everyone was present. Isabel sat with Grant near the bowls lawn. She sat ramrod straight, no twenty-first-century slouch. I needed to call Dr. Milton.

Gertrude poured two more cups of tea. I handed mine to Nathan and helped her pass two more to Helene and Herman.

Herman's eyes looked clouded and young to me. Their expression was not that of the vain, proud Sir Walter Elliot.

"How are you, Admiral Croft?"

"Helene." He whispered his wife's name as if it were contraband. "She called you a different name on our ride. I can't remember it."

"She called me Anne, but don't worry about that. If the names are confusing, don't use any of them. It's only meant to be fun."

He nodded but did not look assured. He shifted to face Isabel. "I don't remember your name either. This is all becoming—" He looked back to me. "Who is she again?"

Isabel didn't hear us, or if she did, she didn't acknowledge Herman's question. She was listening to Helene and the Lottes. It took me a moment to catch on.

"All the common rooms have one," Sylvia was saying. "Gertrude told us about them when we arrived, but you'd never notice. They are so cleverly hidden."

"That might be nice for our rest this afternoon. Herman loves that new BBC mystery," Helene returned to Sylvia. "He's finding it hard to be away from the fixtures, the familiar things from home. I am too, if the truth be told."

"That's understandable. The line can feel too blurry for comfort." Aaron cast a glance to Herman, who was slowly tuning in to the conversation.

"I do miss *Jeopardy*. We watch it over dinner. Do you know *Jeopardy*? It's an American show." Helene directed her question to Isabel but didn't wait for an answer. She smiled to Sylvia. "It's what keeps my brain so young."

"Clara does that for me," Sylvia laughed.

"Can we watch *Jeopardy* too?" Clara asked.

"If Mrs. Mueller finds it, sure. You might find it dull though." Sylvia handed her a napkin to place under her cookie.

Clara. Mrs. Mueller. Real names. I looked to Isabel—half concerned, half relieved—to find her sitting straight. I watched her a moment more. There was something off, too rigid, in her stance, and her eyes were unfocused as if seeing the past rather than any of us.

"Isabel?" I handed her a cup of tea. I wanted to capture her focus. I needed to make sure she was all right. "Isabel?"

She looked at me and . . . She was not all right. There was an almost animal panic in her expression. It reminded me of Grant's description of war. Before I could react or inquire, Clara plopped next to her, almost climbing onto her lap. "Momma said I don't have to play anymore and Gertrude's going to move chairs and pillows into the Day Room and make it like a movie theater this afternoon. We can have popcorn too. Do you want to? You can pick the movie."

Isabel jerked away, and a startled Clara dropped her teacup straight into Isabel's lap. Isabel jumped up, clutching at her skirt to pull it from her legs, and Clara fell to the ground.

I moved first and waggled Isabel's skirt like a fan to disperse the heat as I reached for Clara, who sat wide-eyed and crumpled beneath us. "Are you burned? Are you okay?" One question to Isabel, one to Clara. It was hard to tell who was more distraught.

Grant was beside us in an instant and reached for the gown as well.

"Don't touch me. Get away from me." Isabel's words didn't hold panic. They held anger. They were piercing, guttural, and enraged. She thrashed at Grant, then rounded on Clara. "You ruined it. I knew you would. I said you would. You shouldn't even be here."

I was holding Clara's hand by this time. She slid from my grasp as she sank lower, and I let her go. I was shocked by Isabel. Everyone was.

All the air left our circle. Our camaraderie dissolved. I felt exposed and, as I looked around, it seemed as if everyone else felt the same. We all darted our eyes across the scene as if avoiding a harsh light or the emotions in front of us.

Aaron stepped in front of his daughter and time unfroze. We unfroze. I watched Sylvia's face darken to a low crimson. It was not the red of embarrassment, but the deeper tone of fury.

"What—" Sylvia's one word came out low, but she cut off. Her eyes fastened on me. Whatever she saw in my face stopped her cold. I was unsure what my expression conveyed, but it felt cold, blue, and clammy. All of me felt as if I'd broken a fever. Sylvia's eyes shifted back to Isabel, as did mine.

Isabel paled further, if that was possible, as Aaron scooped Clara up and walked away. We could only see her eyes peeking above her father's shoulder. The tears and confusion there jolted me to action.

"Isabel? Hey—" I grabbed for her as she teetered. She stiffened and pulled from my grasp. Her lips parted, and an odd, strangled sound reached me. I twisted to follow her line of sight. She stared at Nathan.

"Isabel?" He stepped toward us.

She turned and ran.

I looked around at what was left of the group. Herman and Helene had tucked closer together. They were holding hands. Their heads turned in unison to follow Isabel, then turned back to me. Sylvia's focus never left me. Her questions were tangible.

"I'm sorry. I can't explain right now."

Grant stood beside me. He had backed away at Isabel's cry. The only muscle now moving was that small one below his right ear. It flexed as he clenched and unclenched his teeth.

With an "Excuse me," he strode away in the opposite direction Isabel had run.

"I'll find her . . . I'm so sorry." I took off after Isabel, leaving Nathan and Gertrude to explain what they would or could to anyone left.

It didn't take long to find her. Upon entering the hedgerow and the woods behind them, the main path met up with another. Turn right and I would head deeper into the woods to the terraced garden beyond. Turn left and I would drop to the stream. I knew Isabel would always choose water.

She sat on the bench where Nathan and I had blown bubbles only yesterday. I sank beside her, unsure what to say.

We sat a full minute before her words broke the tension. "Mary, I need help."

I swung my arm around her and pulled her close. "I know."

She sank into me. "It was so confusing. I saw Clara, but it didn't feel like her. It felt like me. I remember that age now. I never did anything right. Before the tea fell, I saw it for the first time. We were in our kitchen. The walls were white like the tent and we even had a table with those same knobby legs. Daddy was so angry. I had done something, something about the table, and there were colors. Maybe it was paint, I don't know. Anyway, I'd ruined it, as I ruined everything. He said that's why my mom left. I'd ruined that too." She glanced up at me. "He used to yell a lot when I was a kid, then one day he stopped. I guess I wasn't worth the energy anymore."

"That's not true. And none of it was your fault."

"I think the paint actually was." She offered a sideways smile. "Do you remember when we did that at your house?"

I nodded. It was soon after Isabel and I had met. We had a project for social studies, a three-dimensional map that we'd built together. Our mountain ranges were formed from quick-dry clay and mounted to the foam board, and it was my idea to color them with Sharpies. Ink got all over the table. Dad just laughed, but Isabel almost threw up. She also almost sheared the skin off her knuckles scrubbing the table with Comet before Dad gently but firmly pulled her away.

I remember he was quiet all night. As I was going to bed he asked me, "Is everything all right in Isabel's home?"

I'd answered, "Of course, Daddy. She lives in that new big house on Vine Street. You should see inside. It's super nice."

I closed my eyes and hugged Isabel tighter. Sure, I'd been young then and my blindness had a valid excuse, but how long had I held that narrative?

Isabel continued. "Maybe it was my fault, Mary. All of it."

"You can't rationally think that."

Her exhale was so derisive and self-abasing, I couldn't call it a cry or a laugh. "What about me is rational?"

I squeezed her tighter yet. "Stop."

"An 'I'm sorry' isn't going to cut it back there. That poor child—I didn't even see her, until I did. I saw Aaron first."

"An 'I'm sorry' will cut it, Isabel. Explain it to them, privately. They'll understand."

"That I'm crazy?"

"You're not crazy. You're hurt."

She nodded, then shifted away and twisted to face me. "Nathan Hillam is here."

It was a statement full of questions.

My answer held more. "Yes."

We stared at each other. I broke the tension this time because I couldn't hold on to it. I wasn't angry. It was too hard and too heavy to carry. "He called you, and I answered your phone. He came to help."

"He came for you." Again, a statement full of questions. I didn't answer this time. After a heartbeat, she grabbed my hand and pulled it into her lap. Her dress was soaked and freezing. "I'm so sorry, Mary. That's what I've been trying to tell you about. I didn't mean to do it. I was in the middle of it—" Her eyes widened as if she'd discovered something sour and ugly. "No. I knew what I was doing from the beginning."

I stood. We weren't finished, but I also needed action to help us. "Let's get you changed."

"I can't go back there, not yet. I'm not cold."

"Then at least let's get the dress drying. This way?" I tilted my head farther down the path. "Are your legs burned? That's what Grant was trying to find out."

"Oh." She stood, and I imagined she was remembering Grant and how she'd slapped at him. She touched a finger to her thigh. "They're fine. They sting a little, but I can tell they're not burned."

"Then if you won't go change . . ." I mustered up a smile and looped my arm through hers. "We shall walk. When there are serious matters to discuss, Austen women walk. And it has the side benefit of keeping our figures so light and pleasing."

She choked on a laugh that became a mess of tears before we'd walked five steps.

"I don't want Austen anymore. I don't even want to finish. I . . . I never knew myself, Mary."

"I think that's Austen."

"True . . . I'm not sure I have many original thoughts left." She swiped at her nose. "But Lizzy was right when she lamented her despicable behavior. And I've done the same . . . I've acted so horribly. How did I get here?" She pulled at me. "Do you hate me? Or is the question how long have you hated me?"

"Stop . . . I don't hate you. But I was close, maybe I even did for a heartbeat, when I first heard Nathan's voice on the phone. But not now." I stared straight ahead.

"I'd never heard you talk like that about a guy. You'd always wanted that fairy-tale thing, and then there you were laughing about a guy's faults and quirks—and you accepted them all. You and I—we were written, and then you started changing and I didn't. It was like you were ready for something new and I . . . I didn't know what I wanted. It wasn't planned, honest, but I met him and I was jealous. Can you forgive me?"

We had strolled up the path and out Braithwaite House's front gate. We walked on, and eventually it dawned on me she was waiting. She wasn't pushing me for an answer; she wasn't demanding one. She was awake and waiting.

I broke our silence. "I do forgive you, and I'm sorry too." That spun her head my direction. "I'm your best friend, Isabel, but until this trip I don't think I ever understood, not even when it happened before."

"It can't happen again."

"When we get back to the house you need to call Dr. Milton for his daily update. We've been talking and texting the past couple days. If you hadn't come back by tomorrow, I was to get you on a plane somehow."

"But now?"

"You can ask him yourself . . . And call my dad too. He's been getting practically hourly updates as well."

"I love your dad." Isabel sighed.

"I know." I'd always known. Now I understood.

I felt Isabel stiffen next to me, and I lifted my head to see a small group of women staring at us. I also noticed Bath, twenty-first-century Bath with its buildings and cars—and tourists—surrounding us.

We were standing on the sidewalk of the Royal Crescent, a mile from Braithwaite House, in full Regency dress. And at that moment, three separate families were taking pictures of us.

"Can you pose again please?"

Isabel clapped her hand over her mouth. "What do we do?"

"Smile, then run." I stretched my lips wide.

She grabbed at my arm with both hands, then looked out at the growing crowd. "'For what do we live,'" she quoted, "'but to make sport for our neighbors, and laugh at them in our turn?'"

Three women clapped.

I cringed. "Can we go back now?"

Isabel shook her head. "There's something cathartic about humiliation. Let's walk to the end and back."

"I don't need any more humiliation." As soon as the words escaped, I wished to call them back. Isabel understood that I was reacting to more than the dresses.

"I'm sorry," she said.

"Don't." I looped my arm through hers. "Going back won't help us. I shouldn't have said that. And in the end maybe I'll be thanking you."

"Thanking me?"

"Nathan had left WATT, and you know me. I wouldn't have pursued him—ever. There is a chance I wouldn't have seen him again."

"I will never take credit for that." She tugged me close. "Come on. One lap for good-bye."

Arm in arm, we took our lap. We were stopped seventeen times for pictures—and several groups cut in front of us to take selfies with us as their backdrop.

Chapter 23

Isabel stalled at Braithwaite House's front gate. "I don't want to do this . . . Do I have to?"

"It's a few apologies. The rest we can work out later." I started forward.

She gestured to the path. "This way is faster to the stables. I owe everyone an apology, but I owe him more, Mary. I need to see Grant first."

"Go then."

She gave me a hug and headed down the side path while I continued up the main drive. The sun was behind the house now. Afternoon sent slanted rays across the roofline and shot a warm rose glow off the chimneys.

I didn't want to go back either. Each step felt heavy. I pushed open the front door and found myself alone in the darkened front hall. Sonia had not gone through and switched on the lights or lit the evening's candles.

It was that Regency resting time, the lull between the afternoon event and the procession of the evening. I suspected the Muellers were in their room asleep; Clara was curled up with her iPad with Sylvia nearby; and Aaron, if not comforting his daughter, was outside somewhere with Grant.

I climbed the stairs, intending to change for dinner as was expected. Yet without thinking about it, I found myself pulling on jeans and a sweater. I grabbed my Converse from the bottom of my suitcase.

I stepped into the gallery as Gertrude passed, clutching a high stack of linens.

"Can I help you?" I reached for the toppling tower.

"The cupboard is at the end of the hall." She righted the stack and continued on. I followed. "Is Isabel okay now?"

"She will be . . . I don't think I ever truly understood. I doubt I do now."

"Sometimes you can't see something clearly until you step away from it." Gertrude propped the linens on a display case while she opened another concealed closet. She turned and took in my outfit. "Are you going out?"

"Would you mind if I walked into Bath? I might even skip dinner. I need to clear my head."

"Not at all. Everyone is a little weary tonight. Sylvia asked if Clara could have soup in their room."

"I'm so sorry about her. Isabel feels horrible. She's planning to speak to them, to apologize."

"Kids are resilient. It sounds cliché, but it's true."

"To a degree." I thought of Isabel and I wasn't so sure.

Gertrude touched my arm as if offering condolences. "Go. Take some time for yourself. Do you want Duncan to drive you?"

"Thank you, but I'd rather walk."

She placed the linens in the small closet, then gestured to the narrow stairs I'd found my first day. "Let me get you a coat. It's cooling outside."

We passed through the cupboard-lined hallway to a mud-room. It was stone floored and hook lined. Coats, boots, umbrellas, gardening equipment, and assorted chaos filled counters and bins.

She handed me her own gray waxed coat and opened the side door. "When you come back, if you come through here and up those stairs again, you most likely won't run into anyone. If that's a goal."

"It is tonight. Thank you." I pulled on the coat and set out.

As I rounded the house, Nathan crossed my path. "I've been looking for you."

"You found me." I stalled. "I'm sorry I disappeared. Isabel and I—"

He tucked a strand of hair behind my ear. "Had a lot to talk about. You don't need to apologize or explain. Where is she?"

"She went to find Grant and start her round of apologies. I suspect she'll get to you too."

"How are you?" Nathan's hand slid from cheek to hand and stayed there.

"I'm sorting it all out. She said something on our walk about us being 'written.' She meant the terms of our friendship were fixed, and they were, I agree, but they were fixed on wrong assumptions, if that makes any sense. I pride myself on seeing things clearly, objectively, but I never saw my best friend. Maybe not myself either."

"Don't judge yourself too harshly. Outside math, what's objective?"

I didn't have an answer beyond *nothing* and we both knew it. "You were a pawn, by the way. She never really liked you at all."

Nathan burst out laughing. "I figured that. I mean a Third

Choice Guy can't cause too much heartache, but"—he patted his chest, much like Herman in his fine vest—"I am charming. You never know, it might have gone the other way." He stepped back and took in what I was wearing. "Where are you going?"

"Into Bath." I gave him the same once-over. "And if you're coming, you cannot go dressed like that."

"I'm invited?" He pulled his hand from mine and held it out, fingers spread wide. "Give me five minutes."

At my nod he took off running.

Fifteen minutes later, he joined me down the hill at the house's main gate.

"I thought you'd given up on me and left." He was breathless with the run.

"It took you long enough. If I'd stayed up there, more people might have wanted to come along." I tried to laugh, but it came out flat.

I felt him brush the back of my hand. Our fingers tangled and held.

Nathan was wearing jeans and a quarter-zip sweater and soft brown loafers. His hair looked as if he'd just woken up, or just pulled a sweater over his head. He'd been too hurried—for me. I also noted no five o'clock shadow. He'd shaved. And he had really long eyelashes.

I squeezed his hand, which elicited a questioning glance. "I'm very glad Isabel missed all these charms of which you speak."

"I feel pretty lucky too. Are we walking into Bath?"

"It's only about a mile. I've seen you run on that treadmill. You can handle it." I pointed to a sign ahead. "Sonia told me the Number 12 bus stops there and will take us right to the Roman Baths, if you'd rather."

"Walking is fine." He nudged me. "So you did notice me at WATT?"

"It's clear I noticed you, Nathan."

"Mary Davies." Nathan drew my name long. "It wasn't clear to me. Ever."

He swung my hand in an exaggerated motion like this was exactly what he wanted to be doing and with whom. I willed myself to believe it.

After almost a quarter mile, during which he squeezed my hand, pulled me close, shoulder-bumped me away—generally acted like a sixth grader with his first crush—he pointed to an old car scooting down the street.

"That looks exactly like my first car. My parents helped me buy it a few months after I turned sixteen, and a mechanic my dad knew helped me fix it up."

"I did that too. I inherited my eldest brother's car at seventeen. It was a mess. I did most of the electrical work myself, which might have been illegal. I think all electrical work requires a license."

"You mean except for playing around with it at work?" Nathan bumped me again.

"Yes, but WATT has state-of-the-art counter-fire measures in that lab."

"Thank goodness." He laughed. "I heard you blew up a Golightly prototype."

"That was not a good day. You should have smelled the lab. I was actually on fire, burned all the hair off my right arm."

"You could've been hurt."

I shook my head, recalling the panic of that moment. "I was a little and I was banned from the lab. I may be still. I haven't pressed it."

When we passed a cottage tucked between a gas station and an antique store, Nathan told me how his family rented a house on the coast of Massachusetts one summer and he spent the entire summer cleaning boats and babysitting his sisters.

When we passed a fallen tree, I told him about the fort Isabel and I built in my bedroom when we were eleven—how I sawed branches from a downed tree and wove together a layered roof out of leaves.

"My dad almost killed me over that one. A squirrel nest came in with one of the branches we dragged in, which also scratched up all the paint as it came through. Then the squirrels got loose."

"You're kidding."

"Dad called animal control and hauled out all the branches. They caught the mother squirrel, but not two babies. She was pretty mad and very territorial. So was my mom when she found a baby squirrel in her bed that night and screamed so loud the neighbors heard her. Then Dad really lost it." I glanced at him. "If you knew my dad, you'd know that was a red-letter day. My dad never gets angry. Gentlest man you'll ever meet . . . I got grounded and gathered leaves and random bugs for weeks. It's one of my best memories, though. Before he came home from work and things went south, Mom and Isabel and I crawled inside and told stories the whole afternoon. She could tell the best stories."

"May I ask?"

"You? A question? You never ask questions." I stopped and crossed my arms. Teasing him felt good.

He stopped too. "Tell me about your mom?"

"Isabel never told you about SK's mom?"

He shook his head. "I'd like to keep Isabel out of us, if that's okay."

Us.

"Very okay. My mom was diagnosed with MS soon after I was born, and it moved fast." I scrunched my nose. "Correction—it felt fast. It's a disease with a lot of variance, and it would hit hard, level off, hit again, level, and . . . She died two years ago, just before Christmas."

We walked past The Circus roundabout.

"I'm remembering a lot about her this week. It's the first time I've missed her, really missed her, in a long time. I . . . It sounds horrible, but I think I said good-bye years before she died."

He pulled me close and swung his arm around me. He kissed my temple as we walked and said nothing more.

Within another block we found ourselves in the heart of Georgian Bath. One sign pointed to the Roman Baths and another to the Assembly Rooms. Without making a plan, we strolled in the direction of the latter.

The main room at the Assembly Rooms was larger than I expected. Isabella and Catherine met here constantly in *Northanger Abbey*, Isabella to see and be seen and Catherine to search for Mr. Tilney. In *Persuasion*, Anne met Lady Russell here as well, to tread these same boards and to share news.

When I'd read the books, the Pump Room scenes felt small and tight—intimate. The ladies needed to whisper to keep from being overheard. They bumped into acquaintances rather than simply met them. This room felt too large for that. Even with at least fifty tourists about, I didn't bump into anyone. It made me again wonder what I'd misunderstood, what I hadn't seen clearly.

The walls were painted peach halfway to the ceiling; the next twenty feet were covered in plaster and painted in a faux marble design. I'd have thought it was real marble if not for the weight and the fact that Isabel had explained it all to me when peeling the curtain back on Braithwaite House's plaster moldings.

At one end, columns supported a deep balcony. It, too, was filled with tourists watching the rest of us circle the room below. I fell into step, then noted that the wood floor did not run in parallel slats.

I bisected the room and pulled Nathan with me. "It jigs and jags at odd angles. How did they lay this? How did they get the angles to meet up?"

Nathan pulled me back into the Austen-accepted path. He tucked me into his side and offered a quick apology to an older woman in a bright-pink poncho. "You and angles. You almost knocked her down."

Outside we continued down Gay Street which, with a quick turn on Stall Street, ended right near the Roman Baths and a central market square. The Bath Abbey capped one end in all its Gothic glory, and shops lined the other three sides. There were hanging baskets of flowers; windows bursting with Union Jacks, postcards, Peter Rabbits, and tiny red double-decker buses; and restaurants featuring bright signs offering tea, crumpets, scones, and ale. The buildings were all Georgian and beige stone, changing from pink to gray in the late afternoon light. And . . .

"The Pump Rooms." I dragged Nathan inside the door.

The main room of the Pump Rooms, now filled with tea tables and tourists, was exactly what I expected, minus the tables. I drew in a deep breath and let it out slowly. The space was small, intimate, with a delicate oval balcony at one end. This was where Lady Russell and Anne met. This was where Catherine and Isabella pressed close to whisper so as not to be overheard—though Isabella kind of liked that.

"I thought the other place was where the women met and gossiped, but this is it."

"The other was where they went to listen to concerts and where Captain Wentworth went to show Anne he loves her, but gets the wrong impression and leaves."

"He was kind of dense, especially after she chased after him."

"Really?" Nathan hiked one brow. "So you're saying if someone showed up, you'd understand it was because he loved you? You'd notice and believe it? Turn the tables and chase him, even?"

"I . . . Are we talking about a book?"

He tilted his head as if noting I had not answered any of his questions. But rather than answer mine, he offered a half smirk and walked away. I followed him from the Pump Rooms to the Roman Baths.

Moving from one building to the other, we switched from Regency-meets-modern-commercialism to high-tech-swank-meets-ancient-Rome. The atrium was all glass, steel, and informational kiosks, yet right beyond and through a set of glass doors we found ourselves strolling through ancient stones and past altars to gods I'd never heard of. I paused at the gorgeous central green pool.

I envisioned Roman citizens on expat assignments to England sitting on the surrounding stone slabs, lounging, dipping in the baths, and partaking of the waters with their wine—all while they debated where to send the army next and which culture to pillage and destroy. Maybe this was where they lamented their repeated and failed attempts on Ireland.

Costumed characters stepped out onto the stones. Nathan and I looked at each other, stifled a laugh, and moved to the next room. We'd had enough of costumed characters.

"Come try this." He pulled a cup from a dispenser and filled it at an ornate copper drinking fountain. "Careful."

The paper cup felt soft from the liquid's heat. I touched it to my lips. "Bleh and it's too hot."

He took a sip. "And these are the waters everyone was so mad about?" He tapped the placard. "Forty-four degrees Celsius."

"Why would anyone think they could cure– Whoa . . ." I stared at the sign. "Look at that mineral content—no wonder—and 44 Celsius, that's 111 degrees Fahrenheit. That hot right from the spring?"

"Did you convert that in your head?" Nathan tipped forward and kissed me.

I have enjoyed every moment with you. That is all I wanted. Herman's words to Helene on my gig ride played through my mind. I had thought they were terribly romantic then. Now they made me blush.

"What's that for?" Nathan brushed my cheek.

I took a quick breath and jumped. "I am enjoying every moment with you."

He tipped forward again, with an answering smile. "Okay then." This time his lips touched mine in a lingering brush.

We wound our way out of the Roman Baths complex and onto the square. The restaurants drew my attention. Through one plate glass window I saw sleek metal tables, colored glasses and chairs, and a highly polished wood counter circling the room—and only a few empty tables. I stepped to a menu posted outside another restaurant's red front door. The trendy interior boasted prices to match.

"I haven't really eaten today. Isabel did kind of ruin the tea." I turned back to Nathan. "But to be honest, I'm not up for Celeriac

Soup with Roast Hazels and Hazelnut Oil or Smoked Salmon with Pommery Mustard and Dill Mayonnaise. That's right up there with tea sandwiches and Regency dresses right now. Do you want to find something normal? A beer and a burger?"

"Yes." He smiled like that was the perfect meal—or I was the perfect girl. "Follow me. I saw a place called the Marlborough Tavern on our way to the Assembly Rooms."

Within minutes we were resting on rickety wood chairs at worn unfinished tables. The room felt as if it belonged at Braithwaite House, with its green-painted wainscoting and wallpaper depicting indiscernible purple flowers. Beer taps and wine bottles lined the bar.

The air was heavy with barley, hops, and the tang of red wines and stewed meats. There was a layer of sweet overlaying it all.

"I'll miss this. Life feels slower here . . . I've heard myself think." He opened the menu. His phone buzzed and he glanced at it. "Speaking of thinking, it's Craig. He wants me to call him later."

"I thought you were finished at WATT."

"I am, but I often find it takes a few weeks for everything to settle out. And I like Craig. He's become a good friend. I imagine we'll stay in touch." He laid his phone on the table. "I'll call him when we get back to the house."

"Where will you go next?" I heard my voice lift and hated what it revealed. I wasn't asking about work. He knew it too.

He reached his hand across the table. It grazed mine, before I pulled back. I regretted the action as soon as I took it. I held my breath, hoping he hadn't noticed.

"I'm weighing three proposals; I'll pick one when I get back." His tone was measured. I watched the space between our hands. I didn't have the courage to look into his eyes.

We chatted about silly things over the Posh Kebab Wrap with Autumn Slaw and Yogurt, for him, and the Maximus Burger, with its two patties and a fried egg, for me. It only took egg dripping all over the fries to ease us back to laughter.

As we hit the sidewalk, I felt the burger hit my stomach. "Thank goodness those dresses cinch well above the waist. They almost make me look like I have a chest too."

"So I noticed." Nathan's face was alive with teasing and a glimmer of something deliciously dangerous. There was the question again. I didn't back away this time. I lifted on my toes and kissed him in answer.

He widened his eyes. I only grinned and tilted my head toward another stop, the Jane Austen Center. "We're here. We have to go in."

The "center" was housed in a nondescript townhouse in a row of nondescript townhouses. But the inside was anything but. It was packed with all things Austen: artifacts, writings, placards on the walls. It was like the Braithwaite House gallery on steroids.

We submitted to a costumed guide, as it was the only way to see the full museum. She led us with a perky smile and a dress far inferior to any I'd worn, as she described Austen, her work, and her life in Bath. Our guide concluded the tour in the Tea Room with a coupon for a free biscuit. I could barely contain myself as we politely declined the biscuit and the photo booth.

"Please, no more food." I waved my hand back at the house. "I had it wrong while I was reading. I misunderstood. Austen hated Bath."

We walked up the hill toward Weston Road. I stopped and turned to see the city below us. I couldn't see all Bath, but a good bit of the Georgian part. From this perspective, I saw it differently.

And after the Jane Austen Center, I saw the woman differently too—the writer separate from her books.

"At first reading I thought she loved it. I mean, I'm literal, so I knew I was missing most of the humor people adore about Austen, but Catherine Morland loved Bath, so I thought Austen must have. But she was making fun of Catherine in so many ways—playing on her naïveté, and opening up her eyes and making her question and see things from a different angle. But I didn't understand the . . . not cynicism, but I guess the *realism* there. Isabella Thorpe was Bath for Austen. Bath was like a bunch of Marys to her."

"Marys?"

"She didn't like Marys. They weren't real. They were selfish, all hat no cattle. Like Bath."

We walked on. Nathan was silent. I knew he was cycling through my Texan logic and the Marys. After a few minutes he took my hand again. "You're absolutely right. I do, though. I like Marys, a Mary, very much."

"You liked an Isabella too—or an Isabel." I closed my eyes. I couldn't believe I'd said it. But I couldn't help myself, and if we were going to be anything, I needed to get it out there. It had hovered about me since Isabel's meltdown, or wake-up, and like Wentworth, maybe I was a little dense too. There was certainly room here for misunderstandings and wrong impressions.

Nathan stopped walking.

I looked up and could barely make him out standing only a foot or two away. Darkness had come and I hadn't noticed.

"It's just . . . I was in front of you, Nathan, for a whole year, and if I'm going to be really honest with you, most of that time I was in love with you. I know I missed out that you liked me too, but that had to have stopped at some point, because you dated my best friend and you never actually asked me out or said anything. I get the Isabel thing is between her and me, and who knows how long she and I have been playing out this game, but the fact remains you chose to go out with her. To some degree you pursued her, not me."

I felt rather than saw him step closer. "What must it be like to live in your head?"

"Huh?" I pressed my lips together.

"You and I see things so differently. Please remember nothing is objective. Do you think I bring everyone cupcakes? Coffee? Unpolished stones? What I felt for you never stopped. You gave no encouragement, not any I could see. I was taking your friendship as far as you'd offer it. I only started running this year so I could grab the treadmill next to you at lunch. I spent an entire weekend coming up with a list of reasons why I should shadow you my first months at WATT, why you were the engineer with the most insights on procedure and protocol—despite the fact I already knew you never follow any of them."

"Oh. I didn't know."

"And the second I heard your voice on the phone the other day, I was scared to death. I said last night I almost missed you, Mary, but that wasn't the whole story. You're the one who wasn't able to see me. I hadn't stopped chasing you."

His hand trailed up my arm and held my cheek. I felt his breath the heartbeat before his lips touched mine. His other hand slid around my waist to pull me closer.

Kissing Nathan, really kissing Nathan, was everything I imagined. It was music—layered, nuanced, soul-gripping, and open to endless interpretation. And much better than a fairy tale.

Chapter 24

We entered the house through the mudroom door and climbed the narrow stairs to the gallery. The gallery, open to the hallway below, was filled with soft laughter. Dinner was in full swing.

I caught Isabel's voice. It was light and open. She was telling... I strained to hear. She was telling them about some of Austen's letters to her nieces.

"I think the apologies worked." I looked to Nathan. "Should we join them?"

He pulled me close. "I don't want to share you. Let's go sit by the fire in the Day Room. No one will find us there, and Sonia showed me where she keeps the port."

"Excellent plan. I'll grab a lighter sweater and meet you there. The fire was warm last night."

"I'll call Craig real quick." He kissed me.

I headed to our bedroom; he turned back down the stairway. Within moments, I followed and made my way to the Day Room. I passed close by the dining room and, although I knew I'd be welcome, I was glad I wasn't in there. Isabel didn't need me. This was hers now, whatever became of the visit and the thesis.

Before I reached the Day Room, I heard Nathan's voice coming from the library across from it. The door was ajar, so I pushed it and looked inside. It was a charming little space—a completely interior room with walls fully lined in books. It smelled of dust, ink, old leather, and furniture oil.

Nathan's back was to me. He was typing at his computer, his phone resting near him. I noted the long white cord of earbuds and stepped forward to tap him.

"I disagree. Engineering is not the place for cuts, not when entering the fourth quarter... A sale will never clear that fast and you know it."

He sat back. I stepped back.

"Benson? Rodriguez? Davies? Whom are you planning to sacrifice, Karen? We've run the numbers and WATT's got payroll secured through May... This is precipitous..."

I froze where I was, knowing he hadn't heard me come in.

"She's responsible for 42 percent of deliverables in the past three years... I understand that and I'm not saying it isn't an issue... I don't..."

I backed out of the room completely. *I understand that and I'm not saying it isn't an issue.*

That "she" had to be me. How had it not occurred to me that Nathan would discuss me? That I was part of what was right—or wrong—at WATT? He'd followed me around for a month. He had to have opinions about my work. Was I getting fired? Was he agreeing? Or was he defending me? And if he was defending me—was it because I was good at my job, or because I was now his girlfriend?

"I didn't hear you come down."

I started at his voice. "Just now... How was your call?"

"It was fine." He gestured into the Day Room.

I walked in first and curled into one of the armchairs. "You don't look fine."

"We don't need to talk about it." He pointed to a small silver tray, then handed me one of the two glasses of port resting on it. "I ran into Duncan. He brought these for us."

"We can talk about it if it would help." I waited.

"No . . ." Nathan sat back and watched the fire, seemingly lost in thought. He took a sip. Another. Then he turned to me. "I've asked before, but I don't think I fully understood your answer. Why did you never share your Golightly work with Benson or Rodriguez? They're both solid engineers with different skill sets. They could've helped you."

"It got away from me in a lot of ways, but it also was my job to get it right." I set down my glass. "Craig never pushed me on this. Why are you?"

"Because it's an issue, Mary. It cost a lot of money and, bottom line, he should have. There's no way around that."

"He understood I needed it."

"But as your boss he should have pushed, so there wouldn't be questions now." He flinched as if he'd just revealed something he shouldn't have.

"What are the questions now?" I paused, but he didn't reply. "Are you going to tell me what you're really after? Or do I have to guess?"

"I can't, Mary. Not now, not yet."

I was getting fired. I set down my glass and pushed out of the chair. "I'll see you in the morning."

Isabel was still at dinner or in the ballroom. I looked around our room at the scattered dresses and ribbons, at the silks and wools. This wasn't my world. I grabbed my phone and my computer and I fled.

I headed back to the narrow stairs and the long hallway of cupboards. That first night, while fixing Clara's flashlight, I'd noticed a small room. It had a table, stools, and rows upon rows of jars lining the walls. I assumed it had been the canning room at some point. Tonight it was my hiding place.

I perched on the stool and opened my computer. My hands felt too heavy to move, so I just rested them there. I thought it would hurt more—losing a job after five years, losing a boyfriend after five minutes.

It's just a job. My brothers had thrown out that line countless times over the years—to me, to my dad, to each other. *It's just a job.*

And not even one I'd picked . . . Craig had picked me. Hounded me to join his start-up. He was the one who started the conversation in that elevator and practically grabbed the device I'd created for my professor from my hands in his eagerness. And working in that garage was stifling . . . There were only ten of us that whole year, working eighty-hour weeks and living on Craig's wife's casseroles and Tamarind Jarritos. And the new offices? Always cold and gray. All those divider walls were gray.

It took me twenty minutes and an equal number of data drops to send every remaining scrap on my work to Benson—stuff I'd left off the shared server. Another 13 percent of my hard drive was now free. Golightly and everything else I'd been working on was his.

Why did you never share your Golightly work with Benson or Rodriguez?

Karen had harped on me daily about "collaborative creativity" and "dialoguing across sectors" and "an atmosphere of free data exchange and ideation."

It wasn't that I didn't agree with any of those concepts, once I took out the buzzwords, or that I thought Benson or Rodriguez would steal, ruin, or diminish my ideas. WATT wasn't like that. I wasn't like that. But this one—that's what I couldn't explain to Nathan, but Craig, on some level, had understood—it was asking for judgment on a piece of my soul. I never should have started designing Golightly in the first place. That was my mistake.

But just as Isabel had said today, I was in the middle before I knew that I had begun. I was originally testing my emotions, remembering that movie and even my mom, with some ocular advances the physicists discovered. Then Craig found out, saw the marketability, and pushed me forward. Something tentative, small and private, went above and beyond me before I could balk and call an end to it all. I let it roll me in hopes I'd catch up. I never did.

I scrolled through my e-mails in search of one I hadn't truly considered but also never deleted. MedCore had reached out ten times over the past two years. Maybe it was time to reach back.

I sent a query—just three lines. It hardly took any time at all.

Then I tapped my phone.

"I didn't expect to hear from you." The delight in my dad's voice almost made me smile. It was soft and croaky. He cleared his throat. "I'm taking a coffee break. It's a beautiful day here, by the way, down to seventy-eight degrees . . . I had a good talk with Isabel today."

"I told her to take over the updates. She said she'd call Dr. Milton too."

"She was going to do that right after we talked. I expect I'll hear from her again. She sounds good, strong. You did well, Mary."

"Thanks, Dad. How's the Historical Society building?"

He sighed, either at the change of subject or his surroundings. He was probably stuck in the basement or perched on a ladder in the attic, because electrical wires were never housed in the pretty parts of a building.

"Wait until you see it. All the old woodwork is restored and the wiring is original—1928 knob-and-tube. I saved you a couple of the porcelain knobs. They've got the Benjamin Company stamp right on them."

"That's great. We can build something with them together."

"I bet you didn't call to discuss knob-and-tube."

"Not that I'm not interested, but, no, I didn't. I called to say I'm thinking of a change."

"A change." It wasn't a question. It was a statement of disbelief. "And what are you planning to change?"

"Hey. I change stuff."

"When? What?" Now he was chuckling.

I blew out a breath. This was not going as anticipated . . . So I'd had the same hairstyle since I was seven. I lived in the same apartment I found upon graduation from college, even though I could afford something far better, with a view instead of sitting on a highway. I worked off the same grocery list each week.

"I didn't know I was so pathetic."

"Hey, Peanut. I didn't say that. What's going on here? It's not that you don't change things, you simply go with prevailing winds."

Prevailing winds?

Worse and worse . . . My dad hadn't called me Peanut since my growth spurt in eighth grade shot me from the twenty-fifth percentile in height to the ninety-fifth in six months. Now I'd gotten it several times in as many days. And second, I really was the embodiment of the gloomy page in the center of the bright *Oh, the Places You'll Go!* book. Here was the proof.

"Then it's a brand-new me, Dad. You know that company from Boston? I just sent them an e-mail saying I'm interested. They're working on the next generation of non-lithium dissolving batteries for use in humans."

"I . . . What's going on? You love your job. This feels sudden."

"It's just a job. This company has been after me for a couple years."

"But you never said you were interested; you never said you're unhappy at WATT. That's a big move."

"But now you've got the business up—" I stopped. "I'm ready for something new."

"Of course you want your own life. I'm sorry."

"I didn't mean that." I dropped my head in my hands. I hadn't meant to say that; I wasn't sure I even felt it. I just knew getting pushed out hurt, and I felt pushed on more sides than I knew existed within me—*and* I'd just spread around the pain. "Please, Dad, that isn't why I'm looking for a change at all. I'm just excited about it, about doing something new and different."

I heard a snuffle and a scrape. He was kneading his palm against his chin. I'd seen the gesture for years.

"If that's the case, I'm happy for you and I'm proud of you. Boston's a long way from home, though."

"That's the downside." I felt the urge to see him. Hug him. "Are you free for dinner Saturday?"

"I thought you are in England until the twenty-eighth."

I tapped my computer to look up flights and noted movement in my periphery. Gertrude stood in the doorway, dressed in blue silk, candles in hand. I held a finger to her to wait. "As you know, this trip has taken some unexpected turns." I tried to laugh to lighten the moment. It didn't work. "I'm looking into flights for tomorrow."

"You're leaving Isabel?"

"I'll talk to her tonight. If Dr. Milton hasn't told her to come straight home, I wouldn't be surprised if she wants to stay a few more days."

"Then she'll need you."

"For once, Dad, she won't. She's fine; I promise. Better than you've seen her in years. One look at her and you'd understand. I think we're both better off now."

"Okay. She does sound good." I could sense he was trying to work himself into comfortable. "I love you and I'm happy about all this if you are. We'll talk Saturday?"

Again, another thing rarely said around my house. I felt love from him every day of my life, but the words never came easily to anyone in my family. They were all men. "Yes, and I love you too, Dad."

I tapped my phone to end the call and looked back to Gertrude.

"I didn't mean to eavesdrop, or interrupt." She held out the candles.

"You didn't. I'm the one hiding in your canning room." I held up my phone. "I'm hoping to leave tomorrow."

"I heard."

"I've got some issues at work to deal with and . . ." I looked to the ceiling. "I heard laughter earlier. Isabel will be fine without me, if she stays."

"Your friend is delightful. She is more welcoming than she was your first night here."

"I think time away has done her some good."

"Just like the play in the middle of *Mansfield Park*. Within role play, we find ourselves." She shifted the candles in her arms. "I think that's the true attraction to places like this, as long as you don't stay too long."

"You should share that with Isabel."

"I suspect she already knows." She nodded to her candles. "I had better get these upstairs. Let me know what time you're leaving and I'll arrange a car."

Chapter 25

I woke to soft gray light. Heavy-cloud-cover light. There were no dresses strewn on the floor and Isabel was not already off on an adventure. I looked over to find dark curls spilling across her pillow and blue eyes fixed on me.

"Hello." I crushed my pillow beneath me.

"I woke up a few minutes ago." Isabel pushed herself upright. "Are you sure about all this?"

Late in the night I'd told her my plans. We stayed up until the black had shifted to gray outside the windows talking about all that had gone on—here, at home, and through the years.

She and Grant had gone for another long walk after ours and, upon recounting it, I let her quote one more line. She was bursting with excitement over its "perfect application."

She'd actually held her hand to her heart while delivering it. "'Seldom, very seldom, does complete truth belong to any human disclosure . . . but where, as in this case, though the conduct is mistaken, the feelings are not . . . He could not impute to me a more relenting heart than I possessed, or a heart more disposed to accept his.'"

I had flopped back on my bed and moaned. "That's all you're going to tell me?"

She had perched on her elbows above me with a grin. "One more thing . . . That man can kiss."

She also told me that Dr. Milton had agreed to daily calls and she planned to stay a few more days. Also, Nathan had spent most of the night searching for me. He had knocked on our bedroom door six times. I almost felt guilty for hiding until two a.m. in the canning room—almost.

I'd told her about our walk to Bath, about overhearing his call, and about my plans to move.

Are you sure about all this? I let her present question drift through me. "No."

"Then send another e-mail."

That was another thing I'd told her. In my haste, I'd sent Craig an e-mail resigning. Isabel's shock had confirmed it hadn't been my wisest move.

"And let Karen fire me? She'd love that."

Isabel squished a pillow into her lap. "But you don't know that. That sentence might not have been about you. And you said Nathan sounded like he was against it."

"What about telling me Craig had been wrong all along?"

"So you're the scapegoat. Nathan was probably frustrated that Craig dropped the ball and now you're the scapegoat. Sounds like Karen needs one."

After five years of stories and lots of Friday nights, Isabel knew WATT well.

"Having your 'boyfriend' stick up for you is no better." I made the word *boyfriend* sound ugly to make it easier to let go.

Isabel caught it and let out a long, slow breath. "I see . . . Then I'm sorry."

"For what?"

"Everything. I didn't know how much he really meant to you, and what I did plays into all this. Yes, it's your job, but everything about Nathan and how you feel about all this, I'm in there too. You wouldn't doubt him if it hadn't been for me."

"One has nothing to do with the other." I climbed out of bed and headed to the bathroom.

"One has everything to do with the other," Isabel called after me.

I ignored her and brushed my teeth and hair, dressed in jeans and a cream sweater, and dabbed on a little makeup.

She said nothing further as I darted around the room to finish my packing and slip on my ballet flats. I finally zipped up my suitcase and stood next to her bed. "Call me when you get back?"

She threw the covers back and jumped up to hug me. "You know I will. And if you're serious about all this, I want to throw you a moving-away party. You know your dad will come into town for it. He'd want that."

"You two . . . Don't do that. It's not going to feel like anything worth celebrating." I looked toward the door as if I expected Nathan to knock for the seventh time. "All this got so messed up."

"Not messed up." Isabel slid her hands down my arms and captured my own. "It got real. So don't . . . don't do anything rash until you can see it clearly. Okay?"

Gertrude met me at the bottom of the stairs. "I was coming to get you. Your car is here."

I held out her gray Barbour coat. "Thank you for this. I'm sorry I forgot to leave it in the mudroom yesterday."

"I hadn't thought about it." She laid the coat across the stair's handrail and gestured to the far side of the hallway. It felt like we were in the Pump Room and she was inviting me to step out of the circuit to gossip. She turned as we stepped into a small alcove.

"Before you go . . . I wanted to say thank you. You helped me realize surviving isn't the same as living. This, in many ways, has been my play in the center of *Mansfield Park* too." Her eyes trailed behind me and up the stairs. "I got stuck here somehow, and when the house sold I couldn't move on. But you . . . you played the piano, you forgave Isabel, you risked your heart with Nathan . . . Even what you are doing now."

I found myself unfolding, agreeing, even feeling like it might be true, until she mentioned "what you are doing now." My heart hiccupped. That did not feel like courage.

She dabbed her ringed pinkie finger to the corner of one eye. "My niece lives in France, and she's begged me for years to come be with her family. You showed me last night that I could do it. It's time to go, to move on and be with family. I almost missed my chance." By now she'd stopped dabbing and let the few tears trickle down her cheek.

"I'm happy for you, Gertrude. Will you keep in touch? I'd love to hear about your life there, and your family."

"It won't all happen right away. I'm not that brave. But, yes, I'd like that. I want to hear about your next chapter too."

We'd only known each other a short time, but I didn't want to let her go. Oddly, her story seemed to mirror, inform, interweave, or somehow run alongside mine. It was like music—I'd stepped away before, now I felt almost desperate not to. Some things, some people, I needed to carry with me.

She pulled a tissue from her pocket and gestured to the side hall. "You should go find the others. The Muellers postponed their gig ride and are sitting in the Day Room, and the Lottes are playing chess in the front parlor. No one wanted to leave the house until they'd said good-bye."

I hugged Gertrude, then set off for the Day Room. As I tapped on the Day Room door, Nathan leapt from the library.

"Were you really going to leave without talking to me?" He sounded weary, and a touch angry. He looked both—and hurt.

"No, I wasn't. And I'm sorry about last night . . . Give me a minute?"

Nathan tilted his chin to the Day Room. He said nothing, but his crossed arms spoke volumes.

I pushed open the door. Helene and Herman were squeezed into the armchairs. Both looked up and struggled to stand as I entered the room.

"I wish you weren't leaving us." Herman pulled me to him, then handed me off to Helene in one smooth motion.

She was dressed in dusty blue today, and it matched her pale eyes. She had a red-and-blue woven shawl over her shoulders, and her little mobcap was askew. Her white hair fluffed out at odd angles.

"Dressed as you are, we must seem very silly to you." She pulled me close. There was nothing but warmth in her voice.

"Not at all. You are enjoying a very important anniversary and I loved it, even the dresses. I loved playing the piano, dancing, your wonderful and wise interpretation of Mrs. Jennings, and my gig ride with you both. I won't forget any of it."

"But you must go home. Gertrude said your work needs you." Herman patted my arm.

"We will miss you." Helene pressed her lips together as if she might cry.

"I will miss you too."

"Your . . . your friend is staying. She promised to share with us some little-known Regency customs today." Herman touched his finger to his neckcloth.

"Ask her lots of questions, okay? And be sure to get her to tell some of the behind-the-scenes about the books. She knows all about them—far beyond the characters."

We shared hugs, promises to keep in touch, and a few memories more before I slipped back into the hallway. One step and one deep breath carried me across it and into the library. Nathan was gone.

I returned to the front hall. He wasn't there, nor was Gertrude. The hall felt cold and too large for only me. I stepped into the front parlor and found Sylvia and Clara at the chessboard. Aaron sat looking on. He looked uncomfortable sitting in a needlepoint chair watching chess. He was a Mr. Bingley, meant for the outdoors.

"Are you winning?" I tapped the top of Clara's head.

She grinned up at me. "I am." She slid out of her seat and hugged me.

"I will miss you, Clara."

Sylvia gave me a hug, as did Aaron. "We're sorry to lose you. It won't be the same."

"Who will play the piano?" Clara tugged my sleeve.

"Gertrude said she hired someone who plays even better than I do, and your dancing instructor is staying."

"Safe flight home, Mary." Sylvia pulled me into a final hug.

I headed out the front door and found Nathan at my car, lowering my suitcase into the trunk.

"I told Duncan this job was my insurance. I thought you might try to leave without seeing me."

"I wouldn't do that."

He raised a brow.

"Not after I said I wouldn't."

He shut the trunk and rested his hands on it as if requiring something firm and tangible beneath him. "What's going on, Mary?"

"I overheard you on the phone last night, Nathan. I didn't mean to. But when I tried to ask you about it, you lied. You said everything was fine, and maybe for WATT it is, but clearly it's not for me. You were talking about me."

"I did not lie." He ran his hands through his hair. "There are some things about WATT I can't share. And you wouldn't want me to. It'd be unprofessional. You want me to mix up work and love to satisfy your curiosity? It would diminish both of us. But you've also got to trust me. What are we doing here?" He flapped his hand between us. "What is all this if you don't trust me?"

"Wha— No." *Love?* "I do trust you, but Karen firing me is her decision, not yours. She has made her opinions clear since the day she arrived—in every reprimand, circular instruction, and veiled threat—and you can't defend me because I'm your girlfriend. I'm not saying you said that or think that . . . But if that's what you're trying to do, then WATT is just like you and me, with Isabel sandwiched between us. And I can't have that. That's my job, Nathan, my career. I can't stay there for any other reason than I've earned my spot."

"You and I, and certainly not Isabel, have nothing to do with WATT. Why would you assume I'd champion you for any other reason than you're good at your job?"

I looked back at the house. "Because all the lines between us are too blurry. I'm only realizing now how blurry. I need distance to see them clearly."

"To see me clearly?" He stared at me. I could tell he didn't understand, but I couldn't explain it any better. Isabel hadn't understood either—and to have Isabel and Nathan on the same side of this issue, against me, felt even more confusing. As I'd said earlier, it—everything—simply felt "messed up."

"I'm sorry." I reached up and kissed his cheek. "Can I call you when I land?"

"No."

I stepped back. "Okay."

"I didn't mean that. I'll be in the air." At my expression, he narrowed his eyes. "With you gone, why would I stay?"

"I hadn't thought that far."

"Clearly."

I reached for his hand. He clasped my fingers, but rather than pull me close, he tugged me toward the car door and opened it with his other hand.

I dropped into the seat. "Will you call me when you land? So we can talk?"

"Of course we'll talk." He shut the door.

I sank into the soft leather with the realization I'd been wrong—losing a job after five years and losing a boyfriend after five minutes actually hurt a great deal. I twisted to look out the rear window as the car began its roll down the long drive.

Nathan watched me go. I waved to him. He did not reciprocate.

Chapter 26

I'm going to miss this." I leaned back in one of the Adirondack chairs my dad and I had built from a kit the previous summer. We watched the night sky. Austin, the closest city, was seventy miles away, so there were no city lights to dim the stars. Thousands of them spread before us. "Braithwaite House was like this. There was one clear night and the stars were like a blanket of light." I trailed one line of stars to the horizon, to the trees, to Dad's back-yard, to my feet propped on a large tree stump. "You could fit our whole town into the land on that estate."

"That must have been something." Dad kept his focus on the heavens.

I'd shown up, as I'd said I would, for Saturday night dinner. I brought steaks from Central Market, the makings for a Caesar salad, and potatoes. Dad banked his surprise and let me cook. He did shoo me from the grill when the steaks were done and I showed no signs of pulling them off, and he also gently suggested that the potatoes might be ready after an hour in a 400-degree oven. The Caesar dressing, however, completely homemade, received no helpful input, and had to be redone twice before I was able to add the oil slowly enough to keep the dressing from separating. All in all, it was a good dinner—and my first attempt at real cooking.

I'd told him all about the trip. Isabel, the Muellers, the Lottes. I told him about Gertrude and how it felt like I was looking at Mom or myself and how there was so much I regretted.

"You can't think like that," he said. "She understood and knew you loved her. We all grieve in our own ways and, well, your brothers modeled that for you. It was hard on them too."

I also told him about Isabel's e-mail. She was staying in Bath. Getrude had arranged an interview via Skype with the Stanleys, and they were delighted that an "Austen expert" might take over Gertrude's management role. Gertrude was moving forward with plans to move to France and join her niece's family. And Grant's grandfather was helping Isabel find a local therapist. She hoped to make Bath her home.

"I'm happy for her. There's so much healing in that, and in going to England." Dad gave me a small smile. "Her father will never go back there to live. After moving here, he stopped all work with BP. It's a good bit of emotional and physical distance she's set up. And that man—"

"Grant." I supplied the name. "He's a keeper, Dad, and she loves him." I reached for his hand. "He's everything you'd want for your daughter . . . your other daughter."

I didn't tell him about Nathan.

Now that we were outside, the differences between England and Texas struck me anew. "You wouldn't believe how green it was, Dad. Shades I didn't know existed. Cool too. The temperature, I mean. Dressing in clothing that went out of style a couple hundred years ago will probably never be called cool. But if Isabel stays, you know you'll have to go someday. Maybe for her wedding. You'll love breeches. And those neckcloths? Very you."

Dad chuckled. "We'll see."

"I might get used to a cooler climate. I got to wear sweaters, and a very nice waxed coat, and I loved all the fires."

"You'll get plenty of chances in Boston. You can have fires like this starting in September and probably continuing through April." He added another log to the fire pit.

"I doubt I'll find an apartment with a fireplace, and certainly not a yard with a fire pit." I rolled my head on the chair's high back to face him. "Dad? I have no idea what I'm doing."

I'd arrived home Thursday and hadn't called anyone or done anything for two days. No one knew I was back except Isabel, Dad, and Nathan. Dad hadn't called; he'd assumed I was busy doing whatever it was young people do, and was delighted when I showed up. I didn't expect Isabel to call. We shot off some texts, hers full of heart emojis, but she was happy and occupied with Grant and Gertrude—as she should be.

But Nathan didn't call either, and I wasn't sure what to think about that.

The idea that one's happiness can depend entirely on a particular person—it is not possible . . . Austen's line had returned to me over and over during my two days of sleeping and moping. I hoped she, again, was right.

To be fair, it hadn't all been sleeping and moping. I'd also sent and received a flurry of e-mails with MedCore. Interviews were scheduled for Wednesday, and they booked me a flight out of Austin Tuesday afternoon.

"You can always change your mind?" Dad's statement tilted up into a question laced with hope. He leaned forward with his hands on his knees, as if eager for my answer. Eager for a new answer.

"Too late for that. I've got a hotel booked for Tuesday through Friday. They sent me terms this morning, so I expect Wednesday's interview is a formality. They even hired a relocation firm to help me find an apartment. So next weekend it may come down to packing and going."

"You accepted then."

I shook my head. "I made it clear I was not accepting. When I say it's too late, I mean at WATT. It's changing and my new boss . . . Well, it's time for me to go. But I do need to talk to Craig first. Despite anything else, everything else, I owe him that. I was wrong to just send an e-mail. He gave me ten minutes on Monday."

Dad chuckled. "The same lightning bolt, eh? I'm surprised he gave you more than five . . . But he's going to miss you. Don't forget those days in the garage. Garages are special places."

I smiled. Garages were Dad's treasured places. If you needed to talk to him about something serious or had bad news to relay, you did it in the garage. He had a workbench set up in a corner and it was his creative home. It was also where we connected—Dan, Curt, Scott, and me. If there was one room in the house that had formed us the most, it was the garage.

"Did Dottie order you a cake?"

I snorted and caught myself. "Didn't call to find out . . . I forgot you knew Dottie."

Dad knew all WATT's staff, at least the ones who were part of that original garage bunch. Dottie came on board a couple weeks before we moved into the office building. She had been hired as an office manager, but Craig needed a "garage manager" first, so he brought her on board early. She and Dad had co-managed the packing.

I watched a star shoot across the sky, then realized it was an airplane. It made my eyes prick. I swiped at them. "You wouldn't recognize WATT now. It's got over sixty employees and layers."

"Layers, huh? Rungs on a ladder." Dad sat back in his chair and joined me watching the stars again. "Don't sell yourself short. No matter how much it has changed, that company will miss you. It's made up of all your friends. You were the first engineer; you designed all those gizmos, that kiddie robot that was so hot a couple years ago, that battery, and the—"

"You're right. It was good work." I cut him off. I didn't want to hear about it.

I also didn't want to hear that "the company" was going to miss me. That wasn't true. The company had no feelings, and with its growth rate, WATT was no longer an idea, an enterprise, or a start-up. It was a company. Besides, wasn't that the whole point of *It's just a job?* There was no "missing"—on either side.

"Are you running?" Dad whispered the question.

"Every morning."

That's not what he was asking, and I knew it. He knew I knew it, because he didn't comment or clarify. He waited. I waited too and watched the stars. A few flickered and the sky felt like music. Music required honesty.

"Yes," I whispered back.

Dad reached out and covered my hand with his own, just as I had done to him moments before. He didn't pick it up or squeeze it. He just rested his on top of mine. It was warm and solid and the perfect weight, that reminder that I couldn't escape unseen. I swiped at my eyes again with my free hand.

"I accepted a job to rewire Mrs. Harris's new kitchen."

"Okay..." I choked on a laugh. I had not expected him to follow up with that. "But she's got to pay you more than a chicken. We talked about this."

"She is. I printed cards with the pricing schedule you designed and she accepted it. I standardized the whole thing like you suggested. But I wondered . . . What would you think if I invited her out to dinner sometime?"

"You're asking Mrs. Harris on a date?" I heard my tone. It was almost offensive in the amount of surprise that rippled through it.

I sat up, faced him, and tried again—this time as a sentence, and I smiled as I said it. "You're asking Mrs. Harris out on a date."

Dad kept his eyes trained on the sky. "I don't know that I'd call it a date, but I care about her. She and I have gotten to talking over the past several months, and I'm thinking dinner is a good start—dinner and maybe a movie. Maybe that's too much for one night?"

"I think you could squeeze it in."

"Perhaps I'll take her to La Buona Vita in LaGrange. We went there for your birthday a few years ago, remember?" He slid me a glance. "Isabel ordered that huge cake with the sparklers."

Isabel. She'd seen my dad, my "relational" dad, as she'd called him, better than I had.

"I remember."

"It's a little fancier than what I was thinking for a first date, but the drive will be lovely this time of year."

I leaned back and watched the music. "I agree, Dad. Do that first and save the movie for your second date."

Dad's machine doled out a bag of Skittles every two hours. I let several drop before I circled back each time and swiped the colored rainbow from the catch bowl.

After the third bag, I stood in the center of my studio apartment and surveyed the scene. From the living room, one 360-degree turn exposed every square foot of my home except the shower, which resided behind the bathroom door. The kitchen had been stripped of all superfluous stuff—perishables I couldn't eat, nonperishables I wouldn't, and redundancies. I refused to pack and move six strainers or twenty-seven empty Mason jars.

I'd hesitated over the jars. My old piano teacher sent me three jars of jam every August. The day they arrived always felt like my birthday, and I practically licked each jar clean—all the while pushing aside, and yet cosseting, that little nudge, that pinprick, of the something lost that they evoked.

It was always the music. I could now name it and enjoy it. After my dinner with Dad, I'd driven home and pulled my Lanvin shoe box from the top of my closet. I had also pulled the last jam jar from the fridge, sat on the floor, and thrashed a spoon around its farthest edges. It was delicious.

I turned again. The bedroom was set. Books on the bedside table straightened and every drawer cleared out. The living room, the bathroom, and the small alcove that served as my office—one desk and one chair—were cleared of every broken pencil, every leaky or dry pen, every unnecessary scrap of paper. Three garbage bags and four boxes for Goodwill. Two bags for the Dumpster.

Six hours to clean an apartment. Six hours to ready it to move across the country. Six hours to ponder Dad's question.

Are you running?

Nathan had asked the same question. *Do you ever feel like running away?* Isabel had asked it too—Isabel had lived it. Are we always between moments of running away?

Are you running?

I answered the question. *Not enough.*

I grabbed a pair of shorts and my San Antonio Marathon T-shirt from the perfectly organized drawer, changed quickly, and headed to the Town Lake Trail, my usual route along Lake Austin—which was really a renamed section of the Colorado River. I turned south on Exposition Boulevard, relishing the burn of every hill, and dropped down onto Lake Austin Boulevard to pick up the Town Lake Trail under MoPac.

I passed the Stevie Ray Vaughan statue. *Single-handedly revived blues in the 1980s.* Dad loved that statue and always gave it a salute when we passed. I wondered if Nathan had seen it. He'd love it... I ran on.

I cut back over the river on the Congress Avenue bridge, right over those two million bats. They, too, would be moving soon. They'd head south to Mexico City; I'd travel north to Boston.

It felt as if everyone and everything was on the move. Gertrude. Nathan. WATT. Dad. Time was not static.

I stalled at the end of the bridge. Large white canvas umbrellas covered the patio at the Four Seasons Hotel. They reminded me of Braithwaite House. It felt very close and, in the same breath, a lifetime ago.

And that's when they flew. I looked up as almost two million bats rose into the sky. They came out in waves, an undulating pattern rather than a steady stream. It made me think of Golightly and the power problem. It made me think of WATT: all these individual bats working at the same time, in the same direction. A surge of them rose in the air so tightly I couldn't make out the individuals; it was just a mass of black.

The stream slowed, dark descended, and I ran home.

Chapter 27

The first thing I noticed was the hum. I'd been in my apartment all weekend—the upstairs guy had moved on from Macklemore to Hoodie Allen, my AC unit had chugged away to keep the apartment below eighty degrees, and MoPac had provided its ever-present white noise. But it was here at work that I felt it inside me. There were a variety of computers operating at different frequencies, the AC units, soft chatter drifting in the open space above our cubicles, even a radio somewhere playing Carrie Underwood.

And it was Monday. I secretly loved Mondays. People worked hard at WATT, and it wasn't until Friday they loosened up and relaxed across the cubicles or in the break room or headed to a brewpub to unpack the week. On Mondays we were warming up, heads down and serious, full of promise. This was the week something great would happen.

I felt displaced as the morning passed by. Moira wasn't at her desk. No one needed me. No one stopped by. It was a typical Monday, but I no longer felt in the mix. I had no projects to pursue. This was what I'd wanted, why I'd sent Craig an e-mail, and yet . . .

After about an hour staring at my wire animals, I began cleaning out my desk. It took no time, but more Skittles than my apartment had. Without Dad's controlled distribution system, I power-chomped my way into my third bag before I cleaned my stash from my bottom desk drawer and dropped it all on Moira's neat and still empty desk.

By midafternoon I was stir-crazy and on a sugar high.

"I heard, and not from you, by the way." Moira draped herself over the divider between our cubicles as she always did upon arriving to work. Her now copper-colored hair puddled on my top shelf. "I hate you." Her tone held notes of sarcasm and bravado. Her eyes held hurt.

"Where have you been?"

"I had meetings downtown. I would have told you, but you aren't supposed to be here and you're certainly not supposed to be quitting."

I twirled a finger at her hair. "In my honor?"

"As if. I'm doing nothing in your honor. Copper is simply a good fall color." She hiked her chin. "Everyone was talking about you Friday. Word got out about your e-mail. Really, Mary? An e-mail?" She reached over the wall and dangled a Starbucks cup in my face. "I brought you this. An afternoon pick-me-up. I shouldn't have. But I did, so drink it."

I took the cup, set it down, and walked out of my cubicle and into hers. I hugged her.

She hugged me back. "What's going on? Why'd you do it?" She dropped into her chair and scowled at the packs of Skittles. She didn't comment as I perched on her desk.

"We can't talk here," I said. "We'll talk tonight. For now, let's say I need a change."

"Seems to be a thing around here. We all got called into the staff meeting Friday to say good-bye to Nathan."

"Nathan was here on Friday?"

Moira narrowed her eyes. "Why does that surprise you?"

"Later. But I thought he was finished here a week ago."

Moira nodded. "He came in to wrap something up, but he's gone now. I think. He and Craig were closed up all Friday except for that good-bye meeting." Then she smirked. "He got cake."

"Word is Dottie got me one too. Ten minutes with Craig and cake."

Moira scoffed. Craig's eccentricities bugged her at times. "One of his best employees quits and he only gives you ten minutes? He probably won't even ask why you're going. Why are you going?"

"Later," I reminded her. "And you know him; I'm honored to get ten whole minutes. If he didn't respect me so much, I might only get two."

Moira matched my sarcasm. "Whatever."

"Hey . . ." I shoved at her shoulder. The gesture reminded me of Nathan and his constant happy shoulder-bumping. My false buoyancy faltered. "It's for the best."

"Whose best? You love this job. No one else has got your geeky enthusiasm for everything about this place."

"Mary? Mary?"

I stood. Moira stood too. We found Benson standing in my cubicle looking around as if he might find me hiding.

"He does," I whispered to Moira before calling out, "Over here."

"Oh . . ." He blinked. "Can I talk to you?"

"Sure. Be right there." I turned back to Moira. "Are you busy tonight?"

"All yours."

I put my hand on my heart and left her cubicle. "I'm touched."

"I still hate you."

Benson started talking before I sat. "I've been here all weekend. How are you here? I thought— Have you been here all morning? I would've called you, but I thought you were gone, then Lucas said he saw you. I need to show you this. It's incredible. It works."

Short, compact, and crackling with energy, Benson was my definition of a live wire. He was also the kindest man I'd ever met. He crossed the little hall, pulled a chair from another cubicle with a "Sorry, can I borrow this?" and tucked close to me. "You're brilliant."

I caught back a half laugh and returned the compliment. "And so are you."

He sat straight. "I'm serious." He opened his laptop and pushed it onto the desk in front of me. "I had no idea you were so far along, and then—your idea about the bats."

After my run, I'd sent Benson an e-mail. I'd sent him my notes, but this was more. I wanted his help. There was something about the bats and the waves in which they flew from beneath the bridge that struck me as relevant to Golightly.

"The bats were a great analogy. They come out as individuals, but we see them as waves. Our eyes can't differentiate—mass creates power. I watched a video, and they launch in surges too. You caught the ebb and flow—the sequencing. We need to run the power in dual pure sine waves at alternating rates."

My jaw dropped. It was so simple. Nathan had said it would be. Nathan—

Nathan was gone.

"Here. I came in around four and worked up the schematics

for a prototype. The lab guys are ready when you give the word." He tapped on a different view, then, swiping his finger across his screen, he flew through several diagrams. I barely kept up.

I flicked his hand away to pause on the data sheet. "You did all this since last night?"

"I don't sleep much, and when you sent all your files I got curious. Then last night when you asked for my help . . . You help me all the time, but you've never shared this. I was honored." A red flush climbed his neck. He tapped his screen again and again. "It's all here. Look . . . And this . . . And here."

I glanced at him. Benson was nodding so hard his glasses lifted off his nose. "Maybe you were too close and needed another set of eyes."

"I guess I did."

He poked his screen so hard the colors distorted. "We can do this. You need to talk to Craig." He popped up and looked toward Craig's office. "Is he here today? You've got to take this to him. I haven't seen him. It is Monday, right?"

"It's Monday and he's here." I tapped my phone. "In one minute I've got ten minutes with him. But I sent all this to you because I thought you'd appreciate it. Karen has no interest in it." I stood to go. "We're not going to build it."

"Why wouldn't we?" Benson shoved the laptop into my hands. "Take it. You have to show him."

I tried to shove it back, but he pulled his hands away. "This isn't what I'm seeing him about," I said. "You show him later."

Benson's eyes widened. "We have to design this. This is what we do. Acer wants a device. HP too. And we can get this out the door. Why would they want what's already out there when we've got something better? This is why we're here. It's what we do." He gently pushed the laptop, still in my hands, so that it rested against my chest. There was no handing it back.

Benson dropped his gaze. It darted around my cubicle as if seeing it for the first time. "You're packed up. Are we all switching cubicles again? I just got mine right. Do you know how much time and productivity we lose with each move?"

"No. This is just me." I glanced at my phone. "I'm up."

Benson nodded and pushed on my back. "Will you find me after you tell him? I'll wait. Should I wait here?" He pushed again. "No. I'll wait at my desk."

Moira met me outside her cubicle. "This is a mistake."

"It's not." I kept moving.

"Please, Mary." Her tone stopped me. "You love this job, and I actually don't hate you. I'll miss you."

"I know. Me too."

Moira turned back and I walked on. I glanced in the cubicles as I passed. Each was filled with the unique personality of the person who worked there. Dottie's grandchildren covered every square inch of her gray fabric walls; the finance guy's cubicle—what was his name?—was plastered with pinned spreadsheets overlapping each other. It reminded me of the wallpaper in one of the first-floor bathrooms at Braithwaite House—tiny black dots forming a seascape across the walls. Lucas, WATT's head programmer, had covered all available space within his cubicle with inspirational quotes like *Never Let Go of Your Dreams* and *You Are the Best You Ever.*

I lingered on that thought. Nathan. The piano. Braithwaite House. Dancing. As I passed, I wondered if Lucas might let me steal that last one.

I rapped my knuckles on Craig's office door. Other than the fully enclosed conference rooms lining two of the outer walls, his office was the only real room in our company.

"Come in."

I opened the door and paused, as I always did, to take in his view. Craig's outer wall was full glass and looked out over a fountain and the complex's largest man-made puddle. That wasn't terribly interesting. But on sunny days, especially if there was a breeze like today, sunlight refracted off the droplets of water the fountain shot into the air. The droplets came alive with the full light spectrum. Today it was glorious.

I looked back to Craig. His desk faced away from the wall. I wondered if he ever saw the view.

Eyes fixed on his computer, he started talking before I'd taken a step.

"Mary. Good. You're here. Shut the door and come on in. I'm running late, of course, but I heard Dottie got you a cake. She's a wonder with short notice."

"Yes."

"That's what this is. Very short notice."

"Yes." I sat down.

He pulled his eyes away from his screen and fixed them on me. We called him the Tasmanian Devil, after the old Road Runner cartoon. He moved that fast and often simply spun in circles—his staying power never keeping up with his ideas. But when he stopped moving, he was disconcertingly calm. Like now.

"You heard somehow, didn't you?"

"Nothing firm, but Karen isn't a fan of mine." I hedged. I was not going to tell him about Nathan and England, and I couldn't define what I actually did know anyway.

"It's all gone sideways, so if you're leaving—"

"It's time to move on."

"Is it?" Craig shot straight. He looked upset he'd missed the memo.

"I'll be at MedCore for the final interview Wednesday, but I'm happy to fill out the standard two weeks. I know we're pushing for a strong fourth quarter." The cool laptop, now sitting on my lap, reminded me. "Oh . . . Benson solved the Golightly heating issue and built specs for a prototype if you want to pursue it."

"Benson?"

"I sent him all my data last week." I opened the computer and walked around Craig's desk. "If you look here—"

Craig clamped a hand on my upper arm to silence me. He was a brilliant physicist, engineer, and innovator. He didn't need me interrupting or interpreting. He flipped through the schematics faster than Benson had.

"It's so sleek. Are these numbers right? Is it this compact? This rivals Microsoft's Holo. I had no idea . . ." His voice drifted away as he became absorbed.

Someone tapped on his door. He pointed to it without looking up.

"Come in," I called.

He glanced up, as if surprised the words didn't sound like his voice.

Karen entered.

He flicked his hand to me, eyes back on the computer. "Karen asked to join us, and as you report to her, I agreed it was appropriate. Do you mind?"

Karen's level stare dared me to protest.

"Not at all."

"We've got Golightly." Craig flapped his hand to her now. "Come . . . Come . . . You've got to see this."

Karen walked around Craig's desk on the opposite side and leaned in. He was scrolling so fast I could hardly keep up, and I knew what we were looking at. One glance at Karen and I could tell she was completely lost.

She straightened and backed away. I did the same.

"You did this?" She pointed a finger to me. Craig wasn't paying attention to us.

"Benson did. I sent him my work on Friday and he designed final schematics. He's been awake a few days, I think."

Karen nodded and got lost somewhere in her own thoughts until Craig surprised us both by slapping Benson's computer shut.

"We need a full meeting. Rally the troops. When's that meeting with HP? And—"

"Can we deal with one thing at a time?" Karen nodded to me.

"Right. You're leaving. Why are you leaving again?" Craig swung back and forth in his chair, trying to keep both Karen and me in sight.

To make it easier for him, we circled his desk and dropped into the two chairs facing it.

"Okay, then . . ." Craig pulled a tablet over. He'd already forgotten his question. "I looked up MedCore. Good company, innovative work, and you are right, Karen, it's not in conflict with what we do here. But I'm sorry to lose you, Mary. Four years is a long time . . . Five years. We're at five years . . . You've been invaluable to this company." He looked up. "You've also been a good friend."

I smiled. "We've been through a lot."

"Haven't we?" He blinked, as if just realizing that we held the same fond and frenetic memories. "It's been a ride. Remember that first year when we—"

"That said . . ." Karen paused to clear her throat. "Growth is hard, and not everyone is equipped to handle the challenges. Procedural requirements and streamlining systems can rattle some people. I'm glad you found a company that fits your more fluid style. I think MedCore is half our size?"

"It is. They have a small line. In fact, all resources are focused on one product, a new dissolving non-lithium battery for humans."

"How interesting." Karen's tone said it was anything but.

"Mary offered to see out the two weeks." Craig looked between us. He widened his eyes and held them a few beats. It was his token gesture for *Go figure out the details yourselves.*

Karen bristled. "I hardly think that's necessary. I've had every member of my team catalogue their work, down to the last detail, for the past six months. It was meant to bring me up to speed and highlight inefficiencies, but in both cases now, it serves as a line of sight to past interaction and future projects."

"Both cases . . ." Craig's focus drifted above and beyond us.

Karen squirmed, pushed herself straighter, and rushed on. "The procedures already in place minimize any disruption."

"Fine." Something hardened within Craig's eyes. He dropped them back to his tablet. "Did they throw good money your way?"

I blinked.

"They should. Talk to finance. Moira will know; she can tell you what you're worth." Craig bounced back in his chair. "I certainly haven't been paying you enough."

"Craig." Karen's voice held a warning.

"What? She's an engineer like me and loves the work. They'll pay her less than she deserves if she doesn't know."

Loves the work . . . I found myself nodding.

Craig looked at his watch. "Any last words of wisdom for us?"

"I hardly think that's necessary," Karen interjected.

"Mary's been here for five years. She was my . . ." He looked back to me. "Fourth hire?"

"Fourth hire," I confirmed.

Craig smiled slow and long. "What fun we've had. It's been a good run so far . . . Let me have it. What do we need to do different, better, faster? After all, there's a reason you're leaving."

"Craig—"

He held up his hand. "I contend Mary knows this business almost as well as I do, and I'd like her opinion. We started as a group of engineers. That's what made us great, and if two are walking out my door, I want to know how to prevent number three."

I felt my lips part. Benson was at my desk. It had to be Rodriguez. I glanced to Karen. The skin under her eyes sagged against her glasses. Her mouth was pursed tight.

"Umm . . . I'd be careful not to put too many layers in place. Procedures, while necessary, can curb creativity, especially for your engineers and the physicists." I peeked at Karen. Her face was rigid, but she didn't interrupt.

Craig nodded.

"We're introverts—at least the ones you've got on board now. We need our quiet time to think, but we also need the freedom of uncensored and unmonitored interaction. We work alone, then play off each other to get the best out of our ideas. Until Golightly, I worked that way too. This project, it took over in a way I can't explain." I shook my head. "But back to your question, too many layers and rules make us feel watched and stifled. We know most ideas won't fly, 90 percent, but we need that ninety without feeling the pressure that each one has to justify its existence. Those ninety failures give birth to the ten that make WATT so great."

"To some degree, those 90 percent do need to justify their existence. Every idea pulls resources. We need to keep the lights on here." Karen's voice reminded me of Isabel's when she'd spoken so sharply to Clara.

"Obviously." I spoke to Craig. "But don't make teamwork and all the buzzwords thrown around here a mandate. Let people come together to collaborate on their own. We already do."

I thought about Benson, who always came for help in the afternoons around three o'clock when his energy lagged and, when he relaxed, expanded his conversation topics from science to science *and* Star Trek. I thought about Moira, who handled the financials and teased the engineers and physicists when we began to run a project anywhere close to "red." Her chiding put us on track because we wanted to do things right, not because she rapped our knuckles. She also sang gospel songs under her breath as she worked and made everyone feel better. I thought about Lucas, how he stayed late every Friday, sometimes into the wee hours of Saturday, until his week's programming work was done and he could tap his *You Will Never Have This Day Again So Make It Count* poster on his way out the door.

Craig glanced from me to Karen. He bounced back in his chair. The entire thing lifted off the ground.

I pressed on, leaning toward him. "You're an engineer, Craig, you must have noticed." I paused with the realization that after five years of working with him, I had no clue what Craig did or did not notice. It had been a running joke for years that as long as he had a project, we could move the entire company back to his garage or to Timbuktu and he wouldn't notice. "Nathan did. He noticed. He saw all this."

"Nathan talked to you about changes here? Proposed changes?" Karen's voice cut in.

I pulled back. "When he shadowed me in May, he asked a ton of questions. I realize now he didn't want answers, he wanted to know how I thought about things, make me articulate it, and see it all a different way. He got that WATT was changing, and I think he was trying to help me, help us, be proactive and take ownership of it."

"His reorg proposal makes more intuitive sense now." Craig grinned. I recognized the flash in his eyes—lightbulb clarity had struck.

"Reorg proposal?" Karen's focus shifted.

Craig kept his eyes on me. "I'll miss you, Mary. I sincerely wish you weren't leaving. Is there anything I can do to change your mind?"

I shrugged, recognizing the ambiguity of the gesture but unable to offer anything more. The meeting was over; it was time to go. Karen's elation felt palpable.

She dragged in a breath. "Mary's point is valid, but as we move forward, it's not feasible, even with Nathan's suggestions. With the growth WATT is experiencing, it is impossible to simply give the physicists, the engineers, anyone, their own playgrounds and hope it all turns out well."

She spoke to Craig as if I weren't in the room at all. I stood and headed for the door.

I'd almost reached it when a "Mary?" stopped me.

Karen held her files tight to her chest. Her knuckles protruded bony and white with the strain. "It's probably best you're going, as it sounds like WATT isn't the best fit for you any longer."

You love this job. In my head Karen's snarky tone was replaced by Moira's.

"That's not true. This company has always been the best fit for me." I stepped toward her, enjoying my height. I didn't slouch this time. "I love this place and I've worked hard here—42 percent of all deliverables kind of hard."

Karen's eyes bulged at the number. I glanced to Craig. A look of curious amusement rested on his face, but he didn't comment. I was not about to tell where I'd gotten the number, so I rushed on before either of them could ask.

"You've got twenty-five years of experience, and I get that you've steered larger companies to even greater success, but we're not children playing around 'hoping it all turns out well.' You haven't been willing to see that or see how things really work here. Do you know why the physicists hand-deliver their reports rather than put them on file share? It's because they need that moment. That moment when someone will face-to-face walk through their science—which is their heart song, by the way—and collaborate on its application. After all that alone time, they don't want to send it into the cloud. They need to see it land in someone's hands, watch their eyes light up, and dive into it with them. Then they go back to the computer—yes, and sometimes it's with a cookie. It's their moment of personal connection. It's like oxygen. They've got to have it."

I tilted my head and reconsidered that last point. "We've developed extraordinary trust and friendship here, and that's what drives innovation. Craig was right about the money—I'm sure most of us aren't paid enough, if you broke it down by hours. Benson has been here since four o'clock this morning. And do you know why it's quiet every day around here until Friday? It's not because people hate their work and trudge through the week. We don't work nine to five. Days run together because we're always thinking about this stuff and we don't slow that momentum until Friday. Its makes our workweek longer than you can imagine, and you missed it—you haven't recognized a tenth of the dedication out there."

I stepped back. My flailing hands needed more room. "And, yes, I went sideways with Golightly, and I'm sorry about that." I looked to Craig before facing Karen. "But Craig probably let me because he trusted me to pull through. And I did, by finally talking to Benson. It's not a lesson I'll need to learn twice, but I had to learn it. And an incredible product will come from it—but not if you lose two of WATT's engineers."

I pressed my fingers to my lips to slow myself down and to assess my courage to continue. No one spoke. Karen's mouth was gaping and she was possibly two shades paler, but a crimson spot was beginning to migrate across her cheek. I didn't have the courage to glance at Craig again.

I lowered my fingers and my voice. "You're throwing it all away, the backbone of this company. It's not the batteries and the products we build—that's the output—it's the deep well of creativity and trust that goes into making them. You put us on your org chart and assigned physicists to certain engineers and you quantified a qualitative entity—one of the only truly qualitative aspects here."

Karen's gaze flickered between Craig and me, then narrowed. "I fail to—"

"Karen?" Craig held up a hand. "Will you leave us for a moment?"

"Excuse—"

"Please. I'll come see you later. I need a moment with Mary. Alone."

She slammed the door behind her. She actually had to pull it to make the noise she needed.

I held my hands out without a clue as to what I was offering. "I am so sorry. I just . . . I kept talking."

Craig wasn't listening. He dropped his head onto his desk. It bounced off his laptop and lay there. "What have I done?"

I blinked.

He raised his head and stared at me. "The brain that starts a company, that has that first supernova idea, isn't always the one who can run it. I thought I needed a COO, really a seasoned CEO. Investors wanted it and I, like you, love the creative work. It was the next step ... Rodriguez gave his two-week notice this morning. At least he did it in person."

"Oh ..."

"Exactly. Two-thirds of our designers, the backbone of this place, as you call it. Nathan would have a field day with your fireworks display."

"Nathan?"

"He's been pushing me to fire Karen for six months. Two days after I hired her, almost a month before she stepped foot in the office. That's not true, he fought the hire too. And every reorg discussion with him starts there. Cut our losses with her and move on. He said this morning that WATT is hemorrhaging people and resources ..."

"This morning?"

Again Craig was not listening to me. "He's right. I finally agreed on Friday, but ..." He waved his hand at the door. "Do you know how much I laid out for her? The money? The options?" He dropped his head again. "Do you have any idea how much this is going to hurt us?" His words were muffled by the laptop. He popped up again. "Stay, Mary. You're right about every aspect of this company and you can't leave. What will it take?"

"I'm not sure I understand. You're firing Karen? Did Nathan know this?"

"He's been working for it. It's been our one point of contention and he was right. Other investors raised concerns too, but, like I said, I paid so much." Craig blew out a long breath. "We had a good-bye party for Nathan Friday, then I hired him again to see us through this. No one knows that, by the way."

I plopped into the chair I'd just vacated. Benson's laptop was in my hands. There was a sticker of $E=MC^2$ on the cover.

"You know what I want, Mary. It'll be leaner for a while, but we'll get to do what we do best, even if it's by the seat of our pants. But what do you want to do?" Craig picked up the pen he normally rolled through his fingers and started a helicopter whirl.

"I want to stay."

He stared at me. He deserved more.

"Craig, that was a pretty bad e-mail I sent, and I'm sorry. The five years alone deserved more respect. But the one place I felt good suddenly wasn't mine anymore. At least it didn't feel that way . . . I love my job and I think I do it well. May I stay?"

"Thank you." He closed his eyes as if cycling through a change in plans. "I feel like we're beginning again. Can you feel it?"

I laughed. "Maybe we are. You need to get Rodriguez back too."

"On it right now." He reached for his phone, then flicked it toward the door. "Get out of here and make sure everyone knows you're staying. I'm tired of all the grim faces. And if he's still in Conference Room A, grab Nathan and send him in here."

Nathan? Here?

As I left the room, I heard Craig chuckle. "It's a whole new ball game now."

I leaned against the wall outside Craig's office and took in the entire company before me. Working at WATT hadn't started with a proactive decision; it had started in an elevator with Craig pursuing me. And I perpetuated that fallacy—*I didn't choose the job, it chose me*—for five years. It was false because I'd chosen WATT too—I'd made it mine each and every day as I woke up and brought my best to work. It wasn't just a job. It was *my* job. And these were my people. My home.

I looked toward the office's far corner. Karen's cubicle. She always had an arched reading lamp on when she was there. It was off. I looked across the cubicle walls and didn't see her blond-gray bob and green-rimmed glasses. I didn't see Nathan either. The door to Conference Room A was open; the room was empty.

I walked back toward my own cubicle to find Moira.

"There you are." Moira rounded the corner and met me. "I brought this for you. It's almost gone, and you need a piece of your own good-bye cake."

"Gone?"

"You were in there almost an hour, and when Karen came storming out, people got scared and scattered. Dottie cut your cake up to calm the troops." Moira pulled her lips tight in mock fright. "Word is you were shouting."

"I think I might have been at one point. It was not my finest moment."

Moira lifted her eyebrows as if to say, *Debatable*. I suspected she was weighing the shouting against my e-mail. Both looked bad.

"But I'm staying."

"How? Karen won't forgive you after that . . ." As her statement trailed, she drew a breath. "The Wicked Witch of the West?"

"Can you keep a secret?"

Moira nodded like a small child waiting for cake.

"Going."

She yelped and leapt at me, catching the cake before it toppled. "I can't believe it." Her hug caught me in a half laugh, half hiccup.

"And you said you hated me."

"I already said that was a lie." She pushed me away, then punched me in the arm with her free hand. "Girl, I didn't know how I was going to survive without you, and now . . . It's like Christmas."

"I feel the same." I pulled her into another hug. "Hey—Craig said to send Nathan in. Is he here?"

"He was earlier, I guess. Benson just said he talked to him."

The excitement and the air seeped away. As I stepped back, Moira shot me a questioning glance.

"I wish I'd gotten to see him, that's all, but it doesn't matter. I'll let Craig know he's gone. How late are you staying?"

"I'm not." She glanced at her phone. "The usual suspects are headed to Z'Tejas. A friend of mine works there and is holding a big table on the patio for us. It was supposed to be your good-bye party."

"Go. I'll tell Craig and be right behind you."

"You don't mind? I want to make sure we get our table." Moira hoisted her bag onto her shoulder.

"We'd take two cars anyway. Go."

Moira headed one direction and I the other.

Chapter 28

I arrived at Z'Tejas an hour late.

When I'd told Craig that Nathan wasn't around, I got only a quick wave before he started tapping on his phone. He was most likely calling Nathan—which is exactly what I wanted to do. I sat at my desk staring at my phone for fifteen minutes, ordering myself to call him. I finally gave up. My self-recriminations and MoPac ate the next forty-five.

Moira ordered another round of nachos upon my arrival, and we sat back and listened to Benson tell the team how Golightly was going to set WATT on fire—figuratively this time.

He glanced at me and hesitated. "It's your work, Mary. You should talk."

I shook my head. "It's all you. Moira and I are perfectly content over here."

He grinned and returned to their discussion. Work never ended with this crew—and that was part of the fun.

Moira slid me a margarita. "I ordered it when you said you were looking for parking."

"Thank you." I took a sip of the top layer, which had already melted.

"There's tons to cover here, but first things first. You're staying, Karen's going?"

"So it seems. Craig wants a new CEO. He wants to design again."

She gave me a sideways smile. "Expensive wish."

"He said that too."

"So we take a hit now; it's better than the alternative. And with Golightly, it might not be more than a blip."

I lifted my glass. "To another innovative WATT product."

Moira joined me. "To the Vertex."

I'd forgotten that nickname. We'd called ourselves that back in the garage, back when we celebrated our first product, earned our first paycheck, and knew we would make it—we were the top of the top.

"I need to tell you about England, Nathan, everything."

Moira pulled her neck back. Nathan and England in the same sentence was a surprise. For the next two hours, I told her everything. At some point most of the guys left, and Benson pulled his chair close.

"He kissed you knowing you were getting fired?" That's when I noticed Benson.

"Not quite. I mean it wasn't like that."

"It wasn't close to like that." I looked up. We all did.

Nathan stood behind me. He looked good. Tired, but good. Except his eyes—the dim lighting darkened them. Or anger. I flashed mine to Moira.

"I probably should have mentioned I texted him." She looked between us. "I thought maybe you'd want to celebrate that you were staying, or say good-bye. You weren't in the office for his last day Friday, and you said earlier you didn't see him. But I guess you did, didn't you? Except I didn't know that."

"It's okay, Moira." Nathan spoke to her, but he watched me.

Without another word, Moira scooted to a nearby empty table. Benson followed her.

Nathan pulled her vacated chair farther away from mine and sat down.

"You didn't call. I didn't know you were at WATT." I tapped his knee just to touch him.

Nathan said nothing.

"Are you going to talk to me?"

"I wouldn't be here if I wasn't going to talk to you." He slid his messenger bag to the ground and shrugged out of his jacket.

Moira placed a beer in front of him.

He glanced up and thanked her. I sent her a wobbly smile. She threw me an encouraging one and drifted back to the two-top behind us.

"Why didn't you tell me about Karen?" I scooted my chair one inch closer.

"Nothing to tell until Craig committed, and it wasn't my place once he did. We worked all weekend to restructure around her."

"But . . ."

"I needed time, Mary. What was I supposed to do? Call you and tell you everything was fine now? Beg you not to quit? Beg you to talk to me? To trust me? I already asked those things of you."

"True. And when you put it like that, it doesn't sound good."

"It didn't feel good either. But since you're staying now, I guess I'll need to get used to you. Craig signed me on for a short-term engagement while he finds a new CEO. He'll announce it to you all in a couple days, so please keep it quiet until then."

"That's—" I wanted to say wonderful, exciting, but his closed expression killed my enthusiasm and my hope—and the "used to you" was not encouraging.

Till this moment, I never knew myself.

I laid my hand on Nathan's knee. He didn't shirk away—a good sign. "Nathan? Nothing is what I thought."

"And yet you were so sure." Nathan sank, like all his bones had suddenly softened. "If you'd have talked to me, Mary, and given me a chance, I would've told you something. Not everything, I couldn't have done that, but I was on your side." He took a breath; it came out on a sigh. "You said I didn't see you for a year. But what did you do to me? You had all these ideas in your head, and those were more important to you than trusting me and giving me a chance."

"You're right." I focused on my hand. It was easier than looking into his eyes. "I was so busy licking my wounds from who knows how long ago, and somehow they were all wrapped up in Isabel and Golightly, and life seeped into my work and I couldn't ask Benson or Rodriguez for help. And what's worse? I blamed everyone else, and that didn't feel good. When I heard you on the phone, it felt like the punishment was deserved and I was justified in running away. It oddly felt like the most courageous thing I could do."

I shot Benson and Moira an apologetic look. It was clear they were eavesdropping. They both smiled as if they'd known all along and had already forgiven me. Their grace gave me the courage to continue. "When you share stuff, especially your heart, you can lose it."

Nathan watched me with a look of disbelief.

"I know . . . You know that. It just took me time to understand it was worth it." I glanced back to Moira and Benson, but I spoke to Nathan. "I'm very sorry."

I shifted my chair to fully face him and to cut our audience from my sight line. "Did Craig tell you Benson solved Golightly's power problem? It was as easy as you said it would be."

"He did?" Nathan perked up. Benson shook his head and pointed at me. "You did?"

I couldn't stop my grin. "I was running yesterday, and the bats all flew from under the bridge in a series of waves. Almost two million bats, and at some points, it was just a cloud. You couldn't see the individuals. They were beautiful en masse, and I knew it fit. It fit Golightly and it fit me—and all I wanted to do was share it with you. But after the way I left, I didn't—call you, that is. I did e-mail Benson."

"About the bats?"

"No. Yes. About the fact that they flew out in waves and that I knew it meant something important, that the individuals remained individuals, but were more powerful in a group. That was for Benson. But also, they were amazing and oddly beautiful when together. That's what I wanted to share with you, because I didn't know if you'd seen them or the Stevie Ray Vaughan statue. And I knew you'd love both because . . . I love you and I was sad you weren't running with me to see it all and I was afraid you might be gone."

Nathan cracked a smile.

"What?"

"I'll say it again; what must it be like to live in your head?" Now he was watching me with such a tender look, my bones went soft.

"Again, I'm sorry, Nathan."

"I am too."

I threw my arms around him and kissed him on the cheek.

"You quit your job." He laughed, a mix of exhaustion, exasperation, and affection. "Craig sent me your e-mail, by the way. It was very decisive. I thought you were headed to Boston."

I scrunched my nose. "I know and I would be, but Karen made me so angry I lost it. It wasn't so much about me—I was still heading out the door at that point. It was about everybody else. All your questions came back to me, and I finally understood what you were asking me to see—like the bats becoming one." I glanced over to two implausibly blank faces. I focused on Nathan. "I shut my eyes to all of it and I didn't do justice to anyone, least of all you."

"I took on a new client Friday."

"You just said. WATT."

"That happened over the weekend. I took one in Boston, at half my rate so I could secure the work fast. Three days a week for the next six months."

"Why?" I sat up straight.

He narrowed his eyes.

"No, really, I was horrible. I left you standing there."

"You were. You were stubborn and dreadful and annoying." He chuckled. "But I know you, Mary. I've known you for a year and I love you. I thought some time in Boston might help you believe it."

I threw my arms around him again.

This time he dropped a kiss on my forehead. "What are we going to do?"

"Are you kidding? Skype, FaceTime, phone, text, e-mail, snail mail, and direct flights. We're going to be fine. And you'll be at WATT two days, plus there are weekends. Six months will fly by."

He twisted his chair to face me. "Promise?"

Our knees now wove together. My beige pants. His dark jeans. They looked like piano keys.

I trailed a finger across the colors. "No. At least I hope not. I think I'd like to savor the next six months, if you don't mind—each and every moment with you."

He looped one hand around the back of my neck and pulled me close. He tasted like Chapstick and bubble gum. He pulled a breath away. "Starting now." Then he kissed me again.

There was faint clapping and a whispered wolf whistle nearby.

"Benson," I whispered against his lips.

"Benson," he whispered against mine.

We ignored Benson.

... The wishes, the hopes, the confidence, the predictions of the small band of true friends who witnessed the ceremony, were fully answered in the perfect happiness of the union.

—JANE AUSTEN, *EMMA*

Acknowledgments

Thank you to everyone who makes this journey possible . . .

First, I offer thanks and forever friendship to Daisy Hutton. We started this journey together with *Dear Mr. Knightley* and, though she's moved on to new publishing adventures, she put her mark on this story and my heart. Thank you, my dear friend.

The incredible team at HCCP is next–Amanda Bostic, my new and amazing publisher; editors Becky Monds, LB Norton, and Jodi Hughes; Kristen Ingebretson and the design team; Paul Fisher and the amazing sales team who work tirelessly to get these stories into your hands; Kristen Golden and Allison Carter, who get special shout-outs. Kristen shares her marketing acumen, excellent taste in books, and extraordinary glow and glitter with me–and I'm the better for it. Allison, with her sweet smile and incredible knowledge, gets me out into the world–and I'm the better for that too.

Thanks also to Claudia Cross, agent, mentor, and friend; Elizabeth Lane, first, last, and all-stages-in-the-middle reader; Kristy Cambron and Sarah Ladd, who make each day brighter; and Mason, Matthew, Elizabeth, and Mary Margaret . . . Yes, the players on Team Reay have real names—and amazing hearts—and always pick up what I fail to do with incredible grace.

Last, but never least . . . thank you. Thank you to the readers, bloggers, reviewers, and now friends who have generously picked up these novels and trusted me with your hearts and time. Thank you for joining me and reaching out, meeting me on social media or in person.

Again and again, I'm beyond grateful to share *The Austen Escape* with you.

Discussion Questions

1. At the beginning of the story, Mary is clearly proficient in her work. She gets the job done, but is now stymied by an important project and in jeopardy. Why do you think it has come to this point?

2. Isabel and Mary met at age eight. Is it so unusual for the dynamic of a friendship to freeze within a moment of time? How does that influence how we see the world and our place in it?

3. Is *The Austen Escape* a qualified tribute to Jane Austen and our appropriate of her stories? What would Mary say? Isabel? Gertrude?

4. The idea of perspective and vision—what one can and can't see—is offered time and again. It's given a tangible symbol in Golightly. What can/can't Mary see? What about Isabel?

5. *The Austen Escape* offers up the idea of "hiding places" or escapes. Within stories is one example. What other hiding places does it offer, and how important are such escapes in life? Would you agree with Gertrude that they "can be dangerous"?

Discussion Questions

6. Is everyone in the story "hiding"? What does that say about the need to escape and recover?

7. Mary leaves Braithwaite House not knowing everything and without giving Nathan a chance. Why does she run?

8. Nathan forgives Mary. Does he see her clearly? Do you think he has always seen her clearly, as he states?

9. Was Mary right to stay at WATT? What did Craig see/not see in hiring Karen?

"Katherine Reay is a remarkable author who has created her own sub-genre, wrapping classic fiction around contemporary stories. Her writing is flawless and smooth, her storytelling meaningful and poignant. You're going to love *The Brontë Plot*."

—DEBBIE MACOMBER, #1 *New York Times* bestselling author

An Excerpt from

Dear Mr. Knightley

April 2

Dear Sir,

It has been a year since I turned down your generous offer. Father John warned me at the time that I was making a terrible mistake, but I wouldn't listen. He felt that by dismissing that opportunity I was injuring not only myself, but all the foster children helped by your foundation.

I hope any perceived ingratitude on my part didn't harm anyone else's dreams. I wasn't ungrateful; I just wanted to leave Grace House. A group home is a difficult place to live, and I'd been there for eight years. And even though I knew graduate school meant more education and better job prospects, it also meant living at Grace House another two years. At the time I couldn't face that prospect.

My heart has always been in my books and writing, but I couldn't risk losing a paying job to pursue a dream. Now I'm ready to try. Not because I failed, but because this degree gives me the chance to link my passion with my livelihood.

Please let me know if the grant is still available. I will understand if you have selected another candidate.

Sincerely,

Samantha Moore

April 7

Dear Ms. Moore,

The grant for full tuition to the master's program at Northwestern University's Medill School of Journalism remains available. At the strong recommendation of Father John, and due to the confidence he has in you, the director of the Dover Foundation has agreed to give you this second chance. There is, however, one stipulation. The director wants to receive personal progress letters from you as reassurance that this decision was the right one. You may write to him as you would to a journal, letting him know how your studies are going. He has opened a post office box for this purpose so you won't feel the added pressure of an immediate connection to him or to the foundation. Additionally, he will not write back, but asks that you write to him regularly about "things that matter."

He recognizes that this is an unusual requirement, but the foundation needs to know that its resources are being used in the best way possible. Given your sudden change of heart, he feels it is not too much to ask. To make this easier for you, he will also remain anonymous. You may write to him at this address under the name George Knightley.

Sincerely,

Laura Temper

Personal Assistant to Mr. G.

Knightley

April 12

Dear Mr. Knightley,

Thank you so much for giving me this opportunity. I submitted my application to Medill this morning. I had to use a couple papers on Dickens and Austen in place of the journalism samples requested. While that may count against me, I felt the rest of my application was strong.

If you will allow, I want to honor Father John's trust and yours by explaining my "sudden change of heart," as Ms. Temper described it. When I graduated college last spring, I had two opportunities: your grant to fund graduate school or a job at Ernst & Young. In my eagerness to leave Grace House and conquer the world, I chose the job. Six weeks ago I was fired. At the exit meeting my boss claimed I was "unengaged," especially with regard to peer and client interactions. I did good work there, Mr. Knightley. Good solid work. But "relating" in the workplace is important too, I gather. That's where I failed.

I'm guessing from your literary choice of pseudonym that you are very likely acquainted with another admirable character from fiction—Elizabeth Bennet, Jane Austen's complex and enchanting heroine. At Ernst & Young I tried to project Lizzy's boldness and spirit, but clearly she had a confidence and charm that was more than I could sustain on a daily basis. So now here I am, back at Grace House, taking advantage of the state's willingness to provide a home for me till I'm twenty-five if I stay in school.

Nevertheless, Father John still doubts me and couldn't resist a lecture this morning. I tried to listen, but my eyes wandered around his office: photographs of all the children who have passed through Grace House cover every space that isn't taken up with books. He loves murder mysteries: Agatha Christie, James Patterson, Alex Powell, P. D. James, Patricia Cornwell . . . I've read most of them. The first day we met, right before I turned fifteen, he challenged me to stretch beyond the classics.

"Are you listening, Sam?" Father John finally noticed my wandering eyes. "The Medill program is straight up your alley. You're a great reader and writer."

"'I deserve neither such praise nor such censure. I am not a great reader, and I have pleasure in many things.'" Elizabeth Bennet has a useful reply for every situation.

Father John gave a small smile, and I flinched. "What if I can't do this?" I asked. "Maybe it's a mistake."

He sat back in his chair and took a slow breath. Eyebrows down, mouth in a line.

"Then turn this down—again—and find another job. Pound the pavement quickly, though. I can give you a couple weeks here to get on your feet, then my hands are tied." He leaned forward. "Sam, I'll always help you. But after this, if you're not in school, Grace House is closed to you. This foundation helps a lot of kids here, and I won't jeopardize that support because you can't commit. So decide right now."

A tear rolled down my cheek. Father John never gets charged up, but I deserved it. I should only be grateful to you both, and here I was questioning your help. But help is hard, Mr. Knightley—even when I desperately need it. Every foster placement of my childhood was intended to help me; every new social worker tried to help my case; when I was sent back home at twelve, the judge meant to help my life too . . . I'm so tired of help.

"I'm sorry, Father John, you're right. I want this grant and I asked for it again. I must seem so ungrateful to you, to be questioning again."

"You don't, Sam, and I can understand wanting to stand alone. Even in the best of times and circumstances, it's hard to accept help—"

In the end, Father John believed my commitment. I hope you do too. Here is our agreement: you will pay for graduate school, and I will write you letters that give an honest accounting of my life and school—and you will never write back. That simple, right?

Thank you for that, Mr. Knightley—your anonymity. Honesty is easier when you have no face and no real name. And honesty, for me, is very easy on paper.

I also want to assure you that while I may not relate well to people in the real world, I shine in school. It's paper-based. I will do your grant justice, Mr. Knightley. I'll shine at Medill.

I know I've said more than was necessary in this letter, but I need you to know who I am. We need to have an honest beginning, even if it's less impressive than Lizzy Bennet's.

Sincerely,
Samantha Moore

April 21

Dear Mr. Knightley,

Each and every moment things change. For the most part, I loathe it. Change never works in my favor—as evidenced by so many foster placements, a holdup at a Chicago White Hen, getting fired from Ernst & Young, and so many other changes in my life I'd like to forget. But I needed one more—a change of my own making—so I pursued your grant again.

But it's not of my own making, is it?

Father John told me this morning that he was the one who proposed journalism for me—it was not an original requirement for your grant. I wouldn't have chosen it myself. My professor at Roosevelt College said I produced some of the best work on Austen, Dickens, and the Brontes he'd ever read. I'm *good* at fiction, Mr. Knightley. And I don't think it's right that Father John took away my choice. I'm twenty-three years old; I should be the author of the changes in my life.

I went to Father John and explained all this. I feel he has arbitrarily forced me into journalism—a field I don't know and don't write. "You need to undo that," I pleaded. "They'll listen to you."

Father John closed his eyes. One might think he'd fallen asleep, but I knew better. He was praying. He does that—a lot.

Minutes passed. He opened his eyes and zeroed in on me. Sometimes I feel his eyes are tired, but not at that moment. They were piercing and direct. I knew his answer before he opened his mouth.

"Sam, I won't . . . but you can. Write the foundation's director and ask." Father John stared into my eyes, measuring his words. "Don't lie. Don't tell them I've changed my mind. I have not. I am wholly against a change in program."

"How can you say that?" My own shrill voice surprised me.

"I've known you for eight years, Sam. I've watched you grow, I've watched you succeed, and I've watched you retreat. I want the best for you, and with every fiber of my being, I am convinced that 'the best' is not more fiction, but finding your way around in the real world and its people."

I opened my mouth to protest, but he held up his hand. "Consider carefully. If the foundation is unwilling to alter your grant, you may accept or you may walk away. You always have a choice."

"That's not fair."

Father John's eyes clouded. "My dear, what in your life has ever come close to fair? That's not how this life works." He leaned forward and stretched his hands out across the desk. "I'm sorry, Sam. If I could protect you from any more pain, I would. But I can only pray and do the very best God calls me to do. If I'm wrong about this, I hope that someday you will forgive me."

"'My temper would perhaps be called resentful.—My good opinion once lost is lost forever.'" When Elizabeth Bennet doesn't come through, one can always count on Mr. Darcy to provide the right response. I shook my head and, quoting no one, said, "I won't forgive you, Father John. I don't forgive." And I walked out.

I don't care if that was ungenerous, Mr. Knightley. He overstepped, and he's wrong. So now I'm asking you: Will you let me decide?

Sincerely,

Samantha Moore

April 25

Dear Ms. Moore,

Please forgive me for violating our agreement already, but I felt your question warranted a personal reply.

I understand your anger. It is hard when others hold power over you. Rest assured, your situation is not unique. There is very little any of us chooses in isolation.

Through my foundation, Father John has helped five young adults from Grace House. One attended junior college; another, trade school; one graduated from cosmetology school; and two successfully completed residential treatment programs. Each individual has grown closer to whole.

Father John not only fulfilled all the grant requirements for your application, but wrote me an additional five pages outlining your writing abilities, your gifts, and your determination. His decision to recommend journalism school was not made lightly, as you well know. Remember that, and remember what he has meant in your life. Don't throw away friends and mentors carelessly. They are rare.

I trust Father John's prayerful counsel and judgment, and stand with his original recommendation. My foundation will only award the grant for Medill's master's program.

The choice to accept it or not is yours, Ms. Moore.

Sincerely,

G. Knightley

May 10

Dear Mr. Knightley,

    I didn't withdraw my application. I made my choice and now I sit, waiting for Medill to accept or reject me.

    In the meantime I've settled into my old ways and my old jobs: I resumed tutoring at Buckhorn Cottage (Grace House's cottage for 8-to 13-year-old boys) and I picked up a few shifts at the public library. I've been working at that library for a decade now, even before I moved to Grace House for the first time.

    I was about fifteen when I first arrived at Grace House. Father John took me to his office and invited me to sit. No one had ever done that—invited me to do anything. He chatted for a few minutes, then handed me an Anne Perry novel.

    "Detective Huber got your file for me, Sam, and it's full of references to *Pride and Prejudice*, *Jane Eyre*, *Oliver Twist*, and other great classics. I think you must like to read. So until I get some of your favorites, would you like to read one of mine?"

    The thick hardback had a picture of a Victorian house on the cover. I slowly turned the pages, hoping if I feigned interest in his book, he'd take me to wherever I'd be staying and leave me alone.

    He didn't. "This is one of the first mysteries I ever read. Now I'm hooked. I've got about a hundred titles over there." Father John pointed to his bookcase and waited.

    I looked up.

    "Come to my office anytime you want a new one. I picked that for you because it takes place in England in the nineteenth century, about the same time as your favorites."

    I put the book down, never breaking eye contact. A show of strength, I thought.

    He sighed and leaned back in his chair. "Your choice. I'm sure I can get some classics this week. Or you can go to the public library; it's on the corner of State and Van Buren."

I wanted to say I knew exactly where the library was, but that would require speaking to him, so I simply slid the book into my lap. I wasn't going to admit, even to myself, that I liked the man—and still do. In spite of how angry I am with him at the moment, I know that Father John has always been on my side.

He welcomed me at fifteen and again at eighteen, after I tried to move out. And now at twenty-three, despite my heated words, he's opened Grace House's door once more. So while I'm here, I will listen to his lectures and I will try to do what he asks. I owe him that much.

I'll even try to play nice with Morgan, my new roommate in Independence Cottage . . .

"She's had a rough time, Sam. She turned eighteen a couple days ago and her foster family ended the placement."

"She can go on her own. Isn't that a good thing?"

"Not without her GED. You know how important that is. She's testing next month, then joining the army." Father John stared right through me.

"Why are you telling me this?"

"I'm asking you to be kind. Morgan's defense mechanisms are different from yours, and it may be rough going. Please don't make waves."

"I make waves?"

"Like the ocean, kiddo. Then you retreat before they hit the sand."
Ouch.

So I'm being kind, but Morgan isn't making it easy. We were cleaning the kitchen the other day and I told her about your grant. I was trying to be friendly. She was not.

"You're selling yourself for school? I can't believe you'd give it up for tuition. At least get some money or clothes from the deal."

"Morgan, shut up. You're disgusting. It isn't like that. I write letters to an address in New York and I get my tuition paid to graduate school."

"I bet a lot of girls start out that way." Morgan stopped washing her dishes and stared at me. She smiled slowly, almost cruelly. "Letters will be worse for you anyway. Good luck with that."

"What do you mean 'worse for me'? I can write a few letters, Morgan. That's what I do. I write."

"Honesty will kill you. You're a coward, and you'll lie. That makes the whole deal a lie." She put her plate down and walked away.

She's not right. I'm not a coward, and I will be honest in these letters. Simply because I don't blab my business to the world like Mrs. Bennet doesn't mean I'm a coward. I'm prudent when dealing with people. That's smart. Wouldn't you agree?

But Morgan brings up a good point—her only one so far. Have you read *Jane Eyre*? There's a part when Mr. Rochester meets Jane and asks if she expects a present. Adele, his ward, believes everyone should receive presents, daily. Jane isn't so sure. She replies, "They are generally thought pleasant things . . . a present has many faces to it, has it not? And one should consider all before pronouncing an opinion as to its nature."

You've led me to believe your gift has one face, Mr. Knightley.

I'll leave it at that.

> Sincerely,
> Samantha Moore

P.S. Okay, I can't leave it . . .

If you are truly a "Mr. Knightley," I can do this. I can write these letters. I trust you chose that name as a reflection of your own character. George Knightley is a good and honorable man—even better than Fitzwilliam Darcy, and few women put anyone above Mr. Darcy.

Yes, Darcy's got the tempestuous masculinity and brooding looks, but Knightley is a kinder, softer man with no pretense or dissimilation. Yes, he's a gentleman. And I can write with candor to a silent gentleman, and I can believe that he will not violate this trust.

I admit that if you had a face and a real name—or a nefarious name—it might be different. Morgan might be right. But as I sit here and think about this, I feel comfortable. See what power a name holds?

The story continues in *Dear Mr. Knightley* by
Katherine Reay.

About the Author

Katherine Reay has enjoyed a lifelong affair with the works of Jane Austen and her contemporaries. After earning degrees in history and marketing from Northwestern University, she worked in not-for-profit development before returning to school to pursue her MTS. Katherine lives with her husband and three children in Chicago, Illinois.

Visit her website at KatherineReay.com
Twitter: @Katherine_Reay
Facebook: katherinereaybooks

9 780718 078096